Welcome to San Francisco

San Francisco City smelled of wood and sea salt and the fog that had drifted in again during the night. Sophie's hands trembled as she fastened the top button of the wool coat that had been fashioned from the captain's old blue coat. Her shipmate, Christine, had made the coat and the skirt from the captain's old clothing. He wasn't coming back, but she had no way of telling for certain, since the ship had been deserted and all the lifeboats gone when she wakened from the plague's fever.

SAN FRANCISCO GOLD

ANN ZAVALA

A TOM DOHERTY ASSOCIATES BOOK
NEW YORK

NOTE: If you purchased this book without a cover you should be aware that this book is stolen property. It was reported as "unsold and destroyed" to the publisher and neither the author nor the publisher has received payment for this "stripped book."

This is a work of fiction. All the characters and events portrayed in this book are fictitious, and any resemblance to real people or events is purely coincidental.

SAN FRANCISCO GOLD

Cover art by George Bush

A Forge Book
Published by Tom Doherty Associates, Inc.
175 Fifth Avenue
New York, NY 10010

Forge ® is a registered trademark of Tom Doherty Associates, Inc.

ISBN: 0-812-52360-1
Library of Congress Card Catalog Number: 95-34748

First edition: November 1995
First mass market edition: December 1996

Printed in the United States of America

0 9 8 7 6 5 4 3 2 1

To my husband for everything;
To Mousie, for staying alive;
To Gaby, for the trans-continental editorial comments;
And to all my furry friends who helped in such unusual ways as I wrote this book.

ACKNOWLEDGMENTS

To my editor, Natalia Aponte, for her help and guidance with this project at every stage, and for the feeling of kinship that a mutual love of chocolate brings.

And to the people at the Maritime Museum in San Francisco for help with details of life aboard ships and in the port of San Francisco during the Gold Rush.

SAN FRANCISCO GOLD

1

SAN FRANCISCO CITY SMELLED OF WOOD AND sea salt and the fog that had drifted in again during the night. Her hands trembled as she fastened the top button of the wool coat that had been fashioned from the captain's old blue coat. Her shipmate, Cristine, had made the coat and the skirt from the captain's old clothing. He wasn't coming back, so he would not miss them, Sophie had reasoned. At least she didn't think he was coming back, but she had no way of telling for certain, since the ship had been deserted and all the lifeboats gone when she wakened from the plague's fever.

She fought against tripping on the skirt as she descended the plank to the sandy beach that served as San Francisco's crude wharf area. "Damn, I should have worn trousers and be damned with fashion; at least I wouldn't trip!" Sophie muttered.

"Hey, lady, you for sale or just for rent?" A drunk staggered out from the early morning shadows and almost knocked her over with the power of his breath. He was joined almost instantly by several other men, none of them completely sober.

Sophie felt the man's hands grab her arm. She twisted the man's hands and pulled back on his middle finger just hard enough to make the cartilage begin to crack in the knuckle.

"Don't ever put your hands on me unless you want blood spilled." That should be threat enough. She supposed it wouldn't do to hack someone's hands off within a few minutes of landing in the city without at least one warning.

The drunk didn't listen. He grabbed her again and tried to pull her against him.

"Hey, she said let her go; I'll take her if she doesn't want you. I like redheads." A top-hatted drunk laid hands on her arm, pulling her toward him. "Besides, didn't you hear that we lost Gertrude?"

"Lost her? She died of some disease?" one of the other men asked worriedly. His hands cupped his genitals in a protective gesture.

"No, lost her. She's up and disappeared. No one knows where. So I'll take this redhead for myself instead."

Sophie tried to grab the man's fingers, as she had with the first one, but he was holding on too tight to the woolen material.

Another man joined them, licking his lips as he stared at Sophie.

"Haven't seen a small'un like her for a long time. Reminds me of a girl I was in love with in Minnesota. But she's married and I'm here." Sophie could have felt sorry for him if he hadn't sounded like he was drooling as he stared at her breasts.

"Get away from me this instant," she growled. She wasn't seriously alarmed yet. She was a lot stronger than she looked, she always wore her knife at her waist, and these men were about to get a surprise if they didn't leave her alone.

It wasn't fair, she thought. Cristine had been trying to teach her to be a landlubber lady, a respectable woman, and first off she was going to have to stab a man to keep herself safe. Cristine had been right when she tried to tell her that no self-respecting, proper lady would have set foot on the dock area without a male escort, but there was just one small problem. Sophie didn't have a male escort. The only man who could have taken her ashore was Dominic, and he wouldn't do it because he said no Chinese man should walk as an equal with a white woman, and that had been the end of that discussion.

So it was just her and her knife and she'd have to make the best of it, which probably meant slicing this idiot's hand off at the wrist. She reached to her right side, just behind the pocket of the skirt. The black of the leather belt and sheath blended in with the navy wool and the knife always rode free in the leather, even though the men couldn't see it.

Her hand was just closing on the handle of the knife so she could enforce a little courtesy when the men suddenly spun away from her, scattering in the street and slamming against the building. Two of the men landed facedown in the mud, and the man who had his hand on her arm screamed and went to his knees as the bones in his fingers made an interesting crackling sound.

Arms wrapped around Sophie in a bear hug and she was lifted off her feet and pulled to one side while the men scattered. She struggled against the hug but couldn't break free. Her arms were pinioned to her sides and the knife was out of reach no matter how hard she tried to reach it.

"What the hell!" she swore, kicking against the man's shins. She was rewarded by his grip tightening around her and shifting her body until she couldn't reach his legs again. "Get your buggerly hands off me or I'll slice your balls off and have them for breakfast."

"You don't say. What an interesting idea for a young lady to have," the man said, laughing at her.

Damn, she thought, she'd be willing to bet proper young ladies didn't say things like she just had. So much for Cristine's careful tutelage.

Whoever was holding her ignored her breach of etiquette.

"I think that the lady would like to be able to walk unimpeded, don't you?" The voice was smooth as silk and deep as the ocean and Sophie recognized it immediately.

She was being held prisoner by the pirate who had tried to

board the ship and salvage it while she was recovering from the plague that had left only three people alive on the *Salud Y Amor.* He was nothing but a high seas pirate, a scoundrel.

He was also one of the most beautiful men she'd ever laid eyes on. His image was burned into her memory—every inch of him, dressed in tight canvas pants and the loose cotton shirt. The blond hair, the devilish grin complete with dimples, the deep voice. She'd watched those muscles underneath that shirt and thought what a shame it was going to be to fire a bullet right through that shirt and into the heart beneath, killing him on the spot if he didn't get off her ship.

She didn't finish the job last time; this time might be different.

"Let me go!" Sophie snarled again, even though it wasn't having much effect.

"My dear woman, if I let you go, the other men will continue to make your life difficult, and I'm certain you wouldn't want that to happen, now would you?"

He moved his grip just slightly.

It was all the chance Sophie needed. She smashed her elbow back into the captain's stomach with as much force as she could muster. He responded with a muffled whoosh of breath, his arms opened, and suddenly she was free.

He tried to catch his breath as he doubled over. He wheezed in agony and his handsome face turned an interesting shade of purple as he fought for air.

"Serves you right. You're going to have one hell of a bruise on your stomach by tomorrow morning. Don't go around grabbing ladies when they don't want to be handled," she told him.

Sophie put her hand on her knife as she waited for the captain of the *Flying Angel* to stop gasping. The other men who had been bothering her dragged themselves out of the mud and faded away into the saloons that edged the rough wooden planking that served as a walkway on the beach.

"Ooog," the captain said as he straightened up halfway. His

face was still an odd shade of purple, and his eyes glittered with anger.

Sophie stepped back when she saw the anger, then decided that attack was the best defense and drew the knife, letting the handle rest lightly in her hand. It wasn't exactly a threat, but it wasn't a peaceful gesture, either. "What do you want with me? What did you think you were doing, grabbing me like that?" she demanded.

"I wanted to help you," the captain said. His voice was still slightly strangled.

"I don't need any help, thank you." She shifted the knife and then realized what she'd done instinctively. She'd be willing to bet that Cristine would tell her that real ladies didn't draw knives on men who were trying to help them.

"Those men were going to do unmentionable things to you, you fool."

"Those men were bothering me, and if they'd bothered me for much longer they'd have been minus a couple of fingers. I'm good with the knife; I could have gouged eyeballs or carved other balls and I'd have been fine. I wasn't in any danger."

The captain turned a slightly whiter shade of green as he digested what she'd said, especially about balls. He'd never met a woman who acknowledged that such things existed, much less talked about such things in public, and this was the second time in five minutes that she'd talked about slicing them off. He tightened his legs slightly.

"Don't look so shocked. I've been riding ships with men since I was ten years old. There's nothing of a man's anatomy that's been hidden from me, so I know what I'm talking about. I can take care of myself if I have to."

"Ten years old?" The captain was trying to keep the conversation going until he'd recovered enough to take her arm and walk her away from this dangerous area. Even if she was one of the most uncouth women he'd ever met, she still didn't deserve to be left with the likes of the men who had accosted her.

"My uncle kidnapped my sister and me and for eight years he kept us like prisoners on his ships. We earned our berths, too. I can walk a sail and sew it with the best of the men. Now, if you'll excuse me, I have business."

Ruari was staring at her as if he couldn't believe what he'd just heard. Most probably, Sophie thought, he couldn't. Not many women were able to say that they'd been virtual slaves for eight years and survived it, even if their survival left them a little rough around the edges.

Sophie tried to step past him.

He reached out for her and then stopped his hand an inch from her arm. He looked at her right hand, which still held the knife, and stopped before he touched her.

"You could be in danger. San Francisco isn't like other cities; it's rougher here, more elemental. Even a knife won't protect you from some of the men around here."

"It is exactly like other ports that I've been in. Watch your back, don't let anyone get near you, and keep a weapon handy. I can do all of that."

"I was just trying to help," Ruari said, his voice wounded now that he had enough air in his lungs to be able to make normal sounds again. "I'd have done the same for any woman in distress. There are so many louts around this city that we gentlemen take guarding the women as one of our duties. Especially a woman as delicate and pretty as you are."

Sophie gawked at him, not sure what to say. Delicate and pretty? With her sunburned skin and red hair chopped off an inch from her skull and no figure to speak of? No, he was making fun of her.

"Thank you for the help. Now if you don't mind, I'll be on my way." She sheathed her knife and turned away, walking up the street toward the square.

The captain was taken by surprise and had to run a few steps to catch up with her as she hurried toward the business district.

"Would it harm you to allow me to escort you? I'd be delighted to offer my services. I promise, I am no danger to you." His bright blue eyes were twinkling as he reached out and plucked the knife out of the sheath without her even feeling it. She only knew that it was gone when he ran his fingers over the blade, testing the sharpness.

She grabbed for it but missed, as he kept it just out of reach.

"And don't threaten people unless you mean it; it could get you into trouble," he said.

"I meant to threaten you back there and I meant it when I had a gun leveled at your gut when you tried to take over the *Salud Y Amor.* Maybe I should have shot you while I had the chance, because you reek of trouble."

"No, that's bay rum. I spilled some of the bottle on me this morning. And you are mistaken. I haven't met you before, especially not on the wrong side of a gun. I would have remembered it."

He handed her knife back to her, and she slid it back into the sheath.

"I promise you, we met when you were plying your trade as a pirate."

The captain's eyes narrowed as he stared at her, trying to place her.

"The only ship I've boarded lately was a plague ship. I didn't speak with a woman when I boarded the *Salud Y Amor.* The only person on board that I saw was the cabin boy. Were you perhaps hiding belowdecks watching to see what happened?"

"Fool. You spoke with me."

He measured her against the memory of the barefoot young boy who had accosted him with a gun as he stepped onto the fog-swept deck. That gun had never wavered and he'd never doubted that the boy would have shot him dead if Ruari hadn't decided that prudence was the best idea and headed back to his own ship without the salvage rights that he'd come to claim.

Red hair. Loose shirt that would have hidden any feminine

curves. Lips that appeared just a touch too soft for even a cabin boy.

"No!"

"Yes."

She could see comprehension dawning in his eyes. "I must have been blind not to see that you were a woman."

"It wouldn't have made any difference. I still would have killed you if you'd tried to salvage us. Now will you please leave me alone?" She walked faster, hoping to lose him.

"Where do you want to go first? I'm not going to allow you to walk around the streets of San Francisco without an escort."

"Has anyone ever told you that you are an obnoxious toad? Who the hell appointed you my keeper?" she hissed. She couldn't believe that the man would be so persistent in the face of rejection.

"Has anyone ever told you that you are really quite pretty, even though you shouldn't have cut that beautiful red hair so short? And you do need some clothing that shows off your charms better than heavy woolens do."

Sophie gritted her teeth and started to tell him where he could go and what he could do while he was there, including a few anatomically difficult things, and then thought better of the idea. Even though they were still walking away from the men who had accosted her, she was aware of being watched by almost all of the males that they passed.

She caught expressions ranging from hopeful to wistful to downright sad, and suddenly she understood what she'd heard from the passengers on the ship when they talked about San Francisco. She was a rare commodity. If she wanted to sell herself into marriage, she could do so to the highest bidder and probably become one of the wealthiest women in San Francisco in a matter of a couple of days. It was possible that this man was right; she might be in more danger than she could handle.

"I haven't had the pleasure of a real introduction and there's no one to do the amenities. Besides, we seem to have gotten off on the wrong foot when we first met. Let me introduce myself. I am Captain Ruari McKay of the *Flying Angel.*" He gave a small bow and then grimaced and rubbed his sore solar plexus.

"At least now I know the name of the man who tried an act of piracy against my ship." Sophie stared up at him, her eyes a stormy green.

Ruari grimaced. "You *must not* persist in saying that I tried to take your ship by piracy. I told you then and I tell tell you now, all I was trying to do was help. You could have accepted a few members of my crew on board to bring you into San Francisco and you still would have had control of the *Salud Y Amor.* I meant you no harm."

"As you may have noticed, I didn't want to risk it. And now, if you'll excuse me, I have to find Mr. Thomas Fry's emporium and deliver his order."

"Thomas Fry? His emporium? It certainly doesn't deserve such a fine name, but I'd be glad to take you to Clay Street. You can conclude your business with the man and be out of his establishment within the hour. Believe me when I say that you will not want to be around Thomas Fry for very long, even in the best of circumstances. In fact, may I suggest that you allow me to help you with negotiations?"

"You may walk with me there, but I'll do my dealing on my own," Sophie said firmly. "Damn nuisance, this being a woman," she muttered. If she'd been dressed in trousers and a coat, she could have come and gone through this crowd of men without being noticed. It might be worth a try to pass as a man if everyone kept on staring at her.

"You haven't had a chance to look around the city yet. If you would permit me, I'd be delighted to take you for a carriage ride to acquaint you with the streets and byways. It would be a most enjoyable afternoon if you would say yes."

Oh, those deep blue eyes, she thought. That fine silk voice, the words that should have convinced her that she was wrong and that he was nothing more than the honorable gentleman that he said he was.

She wasn't convinced.

"No. I don't have time. I don't have time for anything except business and finding my sister," Sophie said.

"Yes, all right. Well, perhaps you would allow me to buy you something, a small present just to show you that I mean no harm?"

"A lady doesn't accept presents from a man she doesn't know and doesn't trust."

Ruari looked just slightly deflated. "But if you had a choice, what would you ask for?"

"Besides a couple of pounds of gold or a couple of square miles of prime real estate in the middle of San Francisco?" Sophie hesitated only a second. There was something she'd wanted since she was a small child. She never hoped to own the wished-for things, but it never hurt to ask.

"Two cats, male and female."

She knew that he couldn't deliver them, even should he be disposed to try. Sophie had heard from some of the passengers that cats were extremely scarce in San Francisco.

"I'll see what I can do about pleasing the most beautiful lady I've ever met." Ruari stopped in front of an unassuming little store with dirty windows and a broken slat in the steps leading up to it. "This is the store that Thomas Fry owns. If you need help, call out, and I'm sure someone will come running. Thomas Fry isn't the kind of man that most women want to be around, and I don't think you'll be any exception."

"Thank you, but I won't be needing any help."

"A pair of cats, hmm? That is a most interesting request. I've asked other women what their heart's desires were and had many answers, but this is the first time that felines have been requested. I'll see what I can do. I'll check by the ship a little later to make certain that everything went well with you in San Francisco." Ruari tipped his hat to her and strode off, whistling as if he'd made some sort of conquest.

"Oh, you needn't . . ." Sophie let her voice trail off. It was obvious that Mr. McKay wouldn't hear her, no matter how she protested.

She found, to her dismay, that she rather missed having him at her side, even though she couldn't stand the man. Without someone by her side she felt vulnerable.

It took only a few minutes to discover that Ruari McKay had been correct about Thomas Fry—she really didn't want to be around him, and the faster she could conclude their business the better.

"I'm looking for Mr. Thomas Fry," she announced as the men behind the counter eyed her with expressions ranging from disinterest to lust.

"I am Mr. Fry and how may I help you?" A small, dirty man bustled up to the counter. He obviously tried to make up for his size by wearing the most flamboyant clothing that he could find. He wore a white shirt with ruffles, a red vest heavily ornamented with gold thread, and a watch fob laden with at least a quarter of a pound of gold nuggets. The desired elegant effect was ruined by his greasy hair that fell in hanks around his thin face and by the food stains on the vest and the blackened cuffs of his white shirt.

Worse, Thomas Fry smelled.

Sophie took one sniff of the air surrounding the man and stepped back hastily, almost tripping on the skirt that she hadn't quite gotten used to yet.

She looked around the store and wondered how the man stayed in business. There were almost no goods on the shelves. Not an ax, not a piece of rope, not even red calico. Only a few tins of oysters graced the rough planks that served to hold his merchandise.

"I've come to settle accounts with you on the merchandise being carried by the *Salud y Amor,* captained by Henry Jackson, to be delivered to you as soon as you have paid for those goods."

Fry looked her up and down insolently. He picked at his yellowed teeth with a dirty fingernail and then shook his head.

"Nope, you don't look like anyone having to do with the good captain. Tell him to come in himself."

"I'll be sure to pass on your message the next time I go swimming in the middle of the Pacific. But for now, you'll have to deal with me."

Fry perked up. "He's dead? Well now, that puts a new look on things, doesn't it? You know I'm paid up on those goods and I don't owe you anything. I'll send my men over this afternoon to unload and you'll be finished with the lot of it."

Sophie gasped at the man's thievery. "We will not be finished and you will not unload until you pay the rest of the balance owing on the contract, which is five thousand five hundred dollars." Sophie pulled out the contract that she had found in the captain's desk.

"Got a contract, do you? We'll take care of that," Fry said as he snatched the papers from her hands and threw them into the small stove that was being used to take the chill off the tar-paper and pine-board store. In a matter of seconds her record of the transaction was lost.

Sophie's hand went to her knife, but she didn't draw it because suddenly she was facing a very large and very deadly looking gun that Fry pulled out from under the counter.

"You'll find no one to help you and the knife will only get you killed. You'd best be on your way, and don't try to tangle with the men of this town. They'll eat you alive and spit out the bones."

Sophie stood up as straight as she could. Fry wasn't much bigger than she was, and she hoped she could intimidate him. She knew that he needed the goods from the *Salud Y Amor*, or he'd have nothing left to sell in this miserable store. If other merchants were as desperate for merchandise, she might be able to walk away from Fry and make an even better deal than the captain had.

"I don't think so. If you don't pay me the amount owed, I won't let your men on board the ship. If you try to set foot on the *Salud Y Amor* anyway with your men, I'll shoot them as they try to walk up the gangplank. I've already fought off pirates once on the high seas; it won't be so difficult to fight them off in the harbor with all of San Francisco watching."

Sophie was shaking inside, but she kept her voice steel hard.

"You'd never get away with it. I could pick you off, throw your body overboard, and come and take what I wanted anyway," Fry blustered.

"You could try, but I don't think you'd get very far. If you don't pay me for these goods, I will dispose of them with other merchants. By the time your men come to my ship, I'll have already sold and disbursed them at a much higher profit than a mere five thousand dollars. The only reason I'm offering them to you is because your name is on the contract and I will not break the captain's contract without good cause. On the other hand, give me good cause and you'll never see so much as one tin of crackers from the *Salud Y Amor*."

Fry glared at her. Then finally he snapped, "All right, I'll pay two thousand and that's final."

Sophie shrugged. It was a shame that God had made such a huge mistake as to put the man's ass between his ears instead of where it was supposed to be. "Then you don't get the cargo. And that's final, too." Ignoring the gun that was still pointed at the middle of her breasts, she gathered her skirt, turned, and headed for the door. Her backbone was absolutely straight. She held her head high, and every step she took she expected to feel a bullet plow through that very same spine and exit the front, leaving a terrible gaping hole.

"Wait!" Fry's voice held a tinge of worry. "Three thousand, and it's my final offer."

Sophie's steps never faltered. She reached the door and was almost through it when she heard Fry call her back.

"All right, five thousand five hundred, but it will be unloaded before nightfall tonight."

"It will be unloaded when you have delivered the five thousand five hundred dollars in gold coin."

"Gold dust."

"No, sir, coin. I have heard how difficult it is to find coins in San Francisco and I intend to have them on hand when necessary."

She heard a hiss of irritation. "All right, coin."

"You bastard," she whispered as she tugged at the front door, which threatened to fall right out of the flimsy pine frame. "Tried to get the best of me and lost. That'll teach you."

She stepped out of the shop onto Clay Street and walked to the end of the building, where Mr. Fry couldn't see her. Then she leaned against the unstable wood post that formed the intersection between the Fry building and the building next door. She couldn't tell what was shaking more, the building or herself.

"Hey, Annabelle, you're up early today. I'll see you at the faro table. Remember, my proposal of marriage still stands!"

A man waved at her from across the street, almost as if he knew her.

Annabelle! He thinks I'm Annabelle! It was the first solid indication that she was right when she followed her sister to San Francisco after Annabelle disappeared from on board one of her uncle's ships. They'd always been linked, almost like twins, and Sophie had known the direction in which Annabelle had been taken.

Sophie raised her hand to flag the man down and took a few steps forward. She stopped as he turned a corner. She'd never catch up with him by trying to dodge through the muck that served as streets. But her heart sang. She was right. She'd followed her instincts and Annabelle was here, just as she had expected. It was only a matter of time until she found her sister, and then they could work together to get all the gold in California in their own name.

2

HE SAID HE'D SEE ANNABELLE AT THE TABLE *tonight. The guy was talking about Annabelle dealing him cards. That makes finding her a little easier,* Sophie thought as she left the safety of the building and began to walk through the crowds. She'd look for gaming houses and check them out. Surely there couldn't be that many in a small city like San Francisco. *I was right; Annabelle's using her talent with the cards to earn a living.*

She'd never be able to explain to someone how she knew what Annabelle had been doing in San Francisco, nor why she had been so certain that if she could only reach the city, she'd find the sister who had disappeared in New Orleans. The link that Sophie and Annabelle shared would inevitably draw them back together. They were never completely apart, no matter how many miles there were between them. Annabelle, however, had a little extra gift, one that she had always used when necessary to win money enough to keep them in at least a few of life's amenities. By the time the men on the ships realized that she was more than lucky at cards, she'd already removed a fair portion of their money.

Annabelle had always been able to look at the cards as the men picked them up and instantly know what their hands held. It wasn't marked decks or anything like that, she'd explained one time when Sophie asked her what she saw; it was just that the men thought the suits and numbers of cards so loudly she couldn't have ignored them even if she'd wanted to. And, since they practically gave away the information, she used it to win.

Now all I have to do is find out which gambling emporium you're working with and we'll be back together and safe again.

By the time Sophie had walked two blocks, she knew that it might not be as easy as she thought. There were over twenty gambling parlors, some of them no more than a few feet wide and ten or fifteen feet long, in these few blocks. She could tell that Annabelle was close, but that didn't mean anything when there were so many places that she might be.

"Annabelle, I can hardly wait until I find you," she whispered. "I need to talk to you about Thomas Fry. I don't trust that man as far as I can see him, and you've always been good at outsmarting people like that."

Sophie didn't notice a squat, heavyset man in a red calico shirt and jeans that needed suspenders following her, carefully matching the same turns and twists in her walk through San Francisco.

She stopped short in front of a grocery store. *Lord, look at that! It's a good thing I'm going to have money in a few hours or I'd never be able to afford living in this city!* she thought as she looked at the prices marked on the slate on the store's wall. Eggs were five dollars a dozen; bread was four dollars a loaf. Tinned oysters seemed to be reasonable enough at only two dollars a can, but everything else was so expensive that she could understand why most of the men looked hungry. Even a plate of beans and a piece of bread cost well over a dollar.

"Annabelle! Now you'd better have a good explanation for this, because you turned me down cold when I asked you to come out with me for a bit of dinner over at the new hotel. Here you are standing around on the sidewalk as if you didn't have a thing to do, when you told me you were so busy you couldn't leave the Painted Lady until later this evening for anyone or anything."

Sophie looked up from the menu posted on the board and then forced herself to keep her mouth from dropping open in surprise. She'd never seen what looked like a walking corpse before, but this man definitely fit the bill. He was long and so thin that he looked like he'd topple over from a breath of air if one hit him. His face was cadaverously thin and the shock of yellow-white hair looked like a dandelion on top of his head.

"Oh, Lord, I've known men who needed fattening up, but this is ridiculous!" she muttered in exasperation. Then in a louder voice she said, "I'm not Annabelle!"

"Not Annabelle? Why, look at you; don't be ridiculous. I'd know that red hair and those eyes anywhere, but I must say I've never seen you dressed in such subdued clothing, not since you came here. But yes, you're Annabelle; there can't be two women who look like—" His blue eyes widened and a flush rose over his pallid face. "Good Lord, don't tell me! You're the sister she's always talking about, the one she lost in New Orleans! The one she keeps on saying she's going to go back and rescue just as soon as she has enough money. Sarah, no, Sadie—"

"Sophie," Sophie said. She was getting hungry just looking at the man. He'd be like a python when he swallowed; you'd be able to see every mouthful that he took as it worked its way down that skinny body. "I'm Sophie. I just sailed into town yesterday and I'm looking for my sister and it sounds like you can help me find her."

"Sailed into town? Oh, yes, I heard about another ship landing yesterday, the *Salud Y Amor*, correct? Something about there only being three people on board. A Chinaman and two women. I'll tell you, that brought some comments! A plague ship, someone said." He took a step backward.

"Please don't run off before you tell me where I can find my sister." Sophie didn't want to have to track down yet another person who knew Annabelle and could find the place where she worked.

"First, tell me, was it a plague ship?" the man asked cautiously.

"Yes, I suppose you could call it that. When I woke up after the fever, everyone was gone. The lifeboats had been lowered, the captain had disappeared, and several of us had been left to die. That's why there were only Dominic Tibeau, Cristine, and myself on board. Now, what about my sister?"

"Well, I suppose I can take you to the Painted Lady," the man said doubtfully. "If you don't mind, though, I won't be offering my arm to you. I don't want to catch anything, and God knows there's enough of sickness around here to go around as it is." He drew back and rubbed his long, thin hands together in a washing motion. "But you do need an escort. Why, I just heard last night that another woman disappeared, snatched right off the streets while she was walking down by Dennison's Exchange. Some say it's the Chinese, you know. Me, I just think it's desperate men taking things into their own hands, if you'll pardon the expression."

"I don't think I'm in any danger of being snatched," Sophie said, smiling. She could feel the knife at her waist. She could use it, if she wanted and she wasn't up against Ruari McKay.

"And you are?" Sophie asked.

"And I are?" The man looked blank and then it dawned on him what she was asking. "Oh! Of course; excuse me for my impoliteness. I am Mortimer Abernathy, owner of Abernathy's food and clothing stores, one here, one in Sacramento, one in Sutter's Mill, and soon to be one in Sonora, outfitters to the miners. Best-quality tarpaulins, strongest shovels, best-made rockers available in California." He seemed to be perfectly willing to keep on listing what he did for a living as they walked. "I've been here since the first miners, and I've watched them come and go. Mostly go, because men come in here expecting to make a fortune and only use my store as a place to earn their outfits. Then they go to the mines and come back broke and most of the time sick, too."

"It doesn't sound like it's easy making a living here even with the gold."

"It's not! We've managed to keep the store open, but I do most of the work. Finest mining goods that you can find. There's plenty of gold here, but there's a lot of everything else, too, like gambling and other things a lady shouldn't know about." Abernathy turned the corner and pointed ahead. "Here, down this street to the right and then left at the next corner. You're looking for the Painted Lady. It's one of the places that I supply with comestibles. Belle knows that she can trust me to give her the best that's available, little though that is at times."

"My sister works in the Painted Lady?" Sophie asked, not sure what she'd find when she did reach her sister.

"Work there? Well, not exactly. Annabelle owns it, as far as I can tell," Abernathy said morosely. "Wish I had half of what that woman makes in one night. She's like a beacon, drawing people to her, and it pays off, I'm telling you. It pays and because it pays, she brings in the best women to work with her, at least until they disappear like the last one. Pretty little Frenchwoman, I wonder what made her leave, when she had all of San Francisco interested in her."

Sophie stopped, stunned. She ignored the part about the women as she tried to comprehend that her sister had already managed to buy herself a gambling parlor. Annabelle had disappeared six months ago and in that time she'd progressed to owning her own business? No wonder Sophie had seen Annabelle surrounded by gold when she reached out to find her sister!

Someone bumped her from behind, almost knocking her into the mud. She didn't notice that it was the same heavyset man in the red shirt, who had decided to follow her a little too closely so he could hear her conversation with Abernathy. The merchant eyed the red-shirted man suspiciously and waited until he was well out of earshot before he continued the conversation on their way toward the Painted Lady.

"Don't stop for anything on these streets. These louts aren't too careful about where they put their hands. You could lose a little bit more than just your wallet if you're not careful. We'd hate for anything to happen to you, now wouldn't we? Besides, falling in the dust and mud isn't healthy. It doesn't wash out, and I'd hate to tell you what all is in it. You can smell the worst of it."

Mr. Abernathy elbowed a man out of the way and almost shoved another one off the sidewalk as he escorted Sophie along the walk. She was amazed that Abernathy was able to deal with all the physical aggressiveness without being dumped off the sidewalk by men who looked considerably less frail than he did.

"Suffice to say, San Francisco hasn't got the best methods of waste disposal quite yet. It's something that needs work. If the Romans could do it, then I don't see why modern man can't at least equal, if not better, the ancients' engineering feats. It shouldn't be a matter of engineering for the hills; Rome had hills and they managed quite well."

Sophie stopped to let a couple of men who were coming to blows about something roll around on the dusty ground in front of her. Abernathy grabbed her arm and hauled her past them.

"I told you, don't stop."

Sophie giggled. He'd obviously forgotten that he didn't want to touch her for fear of the plague.

They finally came to a halt in front of one of the hundreds of pine and canvas buildings that lined the streets. The resemblance of the Painted Lady to any of the other buildings stopped there. Sophie looked up at the building and began to laugh. Trust Annabelle to do something entirely different and unexpected to bring people into her place of business. No wonder they called it the Painted Lady; it was a most appropriate name.

The building looked like it didn't exist. To the casual glance, it looked like the canvas walls were rolled up and tied at each pine post. Inside, the patrons bent over the various gambling tables. She saw faro and vingt-et-un and several other games she couldn't name being dealt, and a wheel of fortune spun in place on the back wall. The inside of the place was sumptuously decorated with red wallpaper on the back wall and plenty of candles stuck in fancied-up tin cans for light, and gold mirrors to reflect the light. She could see fine wood floors and a bar that stretched the length of the building. There were two staircases going up to the second floor and even a piano rolled against the side of the staircase. It was just the kind of place that Annabelle would own, a palace compared to other places in San Francisco.

It wasn't until Sophie was within twenty feet of the building that she realized that it was all a hoax. The walls weren't rolled up; they were tightly nailed in place to keep out the dusty wind and eventual rain. That hadn't stopped Annabelle's creative impulses. She'd painted a two-story-high enticement to the adventures that the gamblers might find inside. The second story, Sophie was interested to find, was an advertisement for pleasures with whores, which also didn't surprise Sophie. She and Annabelle might both be virgins, but it wasn't for lack of knowledge of what men would like from them.

Sophie focused on one of the clients that Annabelle had painted and wondered if Abernathy realized that he'd been immortalized as one of the gamblers in Annabelle's palace.

"You finally found a place large enough to have fun with your painting, didn't you, Annabelle?" Sophie said so quietly that Abernathy couldn't hear her.

"It's quite a sight, isn't it? We couldn't believe it when the paintings sprang up almost overnight, but now everyone in the place knows the Painted Lady. It's a good way to draw a crowd in. Can't say as I've ever seen it done before."

"I have," Sophie said. She stepped through the door and was met by the sound and smell of the real bar, and it was nothing at all like the beauty on the outside of the building. Inside there were candles in the tin holders, just as Annabelle had painted them, but it was still dark and smoky. Annabelle had wielded her brush on the inside of the canvas as well as the outside. She had done a fair copy of a red velvet wallpaper with gold friezes along the upper edge. The fake walls were complete with mirrors, bars, and even what looked like a naked-lady statue in one corner. The floor was real wood, but the gaps were half an inch wide and threatened to catch the unwary rambler's heels and the tables were nothing more than pine slabs covered with green cloth. A small stove stood in one corner, just in case it got cold enough to need the heat, but at the moment the Painted Lady was hot with the smell of smoke and men's bodies pressed together too closely and with too little use of soap and water.

"Follow me. Annabelle's usually over here," Abernathy said, leading the way toward the vingt-et-un table where Sophie's near-double sat dealing the cards.

Sophie's heart leaped as she saw her sister. There had been times during the last six months that she'd been positive she'd never see Annabelle again, no matter what her second sight told her, and she'd cursed the uncle who had separated them. She was glad that her worries had been baseless.

"Annabelle, I've brought you a present," the man said, his voice doleful.

Annabelle never stopped dealing. For several seconds her eyes didn't register who was was standing beside Abernathy. She'd taken all the bets, laid down the last card, and begun to scrape in her money when her eyes brightened and her hands started shaking. She folded the deck and took a hesitant step toward her sister.

"I knew you were close; I just didn't know how close!"

She took another step and then grabbed her sister and started hugging her.

"Sophie, I knew you'd come if you could, but there were a couple of times when I thought I'd lost you for sure."

"I knew we hadn't—"

"But it was so close—"

"When I thought I'd die—"

"The heat was terrible—"

"You thought of cool baths!"

The sisters were off and running, speaking their language that no one else in the world could follow because neither of them had to say complete thoughts before the other one could interrupt and hurry on to the next idea.

"I stayed in bed because I couldn't stand up without falling to one side. I thought maybe you were really gone, and this was my body and mind's way of reacting to the shock."

"I wouldn't have left without haunting you."

"I'm glad that it wasn't true."

"I dreamed of walking through the jungle for days on end. Everything itched and the jungle crawled with bugs and I couldn't take a breath because the air was mostly water."

"Bugs, ugh, do you remember—"

"And we killed them all with that herb. Wish I could get more of it."

"The fever was bad; I knew you were so sick—"

"It was only a dream, but there were still times when I thought I couldn't take another breath of the air, it was so heavy and hot. Just when I'd about given up, I'd cool down again and it would be all right for at least a little while."

"I know; I'd wake up gasping with the heat. I'd have some of the men bring me in a huge tub full of cold water and I'd sink down into it. I'd think real hard about standing in a cool stream with the water from a waterfall flowing over my head and down my body and eventually I'd cool down and I could do my work in the bar."

"That's where the water came from—"

"And I kept pulling you this way. I knew you had to come—"

"I almost didn't—"

"I knew you'd make it."

The crowd around them had quieted as the two sisters talked.

"Lord, I didn't think there could be two of them, but take a look; they're both just alike. Twins, I'll bet, and we didn't know it. Listen to the way they talk; I've heard twins do that before." Abernathy's voice was still doleful.

Annabelle heard the comment and shook her head.

"No, we're not twins; there's a year between us. We're just very close." Annabelle hesitated because she couldn't think of a better way to explain the link between her and her sister.

"Two of them, who'd a thought!" one of the other men said.

"I'd like a chance at either of them, but they'd look right through me," one of the other men said.

"Let's get out of here so we can really talk," Annabelle said, pulling her sister along behind her. "Do you know, there were times when I wondered if we'd just imagined it all and we'd never be reunited."

"I knew it wasn't imagination and I knew you were to the west and I had a feeling of ocean and wildness and then smoke, but that could be a lot of places. Oh, and cold, I definitely got cold from you. I knew I'd find you."

The squat man in the red calico shirt who had been following Sophie waited only long enough to see his quarry go into the back room with Annabelle before he left the Painted Lady.

Annabelle pulled aside a piece of calico, and they stepped into what passed as Belle's private room. She hugged Sophie again; then they both sat on the bed facing each other, sitting Indian fashion as they had for years in the past, with each one looking over the other sister's shoulder. For years they'd watched out for each other, most of the time working back to back to make sure no man ever had a chance to touch them. It was a source of pride that no one had ever gotten behind their defenses nor had any man ever been able to touch them, though quite a few had tried.

For the first time in months, Sophie relaxed completely. Annabelle was here. They could take care of each other now, just like they always had.

"This bed is harder than the one on shipboard, and I thought nothing could be worse than that!" Sophie exclaimed when she felt the wire springs underneath her. "Can't you get anything better in the city?"

"Sure, but I don't want anything better. Look at the legs and you'll see what I mean."

Sophie leaned over and looked down at the bed's legs, each of which stood in a water pan that was filled to the brim.

"Bugs?" she asked, her nose wrinkling with disgust. They'd both waged a never-ending war against bugs and rats on board the ships. The men never minded the presence of the critters, but neither Sophie nor Annabelle could abide them.

"Lots of bugs and the biggest rats you've ever seen. I've got men looking for a couple of cats for me, but I haven't been able to find any yet. I think you could make a small fortune importing felines and selling them."

"I wouldn't mind a small fortune. Those men out there were talking about how much they wanted us as their wives. Did you hear the sums they were mentioning as possible bribes to get us into their beds? They'd be terribly disappointed to know that all I want is to be free and rich enough to take care of myself. I don't need a man. They all turn out like Uncle Charles in the end, anyway."

Sophie looked up and saw a strange expression on Annabelle's face.

"Something has changed. Tell me about it."

Annabelle shrugged. "It's men. I think we'd better talk about them and one man in particular when we have the time. I've decided I like them, as long as none of them think they own me."

"Anyone special that you decided you like?" Sophie asked cautiously. She had a strange feeling of disorientation. She'd never expected her sister to decide she liked the opposite sex, not after what they'd gone through while on shipboard. But then, look at the way Sophie herself had felt about Dominic. Not exactly in love, but she sure was interested in the other passenger.

"There are several anyones in particular and they pay very well for my time, too." Annabelle said it so fast that Sophie almost didn't understand her sister.

It took a few moments for Sophie to understand the implication of what her sister had said, and by that time Annabelle had rushed on to other things.

"Do you want something to drink? We've got tea and some coffee, or I could send out for something from one of the restaurants. Are you hungry?" Annabelle started to jump up, but Sophie pulled her back down onto the bed. She'd come back to the subject of men a little later.

"No, first tell me what happened to you. I woke up one morning on Uncle Charles's ship and you were gone. There wasn't anything of yours anywhere on the ship, nothing even to show that you'd ever existed. I thought for a while that someone had killed you. I couldn't think straight for two days and I had a horrendous headache and I kept wondering if this was what would happen when we were finally separated for all time."

"That's because we were drugged. Whatever they used on us was powerful enough that I didn't wake up when they took me off the ship. I only woke up when we'd already left New Orleans heading for the cape. There was no way to get back to you, nothing I could do to tell you where I'd gone. And for a while, Sophie, I wasn't sure that I wanted you to follow me. That voyage was the trip from hell. There were other women on board, not just me, and several of them died when things got especially rough."

"What kind of rough? They didn't . . . rape you?"

Annabelle shook her head. "Not me. I had the knife and even though they kept trying, they were never able to take it away from me. But they did rape the other women. One woman died after the men decided to punish her for fighting back. They dumped her body overboard in the middle of the night. The captain heard about it and suddenly there were a few less crewmen. I think I heard splashes in the night."

"Why would they have killed crewmen for bothering a woman? It's never been a crime before. Look how many times they tried it on us."

"I can't prove it, but I think that the women were going to be sold and the captain lost his investment."

"Sold to who?"

"I never did find out and I didn't wait around for someone to tell me. I decided that the first chance I had, I was going to jump ship."

"You escaped? How?"

Annabelle giggled and leaned forward. "Remember that game we used to play on Uncle Charles's ships when the work got too hard or too monotonous or dirty?"

"You mean the hiding game? The one where we'd find the smallest, most secret place on the ship and then crawl into the space and stay for hours while they hunted all over for us?"

"That's the one. They had me locked in with the other women behind a secret panel in the hold of the ship. They obviously didn't think that anyone would try to escape except through the door, and that was barred so that no one could get out. I shudder to think what would have happened to us all if a fire had started on board."

"Oh, God," Sophie echoed, picking up the picture of flames and women dying because they couldn't escape.

"Anyway, they'd checked the room, but not too carefully. There was a space where the wall met the hull that wasn't tightly boarded in. I could see into the cargo hold that was next to us, and there it was, the way I could escape."

"And that was right through the wall, right?"

"You guessed it. I waited until we reached a port. I didn't even know it was San Francisco; it was just a place where we docked. When the men came to unload the ship, I squeezed through that space and waited. When they were almost done and there were plenty of people on board, I streaked up that gangway, reached the deck, and was down off the gangplank in three seconds flat. I never could have done it if I hadn't been this tiny, because none of the other women were able to follow me."

Annabelle waved at her barely four feet, ten inches of body, which was even thinner than the last time Sophie had seen her. "I tried to tell the men on the docks that there were other women being held prisoner on the ship, but by the time I convinced them that I knew what I was talking about and they decided to storm the ship, she'd already weighed anchor and left. I think they must have headed out and kept going to China. The crowd was plenty angry, I can tell you that. There aren't that many women here, and the thought of women being held captive to be sold to someone else was enough to make most of the men go blind with rage."

"Annabelle," A woman with bright yellow curls tied back with an equally bright blue ribbon stuck her head in through the opening in the calico curtain.

"What do you need, Nellie?"

"Just wanted to let you know that the five of us are having a meeting at eight tomorrow morning. Are you free to come?" The woman daintily bit off the corner of some kind of filled pastry while she waited for Annabelle's answer.

"I'll be there," Annabelle said. "And I want to talk to you about eating up the profits and the possibility of putting a muzzle on you so you don't eat us out of house and home."

"Hey, you promised all the food we could eat when I signed up," Nellie protested.

"That was before I knew that you had the appetite of a pregnant water buffalo."

"I do not. And I'm going to be at that meeting to make sure you don't try to take my food away from me. And if you're thinking of getting in more supplies to serve to the men at the bar, I suggest that you take a look at that new Parisian bakery that opened up on Polk Street. It's got the most delicious little cream cakes. . . ." Nellie drifted off, still munching on her pastry.

"That woman is going to eat us broke," Annabelle said in exasperation.

"She's thin, though; do you think she's got a worm or something?"

"No, she just likes to eat. The problem is, she's one of the women who makes the most money for the Painted Lady, so I can't really complain. She's always busy and she does bring in the customers. We're having to work harder ever since one of our ladies decided to take off. I'd be willing to bet that Gertrude found someone who decided he was in love with her and had a little money and they're setting up housekeeping somewhere up around Rich Bar. But that doesn't help us here; she's got guys coming in asking for her."

Gertrude—wasn't that the woman the men were looking for when she stepped off the ship, Sophie wondered, and then dismissed the thought.

"I hear the business is doing fine. I was surprised to find out that you owned part of the Painted Lady, though."

"We all own part of it, all the ladies that you see. It's different than we ever imagined it when we were riding around on those ships for all those years. Do you know, I've got my first real female friend, a best friend? Josie Santiago found me shivering and wet down by the beach and took me in. I don't know what would have happened to me if she hadn't helped out."

Sophie started to say that Annabelle already had a best friend and that was her, but she bit back the comment.

"It's so different here, Sophie. The women at the Painted Lady all work together; we watch out for each other, just like you and I did aboard Uncle Charles's ships."

"It didn't work too well with us, did it?" Sophie said.

"What do you mean?"

"I'll never forget that morning when I woke up and there wasn't a sign of you anywhere on board. I wasn't able to protect you then, was I, even with all our plans to finally escape."

"That wasn't your fault; it was Uncle Charles's fault. I don't know how he found out we intended to jump ship, but he wasn't going to let a couple of thousand dollars escape. We should have gone when we had the chance, Sophie. We just didn't think he'd work that fast."

"I wish I knew what they put in that tea that put us so soundly asleep. I'd love to use some of it on dear Uncle Charles and then dump him into the ocean where his body would never be found. A little murder here and there wouldn't hurt, wouldn't it?"

Annabelle smiled, knowing that her sister would remember the hours that they'd passed planning the deaths of various people they'd met who needed to die. They'd never carried any of the plans out, but the ideas had given them great satisfaction.

"I knew it had to be the tea. When I woke up two days later and started raising hell about where you'd disappeared to, the captain kept trying to make me drink some more of that loathsome stuff. I'll bet it was drugged and they intended to take me off the ship the same way, nice and quiet so I couldn't make a fuss."

"Red berries crushed up into a dark brown tea?" Annabelle asked.

"That's the one. I kept throwing it over the edge of the ship. Think of the poor fish around the harbor sick from having tasted that mess in their water. Anyway, when they wouldn't tell me anything about you, I started looking for a chance to jump ship and come looking for you. I did it, too, but finding your trail was a lot harder than I had expected it to be. It took a couple of ladies at the Pelado de Oro a long time to trust me enough to tell me you'd been shipped out to San Francisco."

"Whatever happened, I'm glad you're here. Now, where are you staying?"

"On the ship for now. There's plenty of room. Captain Jackson converted a lot of the storage areas into cabins that contained six or eight bunks and then made more money with people wanting passage to San Francisco than he could have made by bringing stoves and top hats. Most of the cargo that we have is supposed to go to Mr. Fry. He's going to pick up all the things that he ordered, and then I've got to find a buyer for the rest of the goods that Captain Jackson bought to sell in San Francisco."

"What kind of goods?" Annabelle brightened perceptibly.

"Nothing very useful, I'm afraid. Fans, fancy women's footwear, silks and satins, and a lot of cast-iron stoves."

"I can use some of it, but I don't know what you're going to do with the rest of that stuff. I'll help you sell it if I can. I'll ask Josie to help out; she's good at finding ways to make something out of nothing, and if there's a market for your things she'll be able to find it."

Annabelle stopped and stared at her sister. "Did you say Fry is going to buy some of your goods? Have you been to see him yet and did he pay you in cash, gold coins, before you ever told him where you are berthed?"

"No, he said he'd pay when he came to have his men unload. And I got him to promise to pay the full amount in gold coins, too."

"Damn, I wish you'd gotten the money right then. I don't trust that man. He's a cheat and a liar and I wouldn't let him have any of the goods until he's paid you in full and you know the coins are actually gold."

"Maybe I should go back to the ship and wait for him?"

"That might not be a bad idea. Come on, we'll both go back to the ship and then we can decide whether you really want to stay on board or not. Oh, I wish Josie were here; I did so want you to meet her. Why don't you come back with me tonight and we'll have a grand time, the three of us?"

Sophie was beginning to hate Josie even before she met her. How dare anyone be Annabelle's best friend except her?

"If the only thing you can offer me in the way of accommodation is a calico curtain between me and a bunch of rowdy gambling men, I can promise you I want to stay on the ship."

The two sisters talked steadily as they walked back to the *Salud Y Amor.* Abernathy trailed them, but his gloomy silence didn't affect their chatter.

They turned the corner on the last building before they reached the *Salud Y Amor* and Sophie abruptly stopped.

The ship looked different. The sails were all still in place, the gangplank was down, but something was different. It took a few moments for Sophie to focus on the waterline on the ship.

"Will you look at that," Sophie said, still not quite understanding what had happened.

"What?"

"The ship is riding a lot higher in the water. Look where the waterline used to be and where it is now." She was silent for a few moments while the implication of what she was seeing sank in. "Oh, Lord, you don't think? I'll kill him!" Sophie snarled as she ran for the ship. The ship's deck was deserted. There was no one guarding the gangplank, and she knew perfectly well what had happened without even checking.

Sophie heaved open one of the hatches to the cargo hold and looked down.

It was empty. Completely and utterly empty.

3

SOPHIE SWORE, USING WORDS THAT EVEN Abernathy had never heard before. She called down calumny on Fry's ancestors and his progeny, should he ever find a woman unlucky enough and ugly enough to inhabit the same bed with him and his pet bedbugs. She named physical attributes that she would permanently change if she found him alone in a dark alley, and she described in great detail fried tidbits she would prepare from the offending parts of his anatomy that she removed in that dark alley.

By the time she finished checking each of the holds, Abernathy had faded into the background, his face a strange shade of green caused by his overactive imagination picturing the curses that Sophie used and by the motion of the ship at the dock.

"Nothing. That pig-faced, flea-balled scrawny little bastard cleaned me out!" Sophie said, gritting her teeth.

"Not out of everything. He didn't touch the galley or the crew quarters or the captain's cabin. At least he left you with something," Annabelle said helpfully.

"I say, is that actually sharp?" Abernathy asked in fascination.

Sophie was flipping her knife in the air and catching it

expertly, the blade gleaming in the late afternoon sunshine. The one time she didn't make a clear catch, the tip nicked her finger and blood spurted out and dripped to the floor.

Abernathy looked at the blood and went even greener than he had been.

"Oh, yes, it's quite sharp. And it's going to do just fine on Mr. Fry when I catch up with him," Sophie said. Her smile made Abernathy blanch.

Sophie was still smiling as she continued talking. "They left the stoves. The miserable sons of bitches left the stoves because they were too heavy, I suppose. That's all I have left of everything I was going to use to make a fortune in San Francisco."

"You have the ship and you have whatever was in the quarters. It looks like there's some nice things down there, and if the captain's dead, it's all yours," Annabelle said. "I'm surprised, though, that Fry was able to find enough men to come and unload the ship that fast. There aren't that many able-bodied gents left in town; they've all deserted for the gold mines. Or if they've gone to the gold mines and come back, they're so sick with scurvy that they couldn't lift a feather."

"Men deserting?" Sophie remembered that Abernathy had mentioned something of the sort, but she hadn't listened closely to him.

"Surely," Abernathy said. "As soon as a ship reaches San Francisco, the crew disappears. Look around you. There's a reason there are four hundred ships sitting in the harbor rotting down to nothing. There's no one to sail them out of the harbor. The only one who has been able to put together a crew and actually get a ship out of the harbor bound for China is Fry, and there are some people who would love to know how he managed it."

"But people could live on the ships, couldn't they? Have you noticed the price of a single room in San Francisco? I was going to see about moving onto shore immediately, but I couldn't afford anything for more than a week at a time and that was when I thought I had five thousand dollars to back me up. The miserable son of a bitch, one of these days he's going to find out whether two parts of his anatomy can be shoved up his nostrils, one on each side, and then I'll pluck his nose hairs—no, I think I'll set fire to them and hope the stench kills him," Sophie said.

"Maybe in addition to torturing him, I'll kill him," Sophie added, continuing with her plans for Fry.

"I have a suspicion that you might actually be rough enough to attempt to harm Fry in retaliation. You must not do anything to him," Abernathy said suddenly. He was still green, which was an interesting contrast to his usual dead white pallor, but he was a little steadier on his legs.

"Why not?" Sophie was willing to listen to Abernathy; then she'd go kill Fry.

"You cannot confront Fry, scoundrel though he is, and never mind that I would like to watch you carry out most of your threats, especially the one about using him as cheap pawnshop sign with only two balls instead of three. But you must believe me, he cannot be touched."

"What do you mean he can't be touched? He came here and he stole my goods and I'm going to make him pay for them if it's the last thing I do." Sophie was getting tired of men trying to tell her what she could and could not do. "I'll take the money out of that dirty hide of his, I'll flay him alive and hang him for the rats, I'll make him go bald, hair by hair as I yank them out—"

"That's quite enough. I agree with you, but there's nothing that can be done," Abernathy said with some asperity. "You will not attack Fry because there's no way that you can prove that you had these goods and that he was to pay you for them and, further more, there's absolutely nothing to prove that he actually stole from you. Didn't you say he burned the contract?"

Sophie quieted down, simply because Abernathy didn't raise his voice and if she continued to scream she couldn't hear what he was saying. "He ripped it out of my hand and threw it into the fire. Everyone in that place must have seen him."

"And everyone in that place is in the pay of Mr. Fry himself. They won't come to your defense, if that's what you're thinking."

"I could ask."

"And you could get yourself killed. If no one will say that he owed you cash for the cargo, then there's no reason to suppose that you can prove that he came and stole the goods. No one saw him come here and take everything off the ship. You can ask around, but I promise you in San Francisco no one will have seen anything. You will just have to suffer the loss."

"I will not," Sophie said stubbornly. "It's my money, my cargo. I saved this ship from pirates and I sailed it to San Francisco and I will have my gold. Don't you understand, it's all that I have!"

"But you can't prove that it was Fry that stole the goods," Abernathy repeated, never letting his voice rise above a moderately sepulchral tone.

"He's the only one who could have known what I had on board. He's the one who said he'd come and pick up his goods. I can confront him. If his shelves are full now, he's the one. Isn't that proof enough?"

"Not really. Suppose we let you go down there and confront him. Suppose he's got lots of new merchandise. Suppose he tells you that none of the cans or cloth or whatever it is he's stocking up with came from this ship. You cannot prove that he stole anything. Even if you get someone to listen, he'll have paperwork, I promise you, and all you'll have is your word. Not very impressive, is it?"

Sophie was near tears as she saw the futility of trying to fight Fry.

Abernathy was relentless. "Furthermore, if he paid anything at all to the captain of this ship, he might just come after you for the price of the goods he already paid for."

"What good would that do him? I don't have it; he took it all."

"Yes, but he could make you leave the ship and take it over for his own use to pay him back for any money advanced on a cargo that he says he didn't get and that you can't prove that he did get. Mind you, I don't think he's smart enough to think of that, but the possibility is still there."

Sophie stared at Abernathy, trying desperately to come up with an argument against what he was saying. She couldn't think of a single thing.

"Don't you see, you *can't* confront him unless you can win. You have to have everything on your side and you have to be powerful and rich enough to carry it off. You are neither. Keep what you have and figure out a way to use it, because you're not going to get anything but trouble from Fry."

Sophie threw herself down on the bench and crossed her arms in front of her breasts. She was so angry she didn't trust herself to speak to anyone, and especially not Abernathy. She knew he was only trying to help her and she knew he was right, but that didn't make accepting the inevitable any easier. Abernathy was right; she couldn't prove anything. The only thing that was within her power was to swear vengeance somewhere, sometime later.

"Just wait, Sophie. You may not even have to do anything to get even with him. You're the last on a long list of people who'd like to have their way with his nasty little body."

"I don't want to wait."

"No, I'm sure you don't, but Abernathy is making sense, isn't he? And if you'll just give me a chance, I may be able to help you do real harm to Fry. Hurting him physically won't make a bit of difference to a person like him, unless we actually kill him. But oh, Sophie, if we can find a way to hurt him financially, that's what would bring Fry to his knees. It's worth a try, isn't it?"

"Why? What can you do?" Abernathy demanded, but Annabelle simply shook her head.

"I'll let you know," she said mysteriously.

"Sophie, can we come aboard?" Cristine's quiet voice startled all three of the people on board. When Sophie had said good-bye to her shipmates that morning, she'd thought that the voyage was over and they'd all go about their lives alone. She'd considered that they might be lucky enough to see each other in San Francisco once in a while, but it had never occurred to her that her shipmates might come back to the ship.

"Cristine? Dominic? I thought you'd be settled in your new homes by now."

"We would have been, but it seems we both encountered troubles we didn't expect," Dominic said. "I need your help."

"I need it, too. I have no place else to turn," Cristine said. She looked completely worn out. Her blue eyes were sad, and her blond hair had lost its shine and curl. She was still the picture of a proper matron, with her pristine black skirt, her black coat with the white trim, and a black bonnet. But the woman who had set out that morning to request help from the Presidio commander because her husband had died en route to his new station had disappeared, replaced by a woman who had obviously not been given what she thought she deserved.

"Who the hell is that?" Abernathy asked, looking up and then up again at Dominic's imposing bulk. Annabelle simply stared at Dominic in stunned silence. It was entirely possible that she'd never seen a Chinese-French man before, particularly not one who stood near seven feet tall and looked like a dark version of someone's garden god standing there on the deck. Whatever the reason for the stares, she was obviously amazed by his appearance.

"Cristine, Dominic, oh, I am glad to see you both! Let me introduce my sister, Annabelle, and her friend Mortimer Abernathy. And these are my friends, Cristine Halladay and Dominic Tibeau. These are the two who made it possible for us to sail into San Francisco instead of dying aboard the *Salud Y Amor* somewhere in the middle of the Pacific. And Cristine is the woman who sewed my nice new clothes. The first skirt and blouse and coat I've ever had, at least since we were kids," Sophie said, running her hand lovingly over the thick wool that Cristine had transformed.

There was a general shuffling and nodding as all of them acknowledged each other; then Sophie decided it was time to move everyone belowdecks before it got much colder. A sharp wind was sweeping in from the bay, and the ship was beginning to bob up and down as it pulled on the anchor.

Sophie noticed that Annabelle was eyeing Dominic. She wasn't sure she liked the intense gaze that took in every one of Dominic's assets, though why she should feel anything at all about Annabelle's perusal of the man baffled her. Dominic was her friend, not her lover, and certainly wasn't destined to be anything more than that.

Sophie heard, as clearly as if she were doing it herself, Annabelle's perusal of the man. His hair was black with a red overtone, something that Annabelle had never seen before, and his eyes were just slanted enough to give his European face an exotic cast. As far as Annabelle was concerned, he was one of the most handsome men she'd ever seen, with his high cheekbones and finely drawn lips. There was nothing about the man that didn't intrigue her.

Sophie decided it was time to get Annabelle's mind off the man.

"Let's all go down to the galley and I'll see if there's something to drink. Some tea would be fine, don't you think?"

"That would be wonderful. I'm parched with thirst and no one would even offer me a drink of water. All they think about in San Francisco is money, and it's the one thing I don't have any of," Cristine said.

"I'll wait up here," Dominic said.

"Now, come down and we'll clear a whole side of the table for you. You can stretch out there and be comfortable, can't you?" Sophie asked.

"I can certainly try," Dominic said, smiling at her. "It's nice to be wanted for the first time today."

It took several minutes to brew the tea and set out the last of the last batch of meat pasties and a quick batch of biscuits from some of the flour left in the barrel. Sophie served the hot tea with fresh lemons that she had found down in the darkest recess of one of the storage bins and plenty of sugar. Cristine looked like she could use some sugar.

"Now, tell me what happened." Sophie addressed the first question to Cristine.

"They won't have me at the Presidio. They were very nice about it of course, all sweet condolences on Kenneth's death while we were at sea and offers of help, but when I told them that the help I needed was in a place to stay and some way to pay the rent and buy food, suddenly they didn't have anything available. They turned me away." Cristine stopped and then smiled bitterly. "The captain did offer to marry me if I was willing. That way I'd have a house and food in return for my favors. He was fifty years old if he was a day and he didn't look any too clean, though no one seems to be clean in this town anyway. I turned him down; then I spent the rest of the day hunting for a place to stay and work to do."

"Did you find anything?"

"As you can guess, there were plenty of offers of a type of work that no self-respecting woman would ever even consider. Why, I'd rather die than compromise my standards."

Cristine didn't catch the look that Annabelle gave her, a slight roll of the eyes that showed just what she thought of Cristine's moral standards.

Cristine continued. "Then there was the housing problem. Oh, Sophie, they were asking three thousand dollars a month for a place no larger than the captain's cabin, and it wasn't even clean. Even worse, they wanted the money in advance. It did no good at all to say that my husband died of the fever and that I should have had an army pension, but they turned me away. No one was in the least sympathetic."

She laughed bitterly. "I've never been treated the way I was today. The people all looked at me like I was touched in the head even to expect the Presidio people to help me. I was told that things are different in San Francisco. Pay or leave, they said, or go get married today. So I'm back and I'd like to stay here for a while. Somehow I'll find money to pay you, but I don't think I can face that city again for a day or two."

Sophie reached over and patted Cristine's plump little hand that was just beginning to take on calluses from the work she'd been doing to help bring the ship into harbor.

"Of course you can stay. Isn't it lucky that you decided to leave your baggage here until you could send for it? It would have been horrible to try to carry that all over town."

"Thank you," Cristine said. "Maybe now that we're in port, we'll have time to resume our conversations about propriety and morals. I did find them interesting, didn't you?"

"Yes, I did," Sophie said. She'd found them fascinating, like visiting a foreign land and learning new customs. She was still trying to incorporate some of Cristine's dictums into her own life, but it was hard work for a girl who'd never even worn a skirt for twelve years.

Sophie turned her attention to Dominic. She watched as Annabelle looked him up and down, her eyes frankly apprais-ing. She was studying him as if she thought he was the most interesting-looking man she'd ever seen, and Sophie didn't par-ticularly like it. She wondered suddenly if her sister was thinking about the same appendage that had interested her so much.

"What about you, Dominic?" Sophie asked.

"I discovered that San Francisco is a little less open toward the Chinese than I had reason to believe when I came here. I was also unable to find a place to stay while I set up my business. Three thousand dollars would have been a welcome offer. The people I talked to were asking for ten and fifteen thousand a month for a place for me to stay. The French accent helps, but Chinese eyes do not aid in finding a safe, respectable address in this town. Several of the people were kind enough to direct me to Chinatown—they said I'd be more comfortable there—but when I walked up Stockton Street, I was stopped at least five times by men who warned me not to stay on the street too long and to be sure to be out of the area by nightfall. The Tong bosses there don't like mixed blood any more than the other people in San Francisco do."

He stopped and then brightened. "However, I did get one interesting offer. Seems that there's a circus somewhere around and I'd be a great sideshow there. Or, as one man told me, I could simply set myself up in a shop and rent out tickets to view myself and bring in plenty of money. Most people here seem to like a sideshow."

"That's not a bad idea. If you ever decide to do that, come to me first. I'd make a nice enough room for you at the Painted Lady," Annabelle said.

"Annabelle!" Sophie was shocked at her sister's forthrightness.

"Don't sound like that. Around here you do whatever you can to make an ounce of gold, and this guy could be a gold mine. I'm certainly not going to let someone else make him an offer first and then wish I hadn't missed out on having him in my place."

Sophie could have acted shocked, but she knew that she'd been just as guilty of sizing Dominic up almost as a sideshow freak herself during their voyage. She'd finally begun to see him as a real person once they'd been stranded on the ship after the plague.

Dominic stayed on the decks even when storms hit, and his massive strength had helped in setting and belaying sails faster than Sophie had ever seen it done. The truth of the matter was, there was no place for Dominic to go and nothing else for him to do except work and stay on deck, because he didn't fit anywhere else. Sophie had felt bad about it, but there was nothing she could do about it.

Sophie caught a stray thought and almost laughed out loud at the way her sister was mirroring her own curiosity. There was one thing that had intrigued her since she'd first met Dominic. His hands and feet were huge, his torso long and well muscled.

But it was what she couldn't see that intrigued her. She was devilishly interested in finding out if he was as big all over as he was in his arms and legs.

One of these days she'd have to tell her sister about the privy on the deck that everyone had used. Sophie had actually tried to catch a glimpse of the appendage that fascinated her so much, but he'd been very careful to observe all proprieties and she'd never had even a glimpse. She also wondered how he pleasured women if he was so large.

From her vantage point as a virgin, she wanted to know if a normal woman like her could accommodate such a man. These questions had burned for the entire voyage, and she had the horrible feeling that she was going to bid farewell to the man without ever satisfying her curiosity. At least if he started work in a circus she might see him in more revealing clothes, revealing enough to give her a chance to soothe her inquisitiveness.

"I decided that the circus, while interesting, wasn't what I wanted to do. I'd rather get on with my legitimate business, but thank you for the offer," Dominic said.

"What is your business, sir?" Abernathy spoke for the first time in what seemed like an hour.

"I have a great deal of experience in importing from China. My father has been in the business for many years, and I learned from him."

"Then why are you not employed with his company?" Abernathy pressed. "You will forgive the bluntness of the question, but there are too many people around here who profess to know about the China trade and then get lost on the way past the Farallons."

"No, sir, I did not say I was a sailor. I said I was an importer. If you can get me to China, I can buy wonderful things for you. Silks and fine carvings and bars for the saloons. Brass and copper work, exotic foods, and everything your trade could desire."

No one seemed to notice that Dominic had not explained why he wasn't working for his father except Sophie, and it only made her more curious about the man.

Abernathy put his thin fingers to his equally thin mouth and said, very quietly, "Men and women?"

Dominic tensed and then obviously decided that the question hadn't been meant to start a fight.

"No, sir, I do not deal in slaves."

The tension between the two men fairly crackled until Abernathy sat back against the rough pine bench and nodded. "Come and talk to me tomorrow. I might be in need of your services," he said. "I have an idea for trade both ways that might be advantageous to both of us."

Annabelle put her hand on his sleeve in a gesture that was almost too familiar as she looked up at Dominic. "Don't forget to come by and look at the Painted Lady. A lot of men use it as a place to make deals. It would be good for you to be known there."

"And it would be good for your business to have a freak in residence?" Dominic said it without rancor.

Annabelle shrugged. She wasn't going to tell him that it hadn't entered her mind what a draw he would be for the bar.

Dominic was already shaking his head. "I don't think I'll be taking any business into public bars. Not until I know how this city works and how difficult it will be for a man like me to be able to survive unscathed. While I was in Chinatown, some of the gentlemen warning me to move on took great delight in telling me what could happen to a Chinaman in the wrong part of town after dark. I think I'd rather not be part of someone's amusement."

"I'm sure things do happen, but not to people such as yourself," Abernathy soothed him. "Then I'll see you tomorrow."

"In the morning," Dominic confirmed.

Abernathy rose. "Annabelle, do you want to come back with me or make your own way back to the Painted Lady? I know you have much to talk about with your sister, but I'm afraid that I need to get back on solid land."

Sophie looked closely at Abernathy and realized that the man was still quite seasick. Even the tea that was guaranteed to settle the queasiest of stomachs hadn't worked on him.

"I do want to visit with her, but it's almost Christmas Eve, and things have been getting rather festive at the parlor. There's been a real increase in business, so I'd best go back and deal vingt-et-un for the rest of the evening. I must see about catching the men with the money who are aching to lose it all before the holidays. It's strange. They miss something they enjoyed back home, so they want to gamble away everything that they have in a kind of orgy of feeling sad for themselves. Remember the sixteen thousand that Black Ramsey dropped at my table on his birthday? I'd hate to miss a chance to make that kind of money again."

Abernathy nodded. He understood making money.

Annabelle put her arm around Sophie's waist as they stood together. "Tomorrow, you and I will sit down over a lovely meal somewhere and talk. Oh, Sophie, I'm so glad to have you back home with me. There are so many things to talk about," Annabelle said, hugging her sister as if she never wanted to let her go.

"Wouldn't you rather stay here in one of the cabins? It would be so much more private," Sophie offered eagerly.

Slowly Annabelle released her grip on her sister. "Thank you, but I have my own place now. I've come to like being on land. The bed doesn't move, the floor doesn't shift with each wave, and best of all, there's always something going on at the bar. Just imagine, Sophie, I can find someone to play cards with me any time of the day or night; it's pure heaven. You know how often I'm up and prowling in the middle of the night. I've never changed that habit, but here's the only place I've ever been able to make money while I prowled."

"She's good at the cards. When she finds someone to play cards with her, she makes it a point to leave him at least enough money for a meal after he's been cleaned out," Abernathy observed. "She's got a reputation for being fair."

Annabelle started to follow Abernathy out of the galley. Sophie noticed that for all her protestations about not wanting to be back on shipboard, Annabelle still automatically adjusted to the ship's movements at the dock, while Abernathy fought to keep his balance. There was a storm brewing in the ocean and the ship was riding high in the water, making the buck and roll even more pronounced.

Abernathy didn't stand on ceremony. As soon as he was back in the open air and in sight of land, he bolted down the gangplank.

"I'll wait for you down here!" he called as he rushed to get his feet back onto stable land.

"Poor Abernathy. He's very nice, but a little strange," Annabelle said as she turned back to Sophie. "I'd better join him though, before the men on that dock decide he's an easy mark. They know me, they'd never try anything because they know I've always got the knife, but Abernathy's different. Besides, I want to tell Josie all about finding you again. She's going to be so happy for me!"

Sophie wished that she could tell Annabelle to stay with her instead of rushing back to this new friend, but she smiled instead and hugged her sister.

They linked arms as they walked toward the gangplank. It was cold and getting colder with the wind sweeping in from the sea. A splatter of raindrops marked the deck and wet down Sophie's and Annabelle's almost matching curls.

"It's so nice to be together again. Tomorrow we'll take more time and really talk about the future. I think you might like to join us in the Painted Lady, once we tell you all about it. In fact, why don't you join us for the morning meeting? I don't think Josie and the others would mind at all," Annabelle said. "Meet me at the place at eight, all right? Once we're finished there, we'll go over to Parker House and celebrate being back together again."

"I'll be there." Sophie watched as her sister ran lightly down the gangplank and joined Abernathy. Within a few seconds the rain had increased to a downpour blotting out the figures as they hurried away from the *Salud Y Amor*.

Sophie stood in the rain and wished with all her might that her sister would come back to the ship and that they would be the way they always had been. They could sit together on the bed and talk about what had really happened since they were separated. They could have their nightly contest of seeing who could throw the knife the most accurately against a wall. Annabelle could tell her what she'd found out about San Francisco and how she'd made such a success of the Painted Lady. They could reminisce about the drawings that Annabelle had done on the inside of their cabin with stolen paints, until the tiny space had appeared to be a lovely glade in the middle of the mountains, with trees and birds and even a cat crouched underneath one of the bunks. Sophie had seen the same cat painted underneath one of the card tables at the Painted Lady, and it made her feel good that Annabelle hadn't forgotten that part of their lives.

She wished very hard that her sister would come back and stay the night with her, talking over the last months that they'd been apart.

Sophie waited until it was clear that not even her most powerful wish could pull her sister back to her. The rain sluiced down over her, masking her tears as she turned to go belowdecks and fix herself a stiff brandy to wipe away the pain.

4

SOPHIE HESITATED FOR A MOMENT OUTSIDE the Painted Lady. The city was coming to life. The windows and doors of the shops were being cranked open or propped open with a barrel, or even, in the case of some of the tents that served as buildings, the canvas was being rolled up to let the wan sunlight in to illuminate the building's contents. Sophie saw a man with two barrels and one plank setting up business as a lending institution and a woman with several pots of beans and at least twenty loaves of bread serving meals on metal plates that were used and reused without benefit of immersion in wash water.

Down the street she saw someone picking up what might actually have been a body and throwing it into a slow-moving wagon.

"Probably just drunk," she decided, shivering. But these were the alleys where men crawled to sleep and it made sense that some of them would die, especially if they'd been up to the mines and come back in such sad shape as Abernathy had described.

Sophie stepped through the canvas opening that had been tied back with a piece of rawhide. The Painted Lady was quiet inside. The gaming tables had only a few desultory players, the bar was open, but there were no buyers, and even the steps to the second story were empty.

"Annabelle, I thought you'd gone to bed." The man sweeping the floor peered at Sophie and then shook his head. "My mistake. You must be her sister. Welcome to San Francisco."

"Sophie, come on up; we're waiting for you!" Annabelle called out from the landing at the top of the stairs.

Annabelle was decked out in the most beautiful dress Sophie had ever seen. It was deep emerald green, cut low in the front and with great sweeping skirts that surely picked up all the trash from the floors. It was cut almost too low, Sophie thought, because her sister looked dangerously close to falling out of the dress. The second thing that caught Sophie's eye was the glitter of gold around Annabelle's neck. Even from the bottom of the stairs she could see that the necklace was made from a heavy gold chain hung with gold coins.

Annabelle saw her eyeing the decoration and laughed. "You're right. I'm never going to be caught without money again. Swimming ashore with nothing but the wet clothes on my back was frightening enough that I never want to go through it again. Some of the women are silly enough to ask for nuggets, but I know the value of coins; they're easier to spend in a tight spot. I even wear it when I'm bathing, just to be on the safe side."

Sophie knew exactly what Annabelle meant. If she ever made any money herself, she was determined to carry at least a good portion of it with her all the time. No matter what happened, she'd have cash for a place to stay and food to eat.

Sophie hurried up the stairs and embraced her sister and then stepped back to look at the necklace from close range. "But how did you make the first coin and then the next one, and enough for that?" Sophie gestured toward the coins, large and small, that hung from the chain. "It looks like you've got about twenty of them, and that's a fair amount of gold right there."

"Come on into my bedroom and I'll explain everything to

you," Annabelle said. "Remember, I said we'd have to talk about men, so now's as good a time as any."

Sophie trailed along, hanging back because for the first time in her life she didn't like the images that were part of the link to Annabelle.

Surely those graphic images couldn't possibly be true. Not after they'd spent their entire young lives keeping men from touching them. After all, Sophie might daydream about someone like Dominic, but the truth was, she'd probably slice off his hand if he tried to touch her. She was curious about things like the size of his penis, but she had doubts that she'd ever be able to let a man do to her what men did to women in holy matrimony. She knew that she'd been scarred by the men who had tried repeatedly to force themselves on her. Eventually she'd been able to recognize the signs of a man in rut simply by the way he walked. No one had ever gotten past her knife and no one ever would. Annabelle had been a little slower with her knife, but no one had ever gotten past her defenses either.

"Now, about how I earned these gold coins."

"I don't think I want to hear," Sophie said faintly.

"Yes, you do." Annabelle moved forward inexorably, pulling Sophie with her. "When I landed here I had nothing except my body. Remember, I told you Josie found me and helped me out? She gave me one of her best dresses, she fixed up my hair, and she told me all about the way she'd been earning a living since she came to San Francisco four months before me. She was earning enough money to keep herself in a nice room, the men were courteous, and she had the choice of who she wanted to sleep with. In fact, I don't believe she ever had more than a couple of men at any one time. They'd pay for everything, just to have the chance to be near her."

"But surely you didn't want to do that!"

"Surely I did. Sophie, I had nothing and no prospects of ever having anything. At first I told Josie I didn't think I could ever do what she did, but she told me that it wasn't nearly as bad as I thought and she was right. I stayed with her two nights, until it was clear that I had to start earning my own way. When I still hesitated, she let me sit down in the wardrobe in her room and watch her while she had one of her men friends up for the evening. I saw everything, things that we'd never even imagined when we talked about what men and women did. By the time I got out of there I was ready to take anyone she brought me. I never knew a woman could want that part of a man's anatomy quite as badly as I did!"

"You watched her? And you liked it?" Sophie asked.

"I did. She helped me find the first man. This is the first gold coin I ever earned, for parting with my virginity." She touched one of the largest gold coins, which held center place on the necklace.

Sophie wondered if she could stop the flow of words if she put her hands over her ears. But she knew better than that; Annabelle was determined to tell her all about it, and when Annabelle was determined to do something, nothing short of an act of God could stop her.

"But you've always hated to be touched! Remember all those times when we kept each other safe from the men who wanted us on the ships?"

"Yes, but this time I had a choice about who I went with. It wasn't like one of those drunk, dirty sailors grabbing us in the dark and trying to force themselves on us. This was my choice and I enjoyed it. Wait until you meet Sandy Ostroyvitch and you'll see why I didn't worry overmuch about losing my virginity, especially not for two thousand dollars. Sex is wonderful!" She grinned at her sister and smoothed the emerald green dress. "And look at what I get to wear. Remember when we used to dream about fancy dresses and fine jewelry? Well, I finally got it."

Sophie wanted to look everywhere except at her sister. She was horrified at the pictures that filled her mind. She didn't care what the reason was; she hated what her sister had done.

"I'm not sure that this is the way we thought we were going to earn all the fripperies."

"What does it matter how it's earned? It's mine now and the business is growing. There are four other women with me and we're all getting rich."

"The others work here doing that, too?" Of course they did; how could she have been so naive?

"Yes, of course, did you think they were just for pretty?"

"But I thought they dealt cards and did things like that. No . . . you know."

" 'You know' is the cause of most of our income. I see that look on your face and I don't know how I'm going to change your mind, but I really do have a wonderful life. I could have starved to death and no one would have cared. There are miners dying out there every day. But I'd gone through so much and lost so much that I wasn't willing to lose everything, including my life."

Sophie thought of the man she'd seen slung into a wagon today. Yes, her sister could have died. She wasn't lying. But Sophie's stomach still did strange things when she thought about what Annabelle did to earn her money.

Sophie couldn't think of one thing to say. Why hadn't she figured this out before? Or had she known and simply buried every possible clue so she didn't have to think about it? Those damned dreams came back to haunt her. She'd known; she just didn't want to acknowledge it.

"At least I don't have to do it."

"No, you don't have to, but I can tell you that you're missing one of the greatest pleasures on earth. I like playing with men; I like having them do naughty things with me. After all those years, I've discovered that a man's body is made for a woman to enjoy."

"I don't believe you!"

"Oh, yes, it's true. Sophie, if you decide that you want to try this wonderful invention out, let me help you get started. You'll be the one in control, you get to choose the man, and we'll promise that he'll be gentle and kind and everything you could want in a lover. We look enough alike that some of the rich men who are pestering me would be delighted to have a chance to court and bed you."

"I don't think so," Sophie said. "I've got some idea of what you've been doing because of the dreams; they were very real, you know."

"What? I didn't know we'd been connected like that."

"I've been dreaming about this and I didn't know where the ideas were coming from." It made Sophie feel better to have identified the source for the almost uncomfortably sexual dreams that she'd been having about Dominic. She had, in those dreams, explored every forbidden part of the man's body, and there had been several mornings when the memories of what had transpired in her mind in the middle of the night had been enough to make her blush every time she even looked at him.

"Yes, I suspected you'd been catching at least some of the fun. It's hard to keep quiet when the world is exploding in ecstasy. Now come on; we've got to get back to the ladies, who all want to meet you."

Sophie didn't know what to say. She'd never expected this. Well, no, that wasn't exactly the truth. She'd had those dreams that were like nothing else she'd ever experienced. She should have known, but she'd tried very hard to ignore the knowing.

"Last night you had to leave because of this?"

"Of course. I couldn't leave my gentleman friend sitting at the bar waiting for me to show up, could I? And I didn't want to say it in front of Cristine or Dominic, either. They've been raised to be proper; who knows what they'd think of my profession? For heaven's sake, Cristine has been married and I don't think she's ever had a night like I had last night."

"Oh, my."

"Think about the offer, Sophie. You wouldn't have to worry about Fry and his cheating you. Get into this business and you'll have more money than him in about a year, I promise you, because you've got what he doesn't and he can't buy or steal it." She pulled her sister up. "Come on and meet the girls. They're in the parlor having tea."

The other women looked up expectantly when Annabelle walked in with her sister.

"Ladies, this is my sister, Sophie. She arrived yesterday on the *Salud Y Amor*. Let me introduce you to Josie, Beatrice, and of course you already met Nellie."

"Welcome, Sophie. So how do you like San Francisco?" Josie asked. She was a startlingly beautiful woman with black hair, black eyes, and the kind of figure that Sophie had always admired, tall and buxom, with a tiny waist that was shown off to great advantage by the tight red dress that she wore. Sophie hated her the moment she laid eyes on her. How could Annabelle have this woman as a best friend? Then she pulled back, startled. What on earth was the matter with her, reacting like that? There was no reason for her to feel that way about Josie; she didn't even know the woman.

She took a deep breath and tried to keep smiling as she answered Josie's question.

"I think I like it, what I've seen of the town, but it doesn't look like there's a building here that's more than two years old."

Josie nodded. "You're right, of course. We're all new here, including this place and Dennison's Exchange next door and all the other buildings and what passes as buildings, except maybe the army outpost and the old mission," Josie agreed.

"Will you be joining your sister here at the Painted Lady?" Nellie asked as she picked up one of the small biscuits from the tray and popped it in her mouth. She was so white that Sophie wondered whether she powdered her face and white blond hair with anything to achieve the look of having been dead a couple of days.

"No, I don't think I'll be joining Annabelle. I have some other ideas for a business."

She was lying. She didn't have an idea in the world about

how she was going to make money to survive, but she wasn't going to become a whore. If her sister wanted to consort with all kinds of men, there was nothing she could do about it, but she was not going to give up the most intimate privacy of her body for a couple of gold coins.

"If you're going to do something else, why don't you open an eatery with some decent filling stews and breads and pies? We've got a Parisian bakery, and we've got a lot of slop houses, but nothing in between," Nellie said.

"We'd get about 20 percent more business if we could offer good food here, so you've got a ready market," Annabelle agreed.

"How much would you pay for good food? Is it really that hard to come by in San Francisco?" Sophie asked.

"Ha," Nellie said, flicking the rest of the crumbs from her fingers. "Food is a real sore spot in San Francisco, because what there is of it isn't that good and it all costs a fortune. I keep thinking of those huge chicken dinners that we used to have back on the farm, you know, with the creamed new potatoes and peas and butter gravy with the fried chicken and then a nice big apple pie with new cream? Oh, what I wouldn't give for a meal like that, but you can't find it here."

"No ingredients?"

"I'm sure the things are available somewhere, but mostly what it has to do with is who has the time to cook like that, and the answer is no one."

"Why are you asking about the food?" Annabelle asked Sophie. "You never learned how to cook, as far as I could see. Mostly what we ate was hardtack and tea."

"I don't know how to make a good meal, but Cristine is a fair hand at making something out of nothing. You heard her; she can't find a place to stay and a job that's not . . ." Sophie stopped and blushed.

"Right, not what we do. Her being an upstanding woman and all, she wouldn't want to do what we do," Annabelle said tartly.

"I can't help the way she is. But I do have all those stoves and it would be nice to earn some money off of them. I'm also thinking of renting out some of the space belowdecks to people who need a place to sleep. I have to use what I've got to earn money or I'll never get started here. Now, if I can convince Cristine to cook for us, how much would you pay for meals brought in for the gamblers?"

"We'd pay a lot, I can promise you. Every time we've had someone who could really cook, they took off for the goldfields and that was the end of them. But Cristine wouldn't do that, right?" Annabelle asked.

"No, I don't think she would. Shall I ask her if she's interested?"

"I think so. Josie, do you have any ideas for items that could be sold to the gentlemen? Sweet cakes, biscuits, even a small dinner pie?"

Sophie noticed how Annabelle asked her friend for ideas instead of asking Sophie, as she always had in the past. It hurt to see the changes that had already crept in between them.

"I'll work on it," Josie said. "But for right now, I've got a grand idea. Why don't the three of us go over to one of the hotels and have a meal there? We could use it as a chance to see if there's anything on the menu that we could steal and have someone else duplicate for the Painted Lady."

"I think that's a fine idea. We'll meet you at Abernathy's in a while and then we'll pick a restaurant. Right now I want to take a little time to talk to Sophie before she has to go back to her ship."

Annabelle didn't even ask Sophie if she wanted to go with them; she just assumed that Sophie would want to be with her sister's best friend.

"It was great to meet you all. I'm sure we'll be seeing each other again," Sophie said brightly and hurried out of the room and down the stairs, trailing behind Annabelle.

The sisters cleared the front doors and walked halfway down the block before Annabelle pulled Sophie to a halt.

"Now," Sophie demanded. "What was all that about?"

"I was afraid you'd—"

"Say something more? No, but I knew I'd said something that you wanted to talk to me about before anyone else caught up whatever idea it was that I had."

"They're all just fine, but they're as money-hungry as I am and they'd latch onto a good idea in an instant. I'd rather that you have a chance to make money from an idea you don't even know you've got yet than give it to those women for free," Annabelle said. She grabbed her sister by the shoulders and turned her around so she was facing toward the bay.

"What do you see out there?"

Sophie shrugged. "Water, ships, and more ships." The bay was clogged with ships that had sailed in and would never leave San Francisco Bay again.

"Ships. That's what I was thinking yesterday while we were on your ship and your friends came back because they couldn't find anything to rent anyplace in town, right?"

"Right."

"And look at all those places out there, just waiting to be rented!" Annabelle said triumphantly.

Suddenly it all came into focus, the idea that Sophie had given voice to, but that her sister had seen the potential of when she heard it. It was the way Sophie was going to make her fortune and wipe Fry off the face of the earth.

"Aha, now you see! The one thing that the people in San Francisco need more than anything else is adequate living space. There's no one around who can build the houses; they've all left for the goldfields. There's no one around to cook and clean; all the cooks have taken off to go panning. In fact, offer any service, even a service like what we offer at the Painted Lady, and you'll get rich."

"And I'll offer a clean, warm, safe place to sleep." Sophie liked the idea more and more as she thought about the possibilities.

"Right! You can buy those ships for pennies because they're not going anywhere and the crews and captains have abandoned them. You might not even have to pay anything, just board them and claim them as salvage. Make them over into places where men can sleep at a premium price until they find something more reasonable on land and you'll have your fortune."

Sophie was beginning to grin. It was the perfect plan. She already had the means to start using the space she owned, and it wouldn't cost her much to buy more ships for even more space. Maybe she'd keep the *Salud Y Amor* only as a bakery and as her own quarters instead of renting out the space.

"It would work. Most of the ships will be for sleeping, but the *Salud Y Amor* can be used to set up a bakery on board."

"Bakery? Yes, in the galley, of course, but there's all that extra space." This time Annabelle didn't follow the line of reasoning.

"No, the *Salud Y Amor* will be a cook's ship, not a sleeper, at least not right now. Remember, the only thing Fry didn't steal was those damned cast-iron stoves. I can use them to turn out enough baked goods to supply the Painted Lady with everything you could need in the way of food, and I'll save back enough of the food to be able to send it over to the sleepers and make even more money off of breakfast. I'll buy another couple of ships, the ones in the best shape, move them close to the *Salud Y Amor*, and use them for sleepers. I could be in business tomorrow if everything works out right. Cristine cooks, I put men up for the night, and maybe there'd even be a place for Dominic in the scheme of this enterprise."

"What could he do?"

"I don't know—if he's already got things settled, then I won't bother him. But if not, there's always things that a man of his size can do."

"Indeed there is," Annabelle said, licking her lips.

"I didn't mean it that way," Sophie said, embarrassed at her sister's innuendo.

"I know, but I did. Now, back to the important things. What about money?"

"That might be a problem." That was the understatement of the century, Sophie thought.

"I've got money and you can have it," Annabelle said. "Today I'll start buying up ships. What do you think, would five be enough to start with?"

Sophie just stared at her sister. It was all moving too fast for her.

"I guess five would be fine. But since Dominic is such a good sailor and probably knows a lot about ships, why not let him check for the basic soundness of the vessels?"

"Oh, I'll gladly have him look over every ship in the harbor and pay him for doing it if he'll take me with him," Annabelle said.

"No," Sophie said suddenly.

"Why not!"

"Annabelle, leave him alone, please? You've got everyone else; leave Dominic out of this. He's my friend, not just another piece of meat."

"He's free to make a choice, Sophie. If he doesn't want to play, he doesn't have to, but you're not his mother; you can't make those decisions for him. Why, are you interested in him and you want me to leave him for you? You don't want any competition?"

Sophie turned to her sister, shocked that Annabelle would say such a thing. They'd never competed against each other because they'd always been too busy protecting each other. This hurt almost as much as Josie.

"Don't look at me like that. I've changed these past few months and you'll change, too, once you've been here for a while. San Francisco is rough and if you live here that's what you become, rough and ready to fight for what you want. It doesn't matter who the competition is; the idea is to win."

"I'll try not to compete," Sophie said. She took a couple of steps toward the bay and the *Salud Y Amor*, then turned to face her sister again. "Can't we?"

"Go back to what it was like before I came here? Oh, Sophie, you have no idea how much I'd like that. To be like two parts of one person, knowing each other's thoughts all the time? It would be wonderful. But when Uncle Charles stole me away, he did more than take my body. He made me survive on my own, without anyone else around to help me. It was hard and I wish things were the way they were, but they're not. It's different now. Just remember, Sophie, however rough and hard you think I've become, I still think of you right after myself. It's a better break than you'll get from anyone else. Now, dear sister, I have to get back to the Painted Lady. I'll come by this afternoon and tell you where we can get the best buys for the supplies that you're going to need to start this new business of yours."

5

DOMINIC LISTENED INTENTLY TO THE IDEA and then took out a rumpled piece of paper from his pocket and began to sketch how her idea for turning ships into hotels could work aboard the *Salud Y Amor*. When she finished, he leaned over and presented her with a cutaway view of the *Salud Y Amor* showing how to put in even more cabins where the cargo had been.

"This is the basic design. It will work with the *Salud Y Amor* or with any other ship that you decide to buy. If you decide to use this ship, we could cut more portholes all around and give the men who rent a space with fresh air, a bunk, and a place to sit. I'd say, looking at the prices on land, you could probably average about one thousand dollars a month per cabin. If you can get the wood, I can give you eight cabins in addition to the ones that already exist."

"Eight thousand dollars per ship each month? I'll be rich!"

"Remember, that's minus the renovation costs."

"That's going to cost me a lot, I imagine."

"I don't know yet. I'll get prices for you."

"I need to talk to you about another idea, but it would mean that Cristine would have to help and I don't know if she'd be interested."

"Tell me what the idea is and I'll plan for it. If she isn't interested, we'll go back to the original drawing," Dominic offered.

"My sister said that she needs baked goods and meals to serve at the Painted Lady. There's no facilities to cook them at the house, but we certainly have the capacity to turn out large amounts of food here with all those stoves that Fry left behind. We can move them up on deck, and if Cristine will cook for us, we should be able to make some extra money from the prepared stuff in addition to renting out the ships."

Dominic sat back and his eyes took on a faraway look as he considered just how to work it all out.

"Yes, it'd have to be on the deck; there's no way to vent that many stoves from belowdecks and the heat would be unbearable."

"We'll keep belowdecks for us. Well, at least for Cristine and me, unless you want us to change around some of the cabins, maybe combine them, to make a place for you."

"Perhaps," Dominic said, but he was more interested in how they were going to move the stoves to the decks. There were already hatches and supply and equipment boxes and a privy on the deck; most of the usable space was already taken for some other purpose.

"I could remove this and this; that would clear some space," he said, indicating his drawings of the cargo boxes that were on the deck. "That will give you some space. I'm sure we could get four of the stoves in place, if Cristine thinks she can handle that many of them at once."

"I don't know whether she'll even agree to cook, but why don't we plan on it and if it doesn't work out then I'll go on to some other plan? If both of these ideas work, we'll be able to provide food and shelter. Both items cost a lot of gold in the city, and I'd like to get a little of that gold to come nest in my pocket.

I don't particularly like being broke, especially since it was a double cross that took away everything."

"I can understand that. I know what it's like to be poor in a strange town. There's nothing very fun about it."

Dominic turned back to his plans. "For just a little more time and effort, I can put up a framework for the stoves. They have to be tied down anyway. There's too much movement and it wouldn't be safe to use them otherwise, so I'm going to have to buy some bolts to keep everything in place. Then we can figure out a way to put up a canvas covering. You'll need something to protect you and Cristine from storms while you're working." He leaned over her shoulder and traced the various points with his finger as he talked. "I think it would work out, though. It's a grand idea."

"Do the stoves first, then. The faster I can get money coming in, the better for all of us. I just wish Cristine would come back so I could talk to her and make sure that she agrees with all of this."

Sophie looked back down at the drawing. "This is exactly what I want, but if what you said yesterday is right about every able-bodied man in the area deserting jobs to go to the gold mines, where will we get the carpenter to do this kind of work? I can do some of the work, but not all of it."

Dominic bowed deeply. "A carpenter at your service, madam. I've worked with wood since I was little. I've always had a talent for working with wood."

"I thought you were an importer."

"I am, but right now it doesn't look like I'll be able to be on a vessel sailing for China for a few months, so I might as well help you."

"Do you really know what you're doing with wood?" Sophie was skeptical that someone as large as Dominic could actually do anything except drive nails with his bare hands. He'd never be able to do careful, precise tiny cuts.

"I'm a very good carpenter," Dominic said, his pride wounded by her obvious distrust of his skills. "I used to have to sneak out of the house to be with the men who fixed up my father's estate outside of Paris. I learned with the best, and I can build fine furniture or a house, depending on what you need. I learned everything those men could teach me about how to handle wood."

Sophie was beginning to think that maybe she was wrong; maybe he could do the work after all.

"Your father must have been proud. That's a fine skill to have." Sophie had developed what little talent she had over the years with men who were willing to teach her to work with wood as long as she took over some of the jobs during a voyage. No one had been proud of her; they'd only been interested in lightening their own load.

"My father hated my interest. He said it was beneath me to learn something so low-class. People of wealth and title don't do such things. He never did explain why working with my hands was so terrible. Despite him, I am a good carpenter. I believe I could make the change with a minimum of fuss and bother. It will at least earn my keep on the ship until I can find another place to stay."

"Earn your keep? You helped sail this ship into San Francisco, and you and Cristine can stay here as long as you want free of charge. You're my friends, for heaven's sake!"

"You'd let me stay here without charging? But I expected to pay!"

Dominic sat down abruptly, almost bumping Sophie off the hatch cover where she'd settled to look at the plans that he'd drawn.

"Of course I would, silly. You just hadn't asked before. I thought you were so sick of the *Salud Y Amor* that you just wanted to get ashore and stay there. I also intend to let Cristine stay as long as she wants, until she finds something she likes better."

Dominic sighed and closed his eyes for a moment. "Thank you, Sophie. No, I didn't know that I could stay here. I thought perhaps for one night, last night when I couldn't find another place to sleep, but not indefinitely. In fact, I walked around the city yesterday looking for a place where I could sleep out in the open and still be protected if it came to that. Do you have any idea how many places won't even think of renting to me because I'm big? I'm sure being a half-breed doesn't help either, but my size is something that people notice right away."

Sophie knew exactly what he was talking about. The first time she'd laid eyes on him, she'd looked up and then up again, just like Abernathy. Dominic had walked aboard the *Salud Y Amor* and she'd thought how difficult it was going to be for him aboard what was a very small ship. "A man like you needs his comfort. You need to be able to stretch out flat without worrying about what you're going to be bashing up against."

"It hasn't been easy, but then living hasn't been easy anyplace except at home, where I helped the carpenters make a bed and sneak it upstairs for me."

"Sneak something into your own home? Why would you need to do that?"

"My father decided when I reached six feet at twelve years old that I was a freak. He was convinced that if I had to sleep in a regular bed, use a regular chair at the table, with everything exactly as it would be for a normal-sized person, I would somehow shrink to fit the rest of the world."

"And you never did."

"No, I never did, much to his disappointment. It was strange. He started out as an adventurer, a person who didn't care what others thought of him. Then, the older he got, the more he began to crave acceptance into society. I don't know why he was so obsessed with those people. I never thought society had that much to offer, but once he'd made his money, he wanted to be one of the elite. It even drove him to throwing my mother out so he could have a young Frenchwoman as his wife so everyone would accept him because of who he married."

"He sounds horrible! What happened to your mother?"

Dominic hesitated an instant before he answered. "He sent her back to her family in China last year. I was gone, taking care of some business in Nice, which is probably why he picked that time to get rid of her. He knew that if I'd been there when he tried to send her away, I'd have lifted him off the rug, hung him from a meat hook, and left him there to rot until he changed his mind about what he was going to do to my mother."

"So he didn't tell you in advance? Smart man, he must have known how you'd feel about it."

"By the time I got home she was on her way back to China. Of course it was almost thirty-five years after he bought her, so her family is almost certainly dead. He was sending her back with nothing, to die in a place that was as foreign to her now as it would be to me."

"What will happen to her?"

"If she actually made it to China, she is probably dead by now. There are no people who would be willing to take her in as part of a family, and without family she could not survive very long."

"You don't think she went to China, do you?"

"No. That's one of the reasons I came to San Francisco. My mother is a smart woman. She somehow figured out what my father was going to do to her long before it happened. She knew that he didn't want to keep her as his 'wife' any longer when he started holding parties that didn't include her because he'd be embarrassed about her accent when she spoke French and because she didn't look like the other women. You must understand, she was raised in an area where French missionaries taught school, and she had a better Parisian accent than my father did. She was also smarter than my father. Over the years she carefully put aside any money that came into her hands. Then, months before my father had the courage to send her away, she stole a large amount of gold and sent it ahead of her to San Francisco so that no matter when she was banished, she would have something to live in comfort on."

"What made her decide to steal so much more at the end? If she'd been sending money steadily, she must have had a good amount of savings."

"My father made her so angry that she decided to retaliate. He was sneaking around behind her back trying to find a wife with some royal blood, and my mother heard about it. She told me the last time I saw her that if he was going to treat her like garbage, then she was going to act in her own self-interest, and she did."

"But if she was actually forced to go to China, she'd never have a chance to retrieve the gold." Sophie knew what it was like to be forced aboard a ship and made to stay there with no choice in destination. That was how her uncle had managed to send Annabelle and her all around the world on his various ships.

"That's right. But I'm certain that she has found a way to come here and get her gold. Just like with your sister, all I have to do is find her."

"When your father sent your mother away, did he also tell you to leave?"

Dominic leaned against the wall as he relaxed. "No. I was away working in a branch of my father's importing business, living in a tiny apartment with almost no furniture because my father wouldn't pay me enough to buy even the wood to make my own. I had come home to tell him that either he had to start paying me or I was going to hire on to his competitors for a living wage. I didn't know that the troubles between my parents had boiled over and left me with nothing until I found him with his new wife and every trace of my mother gone. The servants were the ones who told me what really happened."

Sophie's hands clenched involuntarily. "What did you do? Is he still alive?"

Dominic smiled, but there was little humor in it. "My father is alive only because he was gone when I found out what he had done. There isn't much of the house surviving, though. It's amazing what a man my size can do to destroy things if he's really angry."

"I'll have to remember that," Sophie said. "I wouldn't want you to get angry with me."

"Never, my friend," Dominic said.

Sophie looked at him in surprise. Yes, she guessed that they could be called friends. It was a strange word to think about, *friend*, since she'd never had one before in her life.

"Now, what would be most comfortable for you as long as you stay here? I'd hate to have you think that we were treating you as badly as your father did. Would you like a cabin belowdecks, or a place set aside for you up here?" Sophie asked.

"I can sleep as I have been," Dominic started to say.

Sophie interrupted him. "No, you cannot. It's winter, it's cold, and the fog goes through you like a knife no matter how many layers of clothing and covers you have on. You need a place where you can be safe and warm."

"Perhaps two cabins then, even though it is difficult to walk down there."

"Why not build a cabin on the deck?"

"Because there isn't going to be space, not with all the stoves."

"All right," Sophie said, "belowdecks it is."

Dominic studied her for a moment, searching her face as if there was something in her features that would give him a clue about some mystery. "Why would you offer me this comfort? You aren't part of my family; you owe me nothing."

Sophie shrugged. "Simple. I like you, and you deserve better than you've had here before. Also, if you're going to help me with getting the ships ready to rent out, it pays to keep you happy."

"That is very kind of you," Dominic said, touching her hand lightly.

Sophie leaned forward and sealed the friendship with a quick kiss.

"No!" Dominic said it more as an explosion than as a word. He took her by the shoulders and pushed her away from him.

"No?" Sophie asked, bewildered as she shrank away from him. "What did I do wrong?"

"Christ, woman, what do you want to do? Get me lynched? Get yourself killed? Don't you understand what you're playing with? Look out there!" He turned her roughly so she could see the men working along the wharf. "Look at them and think what they could do to us if they happened to look up at the wrong moment!" His voice was anguished. His hands dropped to his sides.

She stared at the men and then turned back to Dominic.

"Don't worry; they'll never touch us. Besides, none of them care about us; they've all got their own problems."

"And you are incredibly naive if you think that men can't forget their own problems and enjoy a good lynching any day they find a Chinaman stupid enough to kiss a white woman."

Sophie would have liked to argue with him, but she didn't know enough about what people did on shore to be certain that he was wrong. After all, Cristine, who was from a proper Baltimore family, wouldn't even sit down at the same table with Dominic. When he walked past her she averted her eyes as if he didn't exist. When Sophie had asked her about it during the voyage, she'd only been willing to say that nice women didn't acknowledge the presence of such men. It had taken Sophie days to figure out that Cristine meant she didn't like Dominic because he was Chinese.

"Sophie, I like you; you're a very nice woman. But for right now, don't do anything that could get us both killed, all right?"

Sophie nodded, but once again her stomach had that funny unsettled feeling that she got when she realized that living ashore wasn't going to be nearly as easy as she'd thought. There were just too many rules that she didn't understand and too many ways to break them.

6

YOU, BOY, I'M COMING ABOARD MY SHIP. PUT down that wrench and step back before you do any more damage. Just look at what you've done to the deck; how am I supposed to repair that? And you've taken the cargo boxes off. That's stupid. Where will I store my things?"

Who the hell is that fool yelling at? Sophie looked up from wrestling with a bolt that didn't want to be screwed down into the planking on the deck. She squinted against the sunlight to see whom the man was talking to.

She had picked up a bar to bash the bolt past the point where it was stuck when the man started screaming again.

"Put that bar down. I told you, don't do a thing to my ship!"

He's yelling at me?

"Put that bar down or I'll rip it out of your hands and use it on your head, boy."

"I'll use it on your head, you lubber," she said, giving the bolt a smart rap that moved it downward again. The man was more than likely a drunk; they were prone to yelling indecipherable orders at people. The best thing she could do was ignore him.

She wasn't surprised that whoever it was couldn't tell that

she was a woman; she'd gone back to wearing her canvas pants and thick cotton shirt. There was always a cold wind off the bay, so she'd added the captain's old gray work sweater to the outfit, along with a cap to keep her head warm.

There was something awfully familiar about that voice. Even though she couldn't place it right away, she knew it was someone she didn't like.

"Come on, put the bar down," the man ordered again, and she finally got a fix on the last time she'd heard that voice.

"Fry," she whispered. Her grip on the bar tightened until her knuckles were white. She stood up, swinging around to face the man as he headed up the gangplank. He was wearing the same dirty vest and the same trousers that were turned up at the ankles because he couldn't find anyone to hem them to the right size. He'd added a greatcoat of some indeterminate cloth that looked just as dirty as everything else he was wearing and was so long that it swept the debris from the wharf with every step.

She shuddered to think of the dirt and offal that had collected around the hem of the garment. And he still stank.

"Put that wrench or whatever it is down and we'll talk about you getting the hell off my ship. I don't know who sent you here to work, but the job's finished as of this instant. And I'd like to know where the woman is who thinks she owns this place, because she and I have a bit of talking to do."

Abernathy's warning rang in her mind. Damn him for being right! He'd told her that Fry might try to come back and claim everything.

Sophie barred his way at the top of the gangplank.

"Get off of this ship. This isn't yours and I'm not giving you permission to board."

Fry looked her up and down contemptuously. "I'm aboard and I'm going to stay here, so move out of the way."

"You and who else are going to make me?" Sophie challenged him.

"Me and my friend Daniel here." Fry motioned for a man

who had been standing at the bottom of the plank to move forward.

She recognized him; he was one of the men who had been standing around in the shop when she came in to sell the cargo. Her heart dropped as he bounded up the gangplank. While he wasn't as large as Dominic, he outweighed her by a good hundred pounds and was taller by at least a foot. He bowed at her and then lounged back against the ship's rail and crossed his arms, waiting to see what Fry wanted him to do. It made Sophie's blood boil to see him looking like he was at home on her ship.

"Go and get the woman, you know, the red-haired devil. It's time she finished paying her debt to me."

Sophie didn't move. "What does she owe you? You're the one who stole everything from her in the first place."

"That's none of your business. Go find her."

"What if she's not here?"

"Then you'd better head out to town to look for that redheaded little bitch while I search this ship and find out what kind of shape it's in and what else can be salvaged off it before it's towed out into the harbor and allowed to rot."

Fry started to push pass her and go belowdecks, but Sophie stopped him.

"Don't you move one step closer. This is my ship, not yours, and you are standing on my deck. Get off it right now. There's the gangplank and don't come back," Sophie ordered. She took one step forward and was delighted to see Fry back up.

He wasn't finished, though. He tried blustering. "Don't be stupid; it's not your ship any more than my shop in San Francisco belongs to that man over there," Fry said, nodding toward his goon.

"No, I mean it's my ship and I mean that you will leave right now." Sophie pulled off her cap, revealing the red hair that Fry found so objectionable.

Fry's eyes narrowed and his mouth stretched in an ugly grin.

"You! I should have known. You and your sister cooked this up, didn't you?" He was so angry that a collection of spit wobbled on his lips as he talked. "You think you're going to drive me out of business by squeezing me until I'm broke, and you're wrong. I'm going to take everything away from you and then I'm going to work on your sister and by the time I'm done you'll have nothing! Do you hear me? Nothing!" He pushed his face close to hers, spitting as he screamed.

Sophie gagged as his fetid breath rolled over her, but she refused to flinch. Instead she matched him scream for scream.

"I didn't do anything to you; you stole the cargo from me! I'm not wrong; you are. No matter how you try and talk your way out of it, you're trying to steal even more that isn't yours and I'm not going to let you do it! Furthermore, my sister didn't do a damned thing to you, so leave her out of this!"

She punched him on the shoulder with each sentence, knocking him off balance and making him stagger away from her. She wanted him off her deck so she could breathe again without gagging. "Get out of my way; get off my ship and don't you ever come back!"

Fry backed up against a hatch and stayed there only because he couldn't retreat anymore. "Your bitch sister raised the rent on the land under my store so high that I can't afford to pay it; that's what she did to me. Today I got a notice from her that either I pay immediately, including back rent from the first of the month that amounts to almost ten thousand dollars, or she's going to evict me. So I'm moving to this ship and there's nothing you can do to stop me. I figure it's mine, since your good captain had bargained with me for the goods that he was carrying anyway. The order was short, he still owes me money, and this is the way I'm going to get repaid. Now get off it before I have you thrown off, and don't try and come back."

Fry looked her up and down, assessing her charms. "Or I might be able to use you in other ways, if you won't leave voluntarily."

Sophie shivered and then hoped he hadn't seen the small movement. She was sure that he could see everything right through the heavy canvas shirt and men's pants, and it made her sick to her stomach to be looked at that way. Her hand went to her knife that lay against her hip.

He took another step toward her and she was engulfed in the smell that stayed with him, like the smell of a pig that was locked in a pen that was too small and had to bathe in its own urine.

The goon stepped between Sophie and Fry, looming over her. "That's right, missy; just walk off this ship and no one will get hurt. Force me to make you leave and you might not like what happens." He smiled, what was left of his jagged teeth filling his gaping mouth. "I wouldn't mind that one bit; I like that part of the job. And little girls like you shouldn't play around the men; you could get hurt and you don't have anything to fight back with, now do you, sweetie?"

Sophie considered slicing the smile off his face and baiting hooks with his lips. She could do it if she whipped out the knife that he couldn't see in her belt. She decided to leave his lips intact for a few more moments until she knew exactly how hard she was going to have to fight him to retain custody of the *Salud Y Amor*.

She also didn't want to give away any information about how well she was armed. The element of surprise might help her if she had to fight them, though she had no doubt that she could do serious damage to both men before they had a chance to realize what happened to them. No, not the lips. She'd go straight for the goon's heart to get him out of the way so she could get to Fry.

But Fry—oh, Fry she'd kill slowly. First she'd go for the belly and then maybe into the lungs to do a little damage there, cutting them loose and making him cough blood as the tip sliced into the spongy lungs and then finally the heart. She'd probably finish him off before throwing his body into the bay. She'd heard rumors of sharks; she'd like to see if they'd stoop low enough to eat someone like Fry. Just tickle the muscle with the tip of the knife, she thought happily. She'd love every single moment of making him suffer.

"You'd better leave," the goon said, unnerved by her sweetly sinister smile and the faraway look that she had in her eyes. He shifted uneasily from foot to foot, expecting an attack at any moment.

"Throw her off now," Fry ordered the man forward. "You're standing on the deck of my new store, because no one, not you, not your sister, no one is going to try to put me out of business and get away with it."

The goon stepped forward but stopped in midstride when Sophie showed her teeth. It wasn't a smile, it was a threat, and he'd been in enough fights to know the difference immediately. Bared canines made him very wary.

Fry grabbed her wrist, intending to throw her down the gangplank until he felt her soft skin beneath his hand. His thumb began to caress her wrist and he licked his lips. "I'll take you, then. You can keep the ship, but you'll have to keep me, too. How's that for a trade, a ship for my bed?"

"Never!" Sophie tried to pull away from him, gagging from having to be so close to him, but he was surprisingly strong and she couldn't break free as easily as she'd thought she could.

"Don't be so hasty. Think about it. I can take care of you and you'll be wealthy and safe. It's a fair trade."

"I'm not for sale, not for the price of a ship that's mine already," Sophie said.

"Ah, so we've already determined that you are for sale. Now tell me what your price is and we can get on with the bargain." Fry laughed, having trapped her with her own words.

Sophie gasped and closed her mouth. She'd walked right into that one and hadn't even seen it coming.

He reached out one filthy finger and caressed her cheek. It was all she needed to push her over the edge.

"Get your hand off me or you are going to lose it," she said, her teeth still bared. Her voice sounded normal, even slightly sweet, but anyone really listening closely to her would have heard the sharp steel underneath the words.

"Oh, my little darling, you don't have to fight me. I want you and I do intend to have you."

His hand stank just as bad as the rest of him, a mixture of sweat and dirt and things she didn't even want to think about. His nails were black and crusted, and she couldn't even begin to see what his normal color really was.

Sophie stepped back and he followed her. She took another step back and collided with Daniel, who had somehow gotten behind her. His thick arms went around her, holding her in place.

Damn, how had she forgotten the goon while she was dealing with Fry?

She couldn't reach her knife.

Fry leaned closer, his hand cupping her chin so he could kiss her.

She smelled his rotted teeth before his lips clamped against her and she tried to scream and wrench her head away. She couldn't get loose. Fry was about to overpower her and there wasn't a thing she could do about it. Or maybe there was.

She went limp.

Daniel was caught completely by surprise as she dropped out of his arms and crashed to the deck. She began to scramble away from the two men.

"No!" Fry howled, seeing his prize slip away from him. He reached for her, but she bobbed away.

"Come back here or I'll take you to a place where you'll never be found again and you'll still end up doing what I want!" Fry screamed.

He had his hand on her shoulder, pulling at the old gray sweater, when she swiveled on the deck and came up just at crotch level. She hated to do it—it would make her vomit afterward—but there wasn't any other way to make Fry leave her alone.

She bit him in the crotch, grinding her teeth through the filthy pants and hoping against hope that she was seriously wounding or completely emasculating the man.

Fry screamed and began to beat at her head.

She bit harder, until he balled his hand into a fist and smacked her as hard as he could on the side of the face. Her eyes rolled back in her head and she hit the deck, dazed and unable to move. She tried to see through the pain, but she couldn't even focus her eyes, the anguish in her head was so bad.

"Help me," she whispered, but there was no one to hear her plea.

"That'll teach you." The goon's heavy boots smashed into her side and she felt ribs give way under the assault. Blood welled up in her mouth. She couldn't tell if it was from inside her or if she'd bitten her own lips. She tried to reach for the knife, but she couldn't bend her arm back that far without screaming from the pain of the cracked ribs.

Sophie felt the goon lifting her and knew that the next thing she'd feel would be the cold waters of San Francisco Bay closing over her head. Her sister would never know how she died.

Suddenly there was an inarticulate roar and the blows stopped and she sagged back to the deck. She tried to open her swollen eyes, but the blood streaming down from a cut on her forehead turned everything red and opaque so she couldn't see anything.

Fry screamed just once, Daniel swore vividly, and then there was a sound like barrels rolling down the gangplank and a splash at the end of the roll.

"And don't ever set foot on this ship again or the next time I kill you," Dominic said in a low growl.

7

SOPHIE HURT. IN HER DREAMS, THE WILD SEA threw her against the sides of the ship, bruising her with the impact of the blow. She screamed as she tried to turn away from another whack against the hatch cover, but she hit it and the pain cut through her, leaving her gasping for breath. Her head ached from the constant rocking of the ship, and in her dream she wondered why her teeth and jaws were so sore.

It hurt to breathe because every movement of her lungs made it feel like someone was stabbing her side with a very dull knife. Through it all she could hear voices telling her to come back. Annabelle, Dominic, Cristine, she could hear all of them calling, but she couldn't figure out where they wanted her to come back to or how she was supposed to get there. She was caught in the middle of the stormy seas and dark nights and there were no lights to show her where to go.

Occasionally there was an overpowering scent of lavender or attar of rose and voices that she didn't recognize and the feeling of warmth along her face and sides, but for the most part it was simply dark and storm-tossed and painfully frightening.

Gradually the seas calmed and she didn't hurt quite so badly from being bashed against wood and brass.

She opened her eyes slowly. She was still in the captain's cabin, and the ship was still, or a least as still as it could be while in port.

She remembered. She was in San Francisco Bay.

The horrible storm that had threatened to sweep her away and all the pain that she'd felt from hitting the sides of the ship and the brass railing had only been a nightmare.

The nightmare was over and it was time to get up and work. There were changes to be made on the ship, and she and Annabelle had to look at likely ships that they could buy.

She started to swing her legs over the side of the berth and screamed. Daggers pierced her legs, her hips burned with pain, and her head threatened to fall off if she moved it one more inch. Somewhere she'd gotten beaten up by a gang of thugs, that much was obvious, but where and how?

It took a couple of moments for the pain to subside. She realized that she hadn't actually moved more than an inch and that the scream that she'd let out had been nothing more than a moan.

Annabelle sat beside her, oblivious to the world around her as she worked on an intricate drawing of a room where two women sat before a fireplace sipping tea and talking. Two cats lay in front of the flames, their backs to the warmth as they stared into the darkness behind the women. The fire threw shadows across the women's faces and illuminated odd corners of the room behind them where demons seemed to be poised for attack in the middle of the shadows. It was a picture that Annabelle had drawn before when times were difficult for them, but this time the demons seemed larger, their hands grasping ever closer to the women and the danger present in every inch of the room.

"What the hell happened to me?" Sophie rasped. She tried to sit up and then fell back against the pillow as a claw descended on her head and threatened to rip her eyeball out of the socket if she didn't stop moving. She gasped as another claw grabbed her side. Those demons that Annabelle was drawing seemed to have taken up residence in her body.

"Welcome back. We weren't sure you'd survive," Annabelle said, putting her picture aside and gently pushing her sister back against the pillows and blankets.

"What happened to me?" Sophie repeated. She only had fragments of memories of fists and boots crashing into her, but she wasn't sure that they were hallucinations just like the storm had been.

"Fry and one of his buddies happened to you. It's a good thing that Dominic showed up when he did, or you might have been feeding the fish right now. They were about to throw you overboard so they could take over the ship."

Annabelle stopped and smiled, a sweet smile that worried Sophie every time she saw it, because it meant that Annabelle was up to something that probably wasn't going to end well for someone else. It was the same kind of smile that Sophie had used toward Fry right before she tried to emasculate him.

"I'm going to kill him, you know. One way or another I'm going to end up with Fry's blood on my hands, and I'll wash those hands in whiskey and dance on his grave and then go out to eat a celebratory dinner. From the way Dominic was talking, he'd be willing to help out."

"Why?"

"When he saw Fry's man lift you up and start toward the railing to throw you into the sea, he had to save you. He ran up the gangplank, grabbed the man around the neck, and forced him to walk him over to an old sail and had him lay you gently down on the cloth so you wouldn't be hurt any worse than you already were. All the time this was happening, Fry was lying on the deck vomiting. The way I heard it, you almost severed his penis. It made it easy for Dominic to grab the men and throw them off the ship. They never got a chance to do whatever it was that they had planned. You'll have to tell me about the whole mess when you feel up to it."

"Did they hurt Dominic?"

"Ha! He has a couple of bruises where the man landed a kick or two, but the last report I had said that neither Fry nor his henchman was able to walk away from here under his own power. They had to be helped after Dominic rolled them down the gangplank like two tenpin balls. They hit that water and paddled around howling and cursing."

"They hurt me; they deserved to die. It's just a matter of time." Sophie was delighted that the men had paid for their attempted thievery.

"Fry didn't kick you; he was too busy kneeling on the deck vomiting. It was the other man who kicked you. But tell me what exactly did you do to Fry that almost cut his penis off?"

"I bit him."

"You actually laid teeth on him?"

"Only through the clothes. I thought I was going to be sick, putting my mouth that close to his filthiness, but it was the only way to stop that madman. He just kept hitting me, trying to disconnect my head from my neck. He wanted the ship and he was going to take it and he didn't care who got hurt in the process." Sophie stopped talking and raised a hand to her jaw, which ached terribly when she moved it.

"Yes, you took a clop alongside your jaw. Probably Fry was trying to get you to stop biting him. I checked you over and it doesn't look like there's anything broken. I've been using a poultice on it and dripping rum and willow tea into your mouth to help with the pain."

Sophie grimaced. "That's where the strange taste came from. Willow is so bitter that even rum doesn't cover it."

"I know, but aren't you glad that I know about it? What would we do for the pain otherwise, use plain rum like the men do?"

"No, willow bark is nice to have," Sophie agreed. "At least

you didn't have to sew up anything with sail thread, like Hannibal did that time he caught his hand in the winch and almost cut it off."

"God, that was horrible. I wonder if his fingers ever worked again after that. And as for rum, I'd rather use the Chinese remedies to keep you from getting blood poisoning and such. I think I got it right, but let me check. I've been using cherry and wormwood for the fever and putrefaction. It's all I've got; is it good enough?"

Sophie had been a better student than Annabelle, but they both knew enough to manage their own care without having to go to most doctors. "That's what Tsao Liu said worked best, of the herbs that we had on hand. If there's anything else, I don't know about it."

Annabelle handed her sister a small poultice of herbs bound in a piece of linen. "Here, put this against your jaw; it'll take down more of the swelling."

Sophie complied, even though the brew that the old piece of cloth had been soaked in didn't exactly smell wonderful.

"If you think you can sip something, I've got more willow bark and a couple of other things brewed up into a tea, sweetened with honey and rum. How about it?"

"Let me have it, please." It wouldn't have mattered if the mix had been pure bitterroot; she needed something right away to ease the infernal pain along her ribs and jaw.

"What do I look like?" Sophie finally asked, once she had drunk a whole cup of the tea and the pain had begun to ease just a little. She could feel swelling all over her face, and her eyes still couldn't open to more than just slits.

"You look like your face has disappeared into a sea of blue and red flesh, and your eyes are swollen. Your body isn't much better. I stripped off the clothes that you had on. The heavy woolen sweater and the pants protected you some, but not enough. I was worried because one of those ribs could have decided to poke right through your skin and then we'd have been in a mess, but there was nothing except massive bruises all over you."

"Still bad?"

"Still terrible. And I think you should go back to sleep now that the willow will help with the pain."

Annabelle relaxed a little now that Sophie had finally awakened enough to pass all the tests that the herbalists had told her to watch out for. Sophie knew where she was, she remembered some of what had happened, and she was able to focus on revenge. She'd be fine.

Sophie was almost asleep when her eyes popped open again.

"Annabelle, Fry said you owned the land where his business was built and that you raised the rent on him. Is that true or was he lying like he does about everything?"

Annabelle smiled. "Oh, he wasn't lying. I do indeed own the land, and I've raised his rent so high he'll never be able to pay it. He was not making a joke when he said he was looking for other quarters. I'll drive him out by the end of the month and get twice what he was paying from the next tenant."

Sophie was silent for a moment as she digested this information. "How much land do you own?"

"A lot. But it's not a matter of the land or the money or anything else, when you come right down to what I want. What I want is power. I want enough power to never have to worry about anyone else giving me orders. I had enough of that while we were growing up. I've changed, Sophie; I've learned how nice it is to be in charge, and I'll never let anyone make me give up any of the power. Never."

Sophie had always known that Annabelle wanted complete control over her own life, but she'd never realized that her sister might actually be able to do something about making that wish come true, particularly not in the small amount of time she'd spent in San Francisco.

The Annabelle that she saw in front of her wasn't the sister that she'd known so well for all these years. The closeness that they'd had was supplanted by other interests, other dreams that didn't include the two of them together all the time. She would have loved to talk it over with the old Annabelle, to tell her how much it hurt to be shunted aside for new interests. But the old Annabelle was gone and Sophie didn't feel like talking about it with this new stranger.

Sophie drifted off to sleep again, and in her dreams she saw two women, a real one and a ghost, one on top of the other like a mirror image. She wanted to get to the real woman, but the imagine always got in the way. She'd talk to her sister and see the words slide off the image, never penetrating enough to make an impression. In the end she was left weeping over the loss.

Annabelle picked up the drawing and started working on it again, satisfied that she'd done everything that she could for her sister. Now time and healing would have to take care of Sophie. On the other hand, it was time for Annabelle to take care of Fry, starting with evicting him from his store. She'd said that he'd be out by the end of the month, but after seeing the damage that he'd done to her sister, maybe she'd move the date up a little, like tomorrow.

He'd declared war. The fool didn't even know that they weren't the kind of women who folded at the first onslaught of trouble.

Annabelle planned her assaults as she sat with her drawings in front of her, adding infinitesimal details to the scene that she sketched. It was only when she ran out of details that she stretched and shook herself like a dog coming out of water and stood up. She had it all planned out. Now all she had to do was carry out the scheme.

She stared around the room, for the first time really looking at her surroundings. Her attention kept coming back to the corner, until she finally saw what had caught her eyes. The lovely paneling didn't quite meet in one place on the wall.

"Odd," she whispered, and moved closer to see why it gave the impression of not meeting exactly.

She ran her hands over the thick mahogany paneling and noticed a bump in the surface just about where she'd seen a distortion when she was sitting down. She felt the wall give just the slightest bit. Experimentally she pushed inward, and heard a click of a latch.

"What on earth?"

"What is it? Is something wrong?" Sophie asked, surfacing from the dreams that she didn't want to have anyway.

"I don't know yet; I think I just found a secret hiding place of the dear departed captain. I wonder what he's got stashed away in it."

"Gold," Sophie said positively, her voice a little stronger as she tried to sit up in bed and then decided that down was still better.

"Don't be silly; why would the captain have gold on board? It's probably just some musty old ship's books." She stuck her hand into the hole and fished around in the space. Her fingers touched thick leather, and she groaned, thinking that she'd been right; it was nothing but books. Then she felt the small bags tied with heavy leather thongs and her heart began to beat just a little bit more rapidly.

"There's definitely something in here. I need a candle." Annabelle reached over to the table and picked up the tin can with a candle in it that had been serving as a mobile light.

I can't see. . . ." There was a pause. "Oh, my God."

"What?"

Annabelle lifted several small bags out of the hidey-hole and threw them on the bed. The first leather bag caught Sophie on her leg, and she howled in pain.

"Damn it, what's in this? It feels like rocks!" She tried to lift it but couldn't budge the leather bag. She was so weak that lifting anything would have been impossible, but these pouches really were heavy.

"Better than rocks," Annabelle said, and opened the bag and let the coins cascade out in a shower of gold onto Sophie's quilt.

"Gold coins?" Sophie ran her hands through the coins, feeling the coolness in the palms of her hands.

"You're richer than me, I'll bet. You've got coins and all I ever get is gold dust. Oh, Sophie, this is wonderful!"

Annabelle opened all three of the small bags and let everything pour out onto the bed.

Soon there was a mound of gold in the bed, a modest mound, but still enough to see Sophie though hard times in San Francisco.

"What the hell was the captain doing with all this gold?"

"I don't know, but I can tell you that Fry didn't know about it or I would have been dead and buried and he'd have taken this ship apart piece by piece to get this kind of treasure. Without even trying to, I skunked him out of this money!" Sophie began to chortle and then to laugh out loud, even though every breath hurt her lungs and sent her body into spasms of pain. Her laughter began to take on an edge of hysteria.

"What's so funny?" Annabelle asked, beginning to get a little worried at her sister's reaction to the gold.

"I've been racking my brains for a way to earn money. I've been desperate to find a way to be rich, and here it was, hiding behind the paneling in the room all the time. I could go anywhere, I could do anything I wanted and not have to worry about money."

"You still need a way to earn money. San Francisco eats money; it's the most expensive place in the world. This will get you through, it'll give you a start, but you need to earn more instead of just resting on this little bit of money."

"Look at it, a pile of gold. I could go buy a house and live like a queen at least for a year. I could pay you enough gold to give you a chance to start over and never let another man touch you unless you wanted him to. Oh, Annabelle, think of the things that this gold means for both of us!"

Annabelle sat up straight and stared hard at her sister.

"What do you mean, make sure that no man ever touches me again unless I want it?"

She didn't like the sound of that one bit. It meant that Sophie hadn't quite understood that she liked what she was doing. She'd known that eventually they'd have to talk more about her experiences with men and the power that it gave her, but she'd hoped that the conversation could be postponed until Sophie felt better. Still, Sophie had brought the subject up and she was expecting an answer. "No one could pay me that much, enough to give up men."

"What do you mean?"

"I mean that I *like* having men pay attention to me, intimate attention, and I would never give it up, not now that I know how much fun it is. Didn't you believe me when I told you that a man's body is there only to pleasure a woman? I use men, I enjoy them, and I do not intend to give that up without a hell of a fight. Oh, Sophie, can't you see? It's another way of getting what I always wanted. They want me, they give me things, they let me take control of part of their life, and it makes me lots of money. Why would I want to walk away from that?"

"You don't want to stop?" Sophie had a horrible sinking feeling in her stomach, and it had nothing to do with the bitter willow that she'd drunk. Somehow she really didn't understand what had happened with her sister in the past few months. The dream had been right—the person standing in front of her looked like her sister and talked like her sister and even felt like her sister, but it was a mirror image, and the closeness that they'd had was falling away, replaced by something that wasn't nearly as good.

Annabelle shook her head. "I will not stop until I have everything I want, and that hasn't happened yet."

Slowly Sophie began to pick up the coins and return them to the bags. She'd talk to Annabelle about it later. "Would you like to keep some of the coins?"

"I'll keep them for you, but I have enough right now for my

own needs. I don't need these coins for myself. And, Sophie, please understand that I won't take them as a bribe to make me stop having men friends, if that's what you intend." Annabelle was adamant. "Don't ask again until after you've taken a lover and you know what you're talking about. Once that happens, you'll realize why it's impossible for me to stop."

Sophie nodded, but she didn't understand and she doubted that she ever would. She could never let a man get that near to her, and she didn't understand how Annabelle could say she liked it. The very thought made her shiver.

Halfway through the task of putting the coins away, Sophie lay back down and let her sister complete the rebagging and put the coins away in the safe.

"Here, it's back in the safe. You decide what you want to do with it, and then tell me and I'll help you out. Maybe invest in some real estate. I heard that there's a parcel coming up near Job's mercantile. . . ."

Sophie was already shaking her head. "I'm too tired to even think of it now."

Within a few seconds she'd dropped off to sleep, leaving her sister to sit and stare at her pale and bruised face.

Annabelle wished things could go back to the way they had been when she and Sophie had been on their uncle's ships. At least then life had been clear and uncomplicated. Their only needs then had been to stay safe and fed. They'd dreamed about being rich, never thinking that the dreams might become reality.

She touched the necklace with the gold coins. They weren't just money to her; they were proof that she was someone important, that men were willing to pay huge sums of money for her favors. She was rich now, she had her own business, and men came to her for a good time. She'd used that time to talk to them, to learn how to use her money and her body to take even more power.

The dream was imperfect, though. Life had become much more complicated in the past six months, and somehow those complications had changed the closeness that she and her sister had always had.

She closed her eyes and put her head back against the hard wooden upright behind the seat. Strange dreams overwhelmed her, of pain and danger and a link that shouldn't ever have been broken but that had disappeared without a trace, running into a mirror and fading away in the silvered distance.

"Wake up, Annabelle. I'm here to take over for a while," said Nellie. They need you back at the Painted Lady. Something about some man threatening to shoot up the place. Says he knows you and you're trying to run him out of business. Josie said to come get you before she had to take matters into her own hands. She says to tell you he can barely walk and he's still being obnoxious."

"Oh, shit. Fry," Annabelle said, stretching and standing up. "I wish someone would rip his head off and stuff it up his ass and keep on pushing until he turns into a pile of blood and intestines and then let the dogs at him."

"My sentiments exactly. He's horrible, and you'd better stop him before someone does exactly what you're describing. Or don't stop him and let them have their way with him. Except that no one will actually touch him because he's too powerful," Nellie said.

"Not as powerful as he thinks," Annabelle said grimly.

"How's Sophie doing?" Nellie asked, wafting in on a cloud of lavender, followed by the aroma of freshly baked cheese-and-onion pasties. She pulled the warm pastries out from under her purple cape and placed them on the tiny table that also held most of the medicines and poultices that Sophie was likely to need. Nellie wiped her hands on her wispy lavender dress that concealed almost none of her bony body if anyone cared to look closely enough to notice. The dress had other grease stains on it from previous encounters with food.

Nellie smiled rapturously as she bit into one of the crusty

pies. "Cristine's cooking again. She didn't notice when I took two of these just to tide me over."

"I'm sure she noticed, but she's too much of a lady to confront you with your thievery."

Nellie had the grace to look wounded, but she kept on eating.

It was a mystery to Annabelle how Nellie managed to stay so thin that she looked almost transparent while still eating so much food that her bill for comestibles at the Painted Lady was the highest of any of the women working there.

"I'll settle accounts with Cristine. You know you're not supposed to steal; the ladies of the Painted Lady are above that. We own our own place; we're responsible citizens," Annabelle started the lecture and then gave up. Nellie had heard it enough times that she could say it with her, but her need to constantly eat always overcame her law-abiding impulses. When food was present, Nellie was going to have it, whether she had the money to pay for it or not.

Annabelle sighed, carefully tucked her sketch behind the beam that ran across the ceiling of the cabin, and put on her cape.

"Sophie woke up and talked for a few minutes a while back and she was making sense this time. I gave her a poultice and some tea for the pain. Just keep her resting and I'll be back in about twelve hours. There's no trouble if you want to curl up and sleep on the opposite bunk. I'm sure you'll hear her if she moves."

Nellie nodded, but she couldn't answer because her mouth was stuffed full of the pasty. A stray piece of biscuit stuck to her chin as she ate.

Annabelle hurried up to the deck, where Cristine was in the midst of several hundred pasties, all in various stages of preparation. Dominic was working on a small room that he could use if he needed to. He waved a greeting but didn't bother to try to talk, since his mouth was full of nails at the moment.

"I owe you seven dollars. Nellie took two of the pies before she went downstairs," Annabelle said.

"She took three. She ate one before she went down."

Annabelle shook out about ten dollars' worth of gold dust into a piece of paper (she'd gotten very good at estimating gold weights and prices during her months in San Francisco) and handed the twisted packet of paper to Cristine. "I'm sorry; I don't know what happens when that woman is around food."

"She burns it all off with her nightly activities." Cristine obviously didn't approve of those activities.

Annabelle laughed. "She's not that active. Most men are afraid to touch her for fear that they'll break her. Have you ever taken a good look at that skinny little body? Hardly anything for a man to get his hands on, and that's the truth. You, on the other hand, could earn plenty of money with the same activities. Lots more than you can by baking. You do know that, don't you?"

"I will thank you to never speak to me about such a thing again. I am an honest, upright woman, and I would never agree to such an immoral pursuit." Cristine's voice fairly dripped ice, but even that didn't deter Annabelle.

"Sorry, didn't mean to offend you. Just making an offer," Annabelle said.

"No," Cristine said.

"If you change your mind, let me know," Annabelle said as she hurried off the ship and toward the Painted Lady.

Cristine muttered something underneath her breath, something that wasn't quite heard by Dominic, but the tone of the voice carried as much information as what she actually said.

Dominic shook his head. He'd been on the receiving end of enough of those kinds of comments that he knew how hurtful they could be. Cristine, he thought, needed to bend a little and discover that all the world didn't run by rigid Christian morality and condemnation of anyone and anything that wasn't within their purview. He especially didn't like the change that she'd begun to make in Sophie. He liked Sophie the way she was, a little raw, uncultured, but interested in everything and always willing to ask questions and learn. Now Cristine was hemming her in with social restrictions that didn't fit Sophie and would only make her as unhappy as his own father had been, trying to be something she never would be.

If anyone needed to change, it was Cristine, but the chances of her changing were almost zero.

"How is Sophie?" Dominic asked, perfectly aware that Cristine preferred not to talk to him. He hadn't been blind to her habit of going belowdecks when he appeared. But since they were working together on the ship instead of simply sharing the boat during a voyage that would end swiftly with no more than a wave at the end of the voyage as the guests left for their respective lives, he thought it was time that Cristine acknowledge his presence and learn to at least talk to him civilly.

"I have not checked. There is one of *those* women with her now."

"Has she awakened? The last time I asked her sister, she was still unconscious."

"I do not know," Cristine said, still frosty. "My only concern is to get these pasties cooked and out to the places that have ordered them, even the Painted Lady, though I'd rather not deliver there. Then I'll take what's left and go down to Union Square and sell the rest of them. The men seem to enjoy having them for their evening meal. I'm doing what I can for Sophie by cooking and bringing in cash."

"Yes, I can see that you're doing all that you can right now. I'm glad to see that you can use the stoves that I fastened down for you," Dominic said, subtly reminding her that he was the one who had made it possible for her to earn money. "As soon as Sophie is well enough, I'll have to start on the renovation of the ship so it can be rented out. I figure you'll have a lot of wood to burn then, since we're going to enlarge the cabins so more people can sleep in them. I expect that will save a little money instead of having to buy wood ashore for your cooking, won't it?"

Cristine nodded and turned away to extract yet another pan of golden-brown pasties from the third oven.

Dominic waited a minute to be sure that she actually wasn't going to continue any kind of conversation with him and then shrugged and walked away from her. He'd done his best. If she didn't want to talk to him even when they were going to be working together, there was nothing he could do about it.

It was a mystery to him why people like Cristine thought they were civilized when they acted in such a barbaric manner. The trouble with her was that she expected everyone to be pink and blond, Presbyterian, and morally upright according to what her version of morality was. Anything else was both ethically and socially suspect.

In the past few months, he'd decided he hated people like that. They were like his father, and he hated his father because he'd banished Dominic's mother for being "different."

Dominic picked up the hammer, set the next board in place against the uprights that he'd built for a tidy little room on deck, and began to hammer. The handle almost disappeared in his hand, and the force of the blow usually buried the nail with one stroke. While the very delicate carving and finishing work was sometimes difficult for him, he'd long since found that framing and construction were easy and fast when he used his size to advantage with the heavy jobs.

He built at a methodical pace, taking out his anger and frustrations on the wood and nails.

"Hey, you, big guy!"

"What?" Dominic turned and saw Nellie standing on the top step waving to him.

"Come over here, will you?" She stepped up onto the deck and drifted toward the pasties, her eyes glittering as she looked over the display of food.

"No!" Cristine said sharply, stepping between Nellie and the food. "You hand over money before you take so much as a scrap of dough from these trays, do you hear me?" It obviously hurt her to have to even talk to someone like Nellie, but the idea of losing money hurt her even worse.

"It won't cost you anything to be nice," Nellie said in an aggrieved tone.

"It'll cost you one of your hands if you touch that food without giving me gold," Cristine said with unaccustomed heat. She waved her knife in Nellie's general direction, even though she would never have done anything at all actually to harm the woman.

"I'll pay," Dominic said mildly.

"You don't have any money. She does," Cristine pointed out.

"Oh, all right, here's some money." Nellie drew out a poke of gold and daintily placed some in Cristine's hand.

Nellie scooped up another three of the pastries and turned to Dominic, pointedly ignoring Cristine.

"I have a favor to ask, now that Cristine has made me pay out every last bit of gold that I had with me." She looked at Dominic speculatively, her dark lavender eyes glowing as she focused somewhere below his belt.

"How can I help?"

"You can take care of Sophie, since Miss Cook here is too busy to do anything except prepare her wares. I need to earn some money, and to do that I have to be back at the Painted Lady. Can you stay with Sophie for a while?"

Dominic started to say no, thinking of the cramped captain's cabin and how much he just wanted to be able to stretch out and relax after a day of climbing off and on ships looking for the best buys for Annabelle and Sophie. There was no place to stretch out in the captain's cabin unless he wanted to lie down on the floor.

But then, the floor did have a nice rug. He could poke around the cabin and see if there was anything else to cushion the wood. He could go to sleep until Sophie stirred and needed help.

Cristine slammed one of the stove doors so hard that the cast iron almost fell off. "Don't you dare ask such a thing. Why, think of it, a man alone in a woman's room? Shameless, that's what it is! How dare you even think that it was proper and right!"

"Then you take a break and go down and take care of her, because I have to go to work." Nellie took another bite of the second pasty. The first one had disappeared as if a wind had come by and inhaled it.

"I *can't*, don't you understand?"

"Then it's Dominic or she gets left alone. I don't happen to think it's such a horrible thing to have a man in her bedroom, but then that's just my opinion." She smiled at Dominic, making it absolutely clear that he was welcome in her bedroom anytime.

"Oh, hell, I'll take care of her. Go ahead and get going before you miss the pick of the evening," Dominic said.

Cristine winced at the swearword, but she didn't object to Dominic's staying with Sophie because she wasn't willing to give up her business to satisfy her sense of decorum.

Dominic disappeared down belowdecks and Nellie started down the gangplank after having filched another pasty for the road.

"Nellie?"

It was Sophie's voice, weak and trembling.

Nellie turned around. Sophie was standing at the hatchway, her bed dress trailing behind her as she tried to keep her eyes open.

"What on earth are you doing? Get back down there into the bed this instant!" Nellie was appalled at Dominic's lack of understanding about how sick Sophie was. Why was he just standing there letting her ramble on when she should have been in bed?

"I had to tell you to be careful. I had a dream. You are in danger. Someone is waiting for you. Don't take any dark roads back to the Painted Lady. And especially don't go near a place called Sampson's."

"Mr. Tibeau, get her back to bed. Can't you tell when someone is hallucinating?" Cristine ordered him.

"I am not hallucinating. I know that Nellie is in danger," Sophie tried to convince them, but her knees were turning to mush and her head was spinning.

Dominic lunged to catch her before she disappeared in a heap at the bottom of the stairs.

Nellie waited just long enough to make sure that Sophie was tucked securely back into her bed and then hurried down the gangplank. By the time she'd reached the wharf, she'd already forgotten Sophie's warning.

8

ANNABELLE RESTED HER HAND ON HER SISter's forehead. Sophie's skin was hot to the touch, and her eyes had the glazed look of someone who was very sick indeed. It had been over a week since Fry's attack, and Sophie was very sick. For a few days she had done nothing except sleep and drink willow tea. On the fourth day she had begun to walk around the ship and Annabelle had breathed a sigh of relief. Sophie was going to recover just fine. On the seventh day she came down with a fever and lapsed into a semiconscious daze. A fever wasn't at all what Annabelle had expected. She could have used some help, but Nellie had disappeared. It wasn't the first time Nellie had left unexpectedly, but it certainly was the most inconvenient. Besides, four days was longer than Nellie's usual disappearances. She was beginning to worry.

Annabelle had undressed her sister and looked for signs of a wound that might have putrefied, causing the fever, but found nothing except a horrible bruise on the right side of her ribs.

"Maybe that's it. Maybe there's a broken rib in there and that's what's causing the fever," Annabelle said. But if so, how was she going to cure it? She had nothing except the ubiquitous rum and willow bark and the cherry poultice. She knew that cherry poultice wasn't going to work wonders for something going on inside Sophie. She'd need something more to take care of a bad infection.

She felt Sophie's forehead again and swore. Her fever hadn't gone down; it had gone up even higher in the few minutes that Annabelle had been looking for a wound.

"Damn, damn, damn," Annabelle said softly. She was going to have to do something about this. If she didn't get the fever under control, Sophie was going to die. If Sophie died, there were a couple of men who were going to die for what they had done to her.

"Just wait, Fry. Your time is coming, in a dark alleyway or maybe even in your own bedroom with the candles blown out, when you feel the most safe. I'm going to find a way to get even with you."

Someone knocked at the door.

"Who the hell?" Annabelle asked, startled by the sound. She wasn't expecting anyone. She strode over to the door and opened it, peering out into the gloom of the hallway.

"Excuse me? I was told I could find Sophie here."

A man stood in the hallway, holding his hat in his hands and looking very nervous. "I tried to get the lady up on deck to come down and tell you I was here, but there seemed to be some sort of trouble with communications between you and her. . . ."

"Yes, there is," Annabelle said. She'd noticed that Cristine didn't talk to her unless it was absolutely necessary and then it was from as far away as possible. She'd seen it before, upright ladies who thought that something like whoring was catching. Cristine and Annabelle had had an uneasy truce since she'd offered the woman a job at the Painted Lady.

Annabelle didn't mind at all that Cristine didn't want to talk to this man. He was one of the handsomest men she'd ever seen. If he'd shown up at the Painted Lady, she knew who'd have insisted on first crack at him, no matter what he was in the market for. Blond hair, deep blue eyes, not as tall as Dominic, but the cut of his gray trousers left no doubt about his masculine assets. Where on earth did her sister find these men and why hadn't she even mentioned either Dominic or this beautiful god-like creature to her? Chalk it up to just another one of the things that was different between the two sisters. Sophie didn't even notice handsome men, and Annabelle not only noticed them; she used them.

"Can I help you?"

Annabelle looked back to make sure that Sophie was decently covered by the wool blankets before she let him come into the room.

The man peered over her shoulder and into the room. He looked at her, perplexed, and then to the sleeping figure in the bunk. He stared at Annabelle again, obviously comparing the two faces and the identical heads of hair. The two of them still looked enough alike to confuse even people who knew them quite well.

"I think—I want to talk to her?"

He pointed toward Sophie.

"I'm sure you do, but there is a small problem. My sister is really quite ill and cannot have visitors at this time. I'll be glad to tell her anything you want as soon as she's with us again, but for right now, well, I'm afraid your message wouldn't get through to her."

"But I needed to see her about a present." He looked at the still form and began to swallow very hard.

It was a reflex that Annabelle had seen a number of times; big, strapping men sometimes couldn't stand the sight of illness without reacting as if they were even sicker than the person in the bed. Obviously this man was one of the men who could not abide illness of any kind.

"Is she all right? I mean, she isn't dying, is she? I couldn't stand that, not after what I've gone through to get her presents!"

"No, she's not dying. Well, at least I hope not," Annabelle

amended. At this point she wasn't willing to make any bets. "Come on, let's go up on the deck and we can talk there. And you might like to tell me your name, since I don't know you."

The man looked distinctly relieved. "The deck would be delightful, and my name is Ruari McKay, captain of the *Flying Angel.*"

"Just a moment while I get my cape. It's quite warm in here, but when I came down, the winds were scouring the deck like a bristle brush," Annabelle said. Indeed, the winds that had whipped San Francisco for months were back, raising the dust and driving the dirt out over the bay until it hung like a haze over the gray waters.

"It's warmer, but abovedecks is more comfortable for me." The man swallowed again and averted his eyes from Sophie's quiet figure. "Besides, the further away I am from her, the better, at least from her perspective. She already thinks I'm a pirate, no matter how much I've protested that all I was trying to do was help her out of a bad situation."

"What? A pirate? But why would she think such a thing?"

Annabelle followed the man onto the deck. From the rear, as they ascended the stairs, she noticed that he had quite a nice bottom underneath the dove-gray pants.

Once they were on deck, Annabelle and the man sat down on a hatch cover near one of the ovens. The air in the general vicinity of the wood stove's heat was at least tolerable, though a few feet away it felt like the middle of the Arctic Ocean. She noticed that he sat far enough away from her so that decorum was observed, which was a pity.

Wonderful, she thought wryly, *a pirate with manners.*

"Now, tell me what you want and how you came to meet my sister and, most important, why does my sister think that you're a pirate?"

"As I said, I am the master of the *Flying Angel.* We arrived in San Francisco almost the same day as the *Salud Y Amor* and all I ever wanted to do was help." He sounded distinctly aggrieved.

"Yes, I remember that you arrived on the same day. But that still doesn't make you a pirate just for coming into the bay on the same day as my sister."

Ruari shook his head. "No, ma'am, it wasn't because of a chance entrance. We'd met several days before when we saw the *Salud Y Amor* almost on the beach and no one on deck to tend the sails or the anchor. She was riding side on against the waves and was in danger of foundering. I knew that there was no reason for the ship to be there, with no settlements or help nearby, and fearing the worst, we sailed close to her."

"And what did you find?" Annabelle inched a little closer to him. It wasn't purely sexual; she was cold and she hoped that the bulk of his nicely muscled body would deflect at least some of the wind.

"We found the *Salud Y Amor* was a plague ship. I maneuvered my ship close to her, just to see if the ship was completely deserted or there was anyone on board who needed help."

"Of course that would have been your only concern, wouldn't it?"

Ruari had the grace to flush, though the pink cheeks and reddened ears might have been a blush brought on by the cold air. "Well, of course if I'd had the chance, I might have salvaged what I could from the ship. If it was abandoned, of course that would have been perfectly legal."

"But it wasn't completely deserted, was it?"

"No. When I boarded the ship I was met by a person I assumed was the cabin boy. He was holding a gun on me and ordered me off the ship despite my offers of help. I found out later that it was your sister, who was guarding the ship, and there were two other people on board. Naturally, when I discovered that the *Salud Y Amor* was not available for salvage, I offered our help. I had a full crew, while your sister was obviously going to attempt to sail the ship into the harbor using less than a minimum crew."

"And my sister turned you down?" Annabelle didn't think

that this was the complete story. She was almost certain that like most men, Ruari McKay was editing what had happened to make himself look better.

"The only person guarding it was your sister. She mistook me for a pirate and ordered me off the ship, despite my pleas to allow me to help her."

"Right." Annabelle knew all about men who wanted to "help" her in some way. "What did you want to do for my sister?"

"I wanted to leave several of my men on board the ship to help her sail it to San Francisco."

"At what cost?"

Ruari grimaced, though he tried to make it look like a smile. "You and your sister are certainly alike, aren't you? That's exactly what she asked me."

Annabelle smiled. She knew exactly what her sister would have asked. In fact, it almost seemed that she'd been there that dark foggy night when she heard the steps above her head on the deck and knew that they were under attack—of course, she did know it; it was a memory that they'd shared. Sophie had been terrified. She'd known there was another ship close; she'd known that there would be a move to take it all away from her and that there was no one else to depend on to stop the marauders.

"Yes, we are quite alike. At what price did you offer help?" Annabelle asked insistently.

"I didn't say there was a price, nor was I expecting any payment. I was simply trying to help her."

"And when exactly did you offer this help and under what circumstances?"

Ruari had the grace to look uncomfortable. "Well, it was dark when we reached the *Salud Y Amor*, so of course it was dark when I boarded the ship to try and talk to your sister, who I still thought was a cabin boy. I certainly wasn't threatening anyone; I just thought that the faster they could get help, the better it would be."

"Yes. Of course. And what happened?"

Ruari looked down at his hands. If he had been standing he would have shuffled his feet in embarrassment. "I found out she was very good with a gun. As I said, I thought she was a cabin boy and was very angry that she didn't call the captain for me, so I could formally offer help. She turned me down, said something about how having my men on board would mean that I'd salvaged the ship with her permission and she wasn't having any of it. Then she ordered me back to my ship. Well, I didn't want to go, because I thought she was just a cabin boy ordering me about. But I took one step toward her and she shot at me."

He tensed at the memory of the bullet whizzing directly past his ear and embedding itself in the mast behind him.

"She shot at you?" Annabelle hadn't even known that Sophie knew how to pull a trigger, but she guessed that dangerous situations called for learning new skills rather quickly.

"She almost didn't miss. I can tell you, I was back on my ship in a matter of seconds."

"I'll just bet you were," Annabelle said, smiling.

"I still didn't want her to have to deal with being shorthanded and sick by herself, so I stayed within hailing distance of the *Salud Y Amor* for the trip into San Francisco Harbor."

"But she never let you come on board again?"

"No. And it pains me to tell you that I did not find out that the one small cabin boy was a woman until we landed in San Francisco and I approached the *Salud Y Amor* again. She had just left the ship and had been accosted by some rather unsavory characters. I tried again to come to her rescue, and for thanks I got a bruised stomach and the ignominy of being called a pirate in public. It did no good for my reputation, I can tell you that."

"You must have really irritated her if she shot at you."

"I did nothing!"

"Except come aboard in the middle of the night, sneaking around to get whatever you could, right?" Annabelle thought she had the picture now, and it wasn't anything like Ruari McKay had been painting it.

"Both of you have vividly nasty imaginations. Did you know that? She told you about the encounter, didn't she? That's the only way you could have guessed what happened." He sounded distinctly aggrieved.

"She did not. We've had more important things to talk about." She wasn't about to tell him exactly how she knew what had happened that night, because she'd almost been there, the link had been so close between her and Sophie that night. "So what do you want with my sister now, Mr. McKay? There's no use in trying to salvage the ship. Everything that's worth anything has already been stolen by Mr. Fry."

"Oh, don't say such a thing! I certainly am not here to try and take anything from her. In fact, I have presents for her, something that she asked for when I walked her into town that morning. I rather think she'd like them, once she's up and about and able to enjoy them."

"Care to tell me what you're trying to buy my sister's affections with? I mean, if they're diamond earrings I can take care of them for her."

"No." He smiled at her obvious attempt to find out what he was going to give Sophie. "I think these are presents that she definitely has to accept herself once she's recovered from her accident."

Annabelle was immediately alert. "What do you mean, her accident? Who is calling it that?"

Ruari frowned for a moment as he tried to remember exactly who had talked about Sophie's injuries. "I think it was one of the men who works with Fry."

"It was no accident. Fry's the reason that my sister is lying there in that bed trying to die. He beat her so badly that something broke and now she's got a fever that won't come down and I don't know what to do about it; that's what Fry did."

Ruari blanched as she elaborated on her sister's condition.

"I thought he only stole the cargo from you. He bragged about that, you know."

"The son of a bitch. Fry couldn't be content with stealing everything; he had to try and kill her. She's dying in there, Mr. McKay. Dying, and there's nothing I can do about it because I don't think there's a doctor in all of San Francisco who could actually help pull her through this."

"A doctor? Maybe I could help there."

"Do you know any doctors here that we could trust?"

"Well, no. But if you'd give me a day or so, I'm sure I could find the best one in town for her and bring him to the ship."

"She doesn't have a day or two. The only plan I've been able to come up with—did I hear you say you wanted to help out?"

McKay hesitated just a moment before answering. He wasn't sure that he liked the way her eyes had suddenly taken on a predatory gleam, especially when she turned her gaze to him.

"Yes," he said slowly. "Yes, I said I wanted to help. I still feel very bad that she wouldn't let me leave men on board and that she had to do all that work herself. A woman shouldn't have to work that hard. That's what God made men for, to take care of women."

Annabelle liked that train of thought. She'd have to come back to it sometime later, when Sophie wasn't in danger.

"You can help me help her. I need to get to Chinatown and see an herbalist there, Mao Chung. One of the ladies who works with me at the Painted Lady recommended him highly. Unfortunately, she disappeared last week and we haven't been able to talk again about good Dr. Mao's skills."

"Do you think you could actually find him? I understand that finding people in Chinatown is rather difficult sometimes."

"Oh, not so hard. I don't think I'll have any problem. It's just that I don't want to walk down there by myself. I've been told that it's not safe."

"It is not safe for a woman alone, and it's not as safe as we'd like even with a man to escort you. Yes, of course I'll take you. How soon do you want to leave?"

"As soon as I've got someone to stay with Sophie. She still can't be left alone."

Ten minutes later, after a sharp exchange with Cristine that involved a pointed reminder about how much Sophie was helping her by letting her use the stoves and the stores from the ship, Annabelle and Ruari were on their way up to Chinatown.

"How do you propose to find this Dr. Mao if you don't know where he is?" Ruari asked as they entered the narrow mazes that made up most of Chinatown. There were steps down into darkened, dirty apartments, steps up into shops that carried a pungent assortment of goods, most of which Ruari had never seen before, and streets that led off the main streets into what looked like dangerous corridors where anything could happen.

Annabelle stopped and looked around her, cataloging all the different kinds of shops that she saw. She'd been told that Dr. Mao was near the pressed duck emporium and on the street behind the temple that one of the tongs used as a family meeting house.

"I think it's up this way. I seem to remember something about dogs. I think there's a shop around here that sells pressed ducks, and the doctor's place is in that same block." She walked straight up the street toward the temple that had been painted red and yellow and had several carved dogs at the entrance. She patted one of the dogs as she went by, hoping that some of the good luck would rub off on her. Right about now, she thought, she needed good luck if she was going to save Sophie.

There wasn't any sign of a shop with pressed ducks hanging in the windows. She walked all the way around the block and found nothing at all that even resembled such a shop.

"Well, damn," Annabelle said in disgust. This wasn't working out at all as she had expected. She was beginning to get a little worried. She knew that Sophie was getting worse by the minute. She didn't have time to traipse all over Chinatown looking for the elusive Dr. Mao.

Simply by stopping she became the center of everyone's attention. The Chinese men stared at her with open curiosity. Most of them had never seen a woman with red hair before, and there was some pointing and whispering. When her forest-green cape swirled open, revealing her figure in the green dress beneath, they were like any other men as they assessed her possibilities.

She looked up and down the street again, hoping she'd just missed the duck shop. While she looked, she listened to the men, waiting for a clue about how to approach them for directions.

"We could use her," one of the men said quickly.

"No, too unusual. No other women with that color hair here. Plenty of the white ones if we need them."

"But she'd bring a good price," the first man protested. "Even I wouldn't mind bidding on her."

"As if you had the money. Think about what the Mexican one is going to bring. Your share of that wouldn't even buy a strand of this one's so pretty hair."

They stared at her again and it felt for all the world like they were pricing her like a cow ready to be sold.

Annabelle didn't like the tone of the comments, and she particularly didn't like the idea that these men would, in broad daylight, talk about what amounted to kidnapping her. Maybe they were making a macabre joke—she couldn't be sure—but she didn't like it.

Annabelle decided to take the direct approach.

"Where would I find Dr. Mao?" she asked first in English, only to have every single man look beyond her or beside her or through her, but never making eye contact with her. "Dr. Mao? Can you tell me how to get to him?"

None of the men gave any sign that they understood a single word. She was sure that at least some of them understood her.

"They're not very helpful, are they?" Ruari asked. He didn't like this part of town, and he didn't much care for the people, either.

"Not yet. I'm about to change that, though," Annabelle said grimly.

Ruari didn't look like he was having a good time. He didn't exactly fear the people around him, but he certainly wasn't comfortable. There had been some hair-raising stories about some of the gang activity in Chinatown, and while the violence had never been directed toward an outsider, he still didn't feel comfortable. He was just about to put his arm protectively around Annabelle's shoulders when she stunned him into immobility as she started to speak Chinese to the men around her.

The men had the same reaction that Ruari had to her speaking the language. One man dropped a sesame-studded cake that he'd been nibbling on. Another one misstepped and almost sprawled out onto the bricks. No one could believe that this woman with the red hair was using gutter Chinese and some truly terrible words to demand that they take her to Dr. Mao.

"Now!" she ordered, stopping the flow of Chinese with the brusque English word.

"What?" Ruari stepped back and stared at her, his eyes wide. "My God, this is impossible. You couldn't be!"

Annabelle looked at him and rolled her eyes in exasperation. Some men weren't nearly as smart as they were good-looking. "I couldn't be what? Part Chinese? Oh, don't be so stupid! I can speak some Chinese, but nothing like Sophie; she's actually fluent in the language. For years we shipped with Chinese crewmen, and when we had the chance we learned the language, same as we learned French and Spanish and Tagalog. It's nothing special; it was just a way to pass the time."

She let loose another tirade in Chinese, and finally one of the men stepped forward and offered to take her to the estimable doctor.

Ruari followed the man and Annabelle, who continued to converse with their guide in Chinese. He dropped a few steps behind and then a few more.

"You'd better not lag behind. If you get lost, you'll never find your way out of here," Annabelle said as they were led down a stairway to a door covered by a cast-iron grate with a huge lock. The man opened the lock, pulled back the door, which screeched as if it hadn't been opened in a hundred years, and ushered them into a dark little room that was half underground. The room smelled of spices and must and mildew.

The man opened another door at the end of the room and motioned them forward.

"Go in there? Where does it go?" Ruari peered into the dark, twisting tunnel that opened up in front of them and stepped back, almost crushing Annabelle's foot. "I'm not going down in there."

"Yes, you will, because I won't go alone and I have to get to the doctor. So you'd better follow him down the steps, Mr. McKay."

"You actually want to follow him into that tunnel? Do you realize that no one in the civilized part of San Francisco knows where we've gone? We could disappear in there and be lost forever, and no one would know where even to begin looking for us. Besides, there's surely no fast way out of that tunnel if someone decides to harm us. Who knows what they could do? They could murder me and take you off to be a slave girl somewhere, and no one would ever find you."

Annabelle was glad that Ruari wasn't able to understand the comments that the Chinese men had already made about the possibility of kidnapping her. She felt fairly safe because of her hair, but no one was completely safe, at least not in this part of town.

"Don't be ridiculous," Annabelle said, but her voice held just a hint of worry. He was right, of course. If they disappeared, no one would know where they had gone. No, that wasn't right. Cristine knew, but she would be singularly unlikely to be able to do anything about it. If Annabelle and Ruari McKay disappeared, Cristine would wring her hands, she'd wail, and then she'd do nothing at all. She'd keep Sophie comfortable until she died, and then Cristine would probably take over the *Salud Y Amor* for herself and go right on making money with the pasties. She wasn't the kind of woman to come hunting down a lost pair of people that she didn't particularly approve of in the first place.

The Chinese man waited patiently for them to finish squabbling. When Ruari finally realized that there wasn't any other way to get to the doctor, he shrugged and gave in.

"I guess we'd better go, then. You're sure you can't make them tell us about a more direct route, one that doesn't include following someone else?" he asked, still faintly hopeful that she could guide them to Dr. Mao on their own.

"If I could, do you think I'd be down here? I don't like this any more than you do, but it's our only chance, and Sophie needs that medicine."

Their guide led them down more stairs, around in a tunnel that was barely high enough for Annabelle to stand upright in and made Ruari bend almost double.

Ruari swore in a low monotone for most of the time that they followed the man through the narrow corridors that were lit with a few oil lamps. For the most part they were in the dark, and Annabelle didn't much like the sounds that she heard from the other branches of the corridors. There were scuttlings and teeth snapping that made her think of rats. She didn't mind rats too much, as long as they weren't hungry. What she did dislike was the crunching of things underfoot. She had a feeling that she wouldn't want to see what it was she was walking on. It certainly wasn't stone. . . .

She heard whispers around her, but nothing clear enough for her to understand the words. Somewhere ahead of them there was a scream and a moan, but the man leading them didn't even hesitate in his progress down the broken bricks that paved the floor of the tunnels.

There was a sharp rip and another volley of oaths from Ruari.

"My best pants and there they go; I felt it rip the knees. Damn bricks, anyway." He was far beyond worrying about Annabelle's ladylike ears.

"Oh, do shut up," Annabelle said, trying to conceal how worried she was getting at the interminable turns back and forth. She had been following the twists carefully, trying to keep the directions clear in her mind just in case they really did have to get out of here on their own. As far as she could tell, they were almost exactly at the same point they'd been when they went in, but she didn't see how that was possible.

Finally they began to go upward again and the knot in her stomach that had begun to form when it looked like they were completely, utterly lost, despite their guide, began to loosen. They emerged in the sunlight in a courtyard that was filled with plants of all kinds and cabinets with hundreds of drawers. A Chinese man stood in the middle of the place weighing out ingredients for some arcane potion. Ruari let out a sigh that showed just how worried he'd been.

"Dr. Mao?"

The Chinese gentleman turned and smiled at Annabelle.

"My dear, I've been waiting for you. I'm afraid that this is nothing to compare to the surgery in London, but this does quite well for most of my patients," the doctor said in a voice reminiscent of an Oxford don. He waved a hand around the courtyard with the blooms and colors that defied the cold wind that swept the street outside his pharmacy.

"You are from London?" Ruari croaked.

Annabelle laughed at the expression on Ruari's face. The poor man didn't know what to think about a Chinese gentleman who had been educated far beyond what Ruari could ever expect to attain.

"Of course, trained and had my practice there until I decided I wanted a little adventure in my life. This isn't exactly what I had in mind, but it will have to do."

Annabelle grinned. This hadn't been her idea of where she'd

end up, either, but they both had made the best of it.

"My dear, I've been told that you speak Chinese rather colorfully. Would you prefer to continue the conversation in Chinese or English?"

"English is fine, Doctor," Annabelle said. "I don't think you'd approve of my brand of Chinese."

"I neither approve nor disapprove; I just listen. Please tell me, what brings you here and how can I help you?"

"My sister was beaten up by a man. She had bruises on her side at this point." Annabelle indicated on her own body where the man's boots had connected with Sophie's body. "They hit her in the head and she said she was very dizzy and there was another bruise here, on her jaw. She made sense the first few days after the beating, but now she has a fever and I can't wake her up. I know she doesn't know where she is. The fever just keeps climbing higher and higher, and I can't stop it. I've wrapped her in cool cloths, but even that hasn't helped. I've kept giving her willow bark and rum, and I've put a poultice of cherry and couple of other things on the bruise around her ribs, but nothing helps. It just keeps getting worse, and I'm worried about her."

The doctor listened quietly, his eyes following her when she indicated where the blows had hit her sister.

"Has she vomited blood at any time? What is happening with the bruises?"

"There's no sign of bleeding on the outside, no vomiting, but the bruises look like blood has pooled underneath the skin. But it's the fever that worries me. She's so hot and her eyes have a glazed look, like she can't come back from wherever she's gone."

"I think I'd better take a look at her. It sounds like you've been doing all the right things for as much as you know about her condition, but there might be something else wrong that you're not able to diagnose. I'll bring some of the medicines I have that might help.

Annabelle, who didn't realize that she had been holding herself rigid with worry that the doctor wouldn't take her seriously, relaxed. Everything would be all right once he came to the ship and saw Sophie. Annabelle had absolute faith that the doctor would work a miracle and save her sister. After all, he'd stopped the bleeding from Josie, who'd gone to him after an abortion had gone wrong and she'd nearly lost all her blood from a punctured uterus. Nellie had gone to him for something to make her gain weight. Whatever the doctor had given her hadn't stopped her eating, but it had put a few pounds on her here and there. Even Lavonne had given in and gone to see Dr. Mao when she came down with an unmentionable disease. He'd given her medicines to take to build herself up and keep from getting sick again, and they seemed to have worked. None of the men was coming back complaining of leaking penises and chancres on their private parts.

They emerged from the doctor's almost tropical courtyard to the street and Ruari began swearing, but this time it wasn't sotto voce; it was a full-voiced roar that made the Chinese on the street hurry faster to get away from the madman in their midst.

"What on earth is the matter with you?" Annabelle demanded. He was embarrassing her in front of all these people.

"Would you look at where the hell we are?" Ruari's voice ground down to a low growl.

Annabelle looked around and then began to laugh.

They had come out two doors away from the place where the old gentleman had taken them down into the bowels of Chinatown.

9

I CAN'T BELIEVE THAT YOU ACTUALLY ALlowed Ruari McKay to step foot on this ship without skewering him like a ripe piece of meat on a shish kebab. I told you all about him; he's the one who laid in wait for me to make a mistake so he could take over the *Salud Y Amor.* How could you have been nice to him?" Sophie glared at her sister.

"I was trying to get you some medical help. If Ruari McKay hadn't gone with me to Chinatown, I might not have been able to get you the medicines that you needed," her sister said sharply. "Besides, I didn't want to get lost down there, wandering around, when you needed a physician right away."

"You could have asked Dominic to help; he'd have been happy to go with you, and he speaks the language."

Annabelle glared at her sister, completely baffled by her attitude toward Ruari McKay. "Yes, I could have if Dominic had been here. But he wasn't and I didn't want to wait another second to find out if any of the doctors in town could help you. You were burning up and if I got lost or disappeared, like rumors have it that some other women have when they've visited Chinatown, you'd have died before anyone could help you.

Sure as hell we couldn't have depended on Cristine."

"You wouldn't have disappeared—someone with our coloring is awfully hard to hide, even in Chinatown. Especially in Chinatown."

Annabelle considered telling Sophie about the conversation that had been directed toward her by the Chinese men who were assessing her salability but decided not to bring it up. She wasn't sure that she'd understood all of the nuances of what the men were saying, and Sophie was right—someone like her would be awfully hard to make disappear.

She brightened, wanting to share the funny side of her trip into Chinatown, now that she knew her sister was mending. "Sophie, you should have seen the faces on those men when they realized the words that were coming out of my sweet little mouth in their very own language. I think it's a very good thing that Ruari McKay didn't know what I was saying when I threatened to rearrange their intimate anatomy if they didn't take me to the doctor that I'd heard about."

She bounced on the bed, curled her feet up underneath her, and prepared for a long conversation with her sister. She pulled up the blue and red blanket that she'd found tucked away in a cedar chest and wriggled her toes happily in the warmth. It was cold and getting colder abovedecks, and she was glad for the cozy, dark comfort of the cabin. This was just like being best friends with her sister again. It was almost as much fun as talking with Josie when they both had a few minutes off.

Sophie snorted at the image of her sister trying to actually speak sentences that weren't completely composed of a vocabulary that women weren't even supposed to know. "I know what words you learned in Chinese. The only thing that ever appealed to you in any language was the swearwords!" Sophie was laughing at the very thought of her sister being able to do anything except tell the Chinese that she could cause them to be arranged in at least fifteen probably unnatural positions that would do physical harm to themselves if they didn't cooperate with her.

"How did you manage to ask for the doctor using them?"

"I had to work at it, but they got the idea when I kept repeating, 'Dr. Mao, Dr. Mao.' " Now Annabelle was laughing, because she knew exactly what Sophie was thinking and she was absolutely right.

"But there wasn't any way that you could have gone by yourself instead of using Ruari as an escort? Annabelle, I don't think you understand; that man is out to get whatever he can. He has no qualms whatsoever about taking what's available from either of us. He'll rob us blind and then throw us on the dung heap just like all the other men we've ever met. He's no different; he's just more handsome."

"He's definitely more handsome. And do you know, I think you're wrong about him. He was a gentleman, except when he ripped his best dove-gray pants on the bricks in the underground tunnels. Then he swore. But otherwise, I think you've badly misjudged him. He likes you and I think you should give him a chance, get to know him better. Also, he seems to think that we'd be interested in buying a ship of his, the *Mary Kathleen*. It might not hurt to have a look at it when you're feeling better."

"He'd skin us alive on any deal; you know that."

"I don't know anything of the sort and neither do you," Annabelle said, exasperated.

"Annabelle, can we stay far clear of Ruari McKay? I don't trust him, no matter how nice he seems." Sophie tried her best to convince her sister, but she could see from Annabelle's face that she was making no headway at all.

"I think you're being irrational and it's all from that awful fever. We can talk about the *Mary Kathleen* and Ruari McKay later, when you feel better," Annabelle tried to soothe her sister. Maybe it was all the medicines and the awful crack to the head she'd suffered that was making her be so irritable about McKay. Given a little time, she'd most certainly come back to being her normal agreeable self. Dr. Mao's yellow poultice for the broken ribs, and cherry drink for the fever had worked almost immediately.

"Feeling better isn't going to make me change my mind," Sophie said. She lay back against the pillows and gave a small cry. Her ribs still hurt beyond anything she'd ever experienced before, and her jaw was still swollen enough that she didn't want to go out in public. She was recovering, but she certainly wasn't well yet.

"Nevertheless, he is a nice man."

"He's a thief. You just want to see if you can get anything from him. I don't know whether your want sex or power or what, but I can see it in the way you talk about him."

"And would that be such a bad thing? If men are willing to give me dominance over them, if they're willing to give me money, I'm sure as hell not going to turn it down. But I still think you're wrong about that man."

Annabelle shut her mouth, determined not to say another word about Ruari McKay until Sophie had recovered enough to carry on a rational conversation.

There was a loud knock on the door.

Annabelle jumped up to answer it, pulling the door wide. She stared up right into those blue eyes that she liked so much and that Sophie hated.

"Speak of the devil," Annabelle breathed, just loud enough for Sophie to hear.

"Good afternoon, ladies," Ruari said. "I hope I'm not intruding. I asked Cristine and she said that Sophie was much improved, so I decided that perhaps it was time to deliver a small present in the hopes that it will cheer her up."

Ruari McKay stood in the doorway, holding a bunch of flowers and a basket that contained two kittens, one dark orange and white kitten that was making futile leaps in an attempt to get out of the basket and another light orange and white kitten nestled against a pink satin pillow looking sweet and innocent.

Sophie looked at the kittens while Annabelle looked at the

man. Gradually Sophie's eyes were also drawn to Ruari.

Ruari was wearing a dark blue coat, white shirt, and blue trousers, and they fitted him perfectly, outlining the rather nicely muscled body that Sophie remembered having seen when he boarded the *Salud Y Amor* wearing tight pants and a white shirt and not much else. Even as she'd lifted the gun, preparatory to firing it, she'd thought what a nice specimen of a man he was. He had everything in the right place and plenty of it, and it was clearly defined by the pants.

Suddenly she realized that the last thought probably hadn't come from her. Annabelle was obviously interested in Ruari, and it had slopped over into her own thoughts. She shot her sister a warning glance and saw, to her disgust, that Annabelle was indeed staring at Ruari as if he were a delectable piece of cake that she'd like to eat.

Ruari didn't notice Annabelle's interest. He simply stared at Sophie until she began to worry that maybe she had something terribly wrong with her that Annabelle hadn't mentioned.

Sophie smiled. It was funny; she disliked Ruari and he was concentrating on her and ignoring Annabelle, who obviously liked him very much.

"I *was* beaten, you know, if that's what you're looking at," she said sharply, jolting him out of his reverie.

"I'm sorry, I didn't mean to stare; it's just that I've never seen a black eye quite that color before. I've very glad that you seem to have almost permanently disabled the man who did it to you." He smiled disarmingly.

"Yes, it's nice to know," Sophie said. She was glad she'd hurt him, but her stomach did a queasy little dance every time she thought of getting that close to that disgusting man.

"The rumor is that Fry is going to walk with a severe limp for the rest of his life and will never father children. I heard a rumor about what might have happened to him, but I gave it no credence at all. You *couldn't* have done it."

Sophie nodded. "But I did exactly what you heard and I'd do it again, only this time I'd like to have a knife handy for the carving instead of having to dirty my mouth," Sophie said grimly. The taste still lingered in her mouth, even after days of being sick. Nothing could wash away that filthiness. "I just hope I don't get some terrible plague from having touched that man." She shuddered delicately. She tried to be nice, but her attention wasn't on either Fry's condition or Ruari McKay in her bedroom. She couldn't take her eyes off the kittens in his arms.

She remembered telling him how much she wanted a pair of cats, but it was like hoping for the moon. If he'd brought them just for a visit, to gloat that he had two cats while she had none, she'd think seriously of doing to him what she'd done to Fry; only this time she'd make it a total emasculation.

Annabelle suddenly realized that she hadn't invited Ruari in to sit down. The unstated fireworks between her sister and McKay had completely washed her manners away.

"Please do come in and sit down. We're delighted to see you," she said, sending a quick look at her sister that dared her to contradict her.

"Thank you. I'd be delighted to sit for a while."

Ruari placed the basket, which in addition to kittens also had a container of milk, a tin of oysters, and four eggs tucked into a safe compartment away from exploring paws, on the end of the bed.

The adventurous dark orange kitten, sensing a chance to escape, hopped onto the bed and then stopped, wide-eyed, not sure where to go from there. The other kitten yawned and looked around but didn't bother to move from the comfortable pink cushion in the basket.

Sophie couldn't think of a single thing to say as she looked at the little animals. She'd wanted a cat for so long that the idea of actually owning one was a little overwhelming, and two were definitely heaven. She reached out and touched the darker orange cat on the forehead and was delighted when he rolled over and presented his tummy for a quick rub.

"Oh, the darlings," she breathed.

Ruari watched her face anxiously, trying to read her expression.

"It is all right, isn't it? There isn't any reason why you can't take care of them? I mean, you said you wanted a cat . . ." Ruari began to search for something more to say. The adventurous cat decided that maybe it wasn't so dangerous after all, out there on the bed, and jumped straight up Sophie's legs, almost upsetting the basket with the precious eggs and milk. Ruari grabbed for the basket, caught it as it was tipping, and in the process dumped the other kitten onto the bed.

Both of the animals tussled for a moment and then looked around as if searching for something. It only took a moment for them to head purposefully toward the half of a pasty that Annabelle had left on the bed. They attacked it with tiny teeth and claws, ripping off bits of the meat and biscuit and growling tiny kitten growls as they ate the food.

"Do you like your presents?" Ruari finally asked, unable to wait another second to hear what Sophie thought of the babies.

Sophie stared up at him, her green eyes wide. "My presents? You mean you're giving them to me?" she asked in disbelief.

"Of course. Why else would I be here? I felt sorry about what happened to you and I wanted to do something to make you feel better. Just going to get medicine in Chinatown didn't seem to be enough, so I decided you needed these two to keep you company while you mend."

The cats finished tearing the pasty to bits and began hunting for new prey. The pink ribbon on the basket was a likely target, and within seconds they had sent the eggs rolling toward the edge of the bed.

"Oh, you little darling," Sophie said, scooping up one kitten and grabbing at one of the eggs before it fell off the bed. "You're going to be several handfuls to take care of, aren't you?" She didn't care that her side ached and that talking made her teeth feel like they were going to fall out. She'd never been so enchanted with anything in her life.

"I didn't know they'd do this," Ruari apologized, trying to scoop the eggs back into the basket. In the process, his hands connected with her covered knees and they both jumped back as if they'd been struck by lightning.

Sophie stared at Ruari in surprise, trying to figure out what had made her body give that response to him. She did still hate him, didn't she?

"How much do you want for them?" Annabelle asked, always practical. She knew how Sophie was about animals. She would give away all the gold she had on the ship just to keep these two cats, and Annabelle wanted to make sure that they hadn't misunderstood Ruari about giving them away to Sophie.

Pets had always been a sore spot between the two sisters. Annabelle didn't particularly like animals, while Sophie loved every animal she'd ever met. She had once made a pet of a rat aboard ship, feeding it until it would run out at the sound of her footsteps and beg for food like a dog. She'd cried inconsolably for days when she'd been forced to leave the rat behind as they moved to a different ship, and she'd vowed that one day she'd have all the animals around her that she wanted.

"They aren't for sale. They're a present."

"I don't believe you; I know that people have been advertising for cats and are willing to pay several hundred dollars. Why would you just give these away?" Annabelle challenged him.

Ruari looked at her in exasperation, the tiniest frown creasing his perfect face as he explained. "They didn't cost me anything because my cat on board the *Flying Angel* had kittens and these two were left over. I thought Sophie might like them."

He turned to Sophie, pointedly ignoring Annabelle. "The last time we met, I was hoping to talk with you about the *Mary Kathleen,* but that little Chinatown adventure disrupted any kind of discussion. Why don't we all go down and take a look at the *Mary Kathleen* when you feel better? She's well built, a fine craft. Her captain wanted to get out to the goldfields and lost her in a card game the night after he'd landed. Said something about having gotten the most important cargo off, and that he had no more use for her. I won her for one thousand dollars and I'll let you take her over for the same price plus 10 percent."

Annabelle was seething. How dare he act as if she weren't there? No man did that and got away with it, not if she had anything to say about it. Besides, his blatant offers of things that Sophie wanted were beginning to irritate her. First cats, then a wonderful ship for a pittance? Why wasn't he offering all of that to her instead of her sister?

Sophie seemed to be oblivious to her sister's anger. "Mr. McKay, I understand that you are trying to do me a favor, but please tell me something. Why would I pay you eleven hundred dollars for the *Mary Kathleen* when there are all kinds of ships just rotting away in the harbor?"

"Because they *are* rotting. I know this ship; she's a good one and worth your money. Or you can pay a hundred dollars eleven times over to buy ships that will go down in the first real storm. You haven't seen any storms here yet; they don't hit until January or February. When that wind comes racing in through the bay and up the hills, carrying the rain with it, those ships will sink, carrying every man jack aboard down with them, and you'll be responsible for their deaths because you bought the cheapest and worst."

"She's actually that good of a ship?"

Ruari nodded. "One of the best I've ever seen."

"I can't get out to look at her or to buy her right now," Sophie said, indicating her battered body with a sweep of her hand. In the process she dislodged one of the kittens from her knee and he rumbled sideways, squealing with indignation.

"I don't expect you to try and examine her until you feel better. I'll hold onto the *Mary Kathleen* until you feel well enough to visit her. I'll sell her to you on those terms as long as you make certain that she isn't ruined. I hate to see a good ship left to rot, and I know you'd take care of her."

"Why does it matter so much to you?" Sophie asked.

Ruari hesitated. "I guess because I come from a shipbuilding family. For the first twenty years of my life I lived, dreamed, and worked on ships. If you've ever heard of the Boston McKays, well, that's my family."

"McKays? Yes, I've heard of them."

"So has anyone else who has ever been involved with shipping. And I can tell you that it was a wonderful boyhood, immersed in the best of shipbuilding. I even had a hand in designing a hull for a ship that raced from Boston to England and garnered a prize for being the fastest ship on the seas."

"But if you are from that family, what are you doing out here?" Sophie asked, intrigued in spite of herself. "Why aren't you back home working in the family business?" She hated being interested in him, but she could feel her entire attitude toward him shifting. Maybe, just maybe, he wasn't so bad after all.

"Because there isn't a family business anymore."

Sophie looked at him sharply. There was a lot of anger in that response, and it seemed to be the same kind of anger that she still harbored toward her uncle.

Ruari continued. "My father died when I was eighteen, my mother remarried with unseemly haste, and my stepfather took over the yards. Within two years he'd gambled everything away. The only thing I managed to salvage, because she was registered with me as captain and owner, was the *Flying Angel.* I came out here to make another fortune, one that my stepfather couldn't touch."

"And here you are in San Francisco and the *Flying Angel* is becalmed. What are you going to do?"

"I'm looking for a chance to sail to China. That is where the money is flowing, in the China trade. If I can find someone to sponsor a trip, I'm sure that I'd come back with enough of a profit to make the next voyage on my own." Ruari leaned forward, obviously delighted with the chance to talk about his dreams to someone new, especially a very pretty someone new.

"Who would you be working with?"

"There are several groups of people who are trying to organize the shipping to China. At the moment I seem to be dealing with a group of men who are forever in meetings or away from their buildings or engrossed in other activities. It's like trading with ghosts. But I will get the deal eventually and I'll be back on the seas before the spring storms. Until then, though, I've got to stay alive, and to do that I need to sell the *Mary Kathleen.*"

Sophie petted one of the kittens, who had decided to nestle against her side and drift off to sleep. She was satisfied that Ruari had a good reason for selling the ship to her and was fairly sure that he wouldn't lie about the ship's condition.

"What do you know about the cargo that the captain left?" she asked, her voice quieter than normal because she didn't want to disturb the kitten.

"Almost nothing. It must not be valuable or someone would have bought it before the captain turned the ship over to me. I expect that there are foodstuffs and perhaps trinkets, but nothing of great value." He discounted the cargo completely.

Sophie was glad to have the offer of the ship, but she was also wondering about that cargo that had been left intact on the ship. What was there? What could she use and what could be sold? Would it be possible to make up for the loss that she'd suffered at Fry's hands if she was just a little bit creative with the contents? She'd have the space on the ship that could be rented out, but it would be even better if she could sell cargo as well for the maximum profit for her money.

The other kitten clambered up Sophie's knees to her stomach and proceeded to knead a soft spot to lie down on. The purring filled the room.

"Are you sure you want to give away these kittens? I know

that they're worth a lot of money on the street in San Francisco. Are you sure you don't want something in exchange for the kittens?"

She wouldn't tell him, but she was so enamored of the little beasts that she would have given him almost anything that he asked for.

"I'd like your company for dinner and a theater show, whichever show you'd like to go to, as soon as you're well."

He looked straight at Sophie, and his smile was disarmingly sweet, almost as sweet as the kittens. He knew how to use that gorgeous face of his; he'd mastered all the right expressions to make women like him instantly. The smile. The quirk of the eyebrow, the dimple at the side of his mouth that deepened as he laughed. Those deep blue eyes that seemed to sparkle as he talked, the windblown blond hair that curled despite his best efforts to control it. Oh, he knew what he was doing, all right, but she wasn't impressed. He was still a pirate.

Sophie thought about saying no, but she had no idea whether he'd take the kittens back and depart forever if she didn't accept his invitation, and she didn't particularly want to find out. Besides, the kittens had worked a change that nothing else could have done. She was beginning to think that maybe Annabelle was right; maybe he wasn't so terrible after all.

"All right, I'll go with you."

She was suddenly overcome by a desire to yawn. She tried to squelch it, clenching her teeth and pursing her lips, but it was obvious that Ruari saw what was happening.

"Oh, good for you, Sophie. I'm so glad you're going to go with him," she heard Annabelle mutter sotto voce. It was low enough that it was probably their own private communication, and he wouldn't have understood even if he'd heard her talking. "I wish you'd given me a chance with him."

The smile that lit Ruari's face had to be genuine. No one could turn on that kind of power if he didn't mean it. "I'll come back in a couple of days. By that time you should feel better and we can walk around the deck a few times to help you get your strength back."

He was bouncing around like a kid who just got a present he hadn't expected. "Would you like me to bring you some more eggs so you can have a nice thick drink made from them? Or perhaps a custard? My ship's cook is back from the goldfields, where he went broke, and he makes a fine custard—yes, that's what I'll bring next time!" He waved good-bye without waiting for Sophie to tell him whether or not she wanted ten-dollar eggs used in a custard for her and hurried up the stairs to the deck.

Annabelle rushed after him. "Ruari, if you're going to be in the area tomorrow, please drop into the Painted Lady. I've got to go back to Chinatown for some more medicine for Sophie, and I'd love to have you walk with me."

Ruari muttered something that didn't sound complimentary about the possible visit to Chinatown, then sighed and nodded. "In the afternoon, if that's acceptable. I'd be delighted to help out with anything that Sophie needs."

"Fine. I'll wait for you tomorrow," Annabelle said. Well, she thought, that put her in her place, which was definitely second to Sophie with this man. She felt something stirring within her that had never been there before. She felt like she was in a competition with her sister for this man, and in one selfish second she decided that Sophie would not have Ruari McKay.

10

THIS IS SUCH FUN. TOMORROW NIGHT WE can figure out just how many ships we want to buy. I think five should be enough, don't you?" Sophie said. "I'll ask Cristine to make some of those new chicken pies and you can stop by for some of those delicious chocolate crèmes. Doesn't that sound good?"

"Oh, not tomorrow night. We'll have to finish the discussion some other time," Annabelle said.

"Not tomorrow night? Why not?" Sophie was surprised that her sister wasn't going to come back to the ship as she had every day for the past week. For the last two days, with their nightly hour or two spent together, it felt almost like old times. Of course Annabelle had to leave before the evening crush started at the Painted Lady, but they still had enough time to talk about important things like the ships they were going to buy.

"Because Josie and I are going out shopping for some new cloth for dresses. Then, later on, I'm going to have a very special meeting with Ruari, so there's no time tomorrow and maybe not the next day either, if Josie and I decide to go for fittings."

"New dresses? Oh, how exciting," Sophie said. "I haven't

anything except the skirt and coat that Cristine made. Maybe I should get some new clothes, now that I know I have at least a little money set aside."

Sophie waited for the invitation to go with Annabelle and Josie, but it didn't come. The silence lengthened until she realized that Annabelle had no intention of taking her around to the various shops to look for cloth.

"Well, I guess you and Josie wouldn't want me along anyway," she said, sitting back against the bed. She struggled not to show just how much her sister's rejection hurt. "I suppose I could always ask Cristine to take me around. I'm certain she's found the proper stores for a gentlewoman to buy from by now. She's very good at that, you know."

Annabelle wrinkled her nose at the mention of Cristine. "She's no good for you, you know. She's trying to make you into something that you're not, and you're never going to be the perfect paragon of manners that she wants."

"And who do you think I should go with to pick out clothing? You don't like Cristine, you don't want me with you, and you've got Ruari in your pocket for any other time that might be available. That doesn't leave me with a lot of choices, does it? Or is it that you'd rather see me stay in the woolen outfit so I don't give you any competition as you roam the city looking for the next victim, or should I say lover, who can give you just that much more control, that much more power, and, just incidentally, that much more sex?"

Annabelle cocked her head and looked at Sophie. "My, a little touchy tonight, aren't we?"

"We aren't anything. It's down to you by yourself or with Josie and me by myself or with Cristine. We aren't a team anymore, I guess, even though I thought after this last week things were getting back to normal, the way they had been on the ship."

Annabelle rose slowly. "I'm sorry if I gave you that feeling. I've been here because you were terribly ill and I wanted to take care of you. But that doesn't mean that my life is going to change back to the way it was before I came to San Francisco. We don't have to be inseparable, like we were. In fact, we cannot possibly be the same as we were, not and live our own lives."

"Then why are we considering buying ships together and renovating them? You don't really want to be partners with me if you feel like I'm hanging onto your apron strings so you can pull me along. God knows I'd never want you not to live your own life."

Sophie's hurt was beginning to be supplanted by anger.

"I suppose you could say that, though I prefer to think that all I'm doing is helping you through the rough first couple of months in a new city," Annabelle said. "Look, I'm not trying to hurt you, but we can't look out for each other the way we used to. We need to be apart, with different friends and different interests. You don't want to be with Josie and me; you wouldn't have fun. You don't even want to be with Ruari and me, because you don't really like him, and besides, I don't want another woman around when I'm with him."

Sophie started to tell Annabelle that she'd like a chance to see whether she'd like to be with Josie and her when they did things like shop for dresses, but she knew from the way that Annabelle's jaw was set that she wouldn't be able to change her sister's mind. Instead, she focused on Ruari and her sister.

"Doesn't it bother you that he really isn't interested in you? He comes here every day, you know, bringing me sweets or something for the cats, or just to talk. I don't trust him completely, but he's not nearly as bad as I thought he was when I first saw him on board the *Salud Y Amor*." Sophie was genuinely curious about how Annabelle could feel good about chasing after a man who wasn't interested.

"He's interested. I can promise you that. He comes to visit you because he feels sorry for you. He doesn't feel sorry for me," Annabelle said, preening.

The look that Annabelle gave her was enough to make Sophie want to throw up. That, in combination with the sinking feeling in the pit of her stomach when Annabelle declared that Ruari only came to see her because he felt sorry for her, made her ripe for a fight.

"You don't have to try and make me jealous, you know. Whatever the reason, Ruari McKay comes here every day to visit me. He's been the perfect gentleman, and I must admit, my initial feelings of loathing have definitely changed. But as for his feeling sorry for me, you are wrong. Remember, Annabelle, you've always been good with the cards. You could read them no matter who held them, and it helped you make money every time you could sucker someone into playing with you. But I've always been the one who could read people, and I can tell you that Ruari isn't interested in you and he isn't sorry for me."

"Then why do you think he takes me to bed?"

Sophie fought to control the urge to slap her sister silly. She gritted her teeth and put her hands behind her back. "I don't believe he does, and if he does, I don't care. He still does not feel sorry for me." It was a lie. She did care, not so much because Ruari meant anything to her, but because Annabelle was being so mean to her.

"Yes, of course, you'd know about things like that, wouldn't you, you and your miss prim and proper best friend. Silly you, not only don't you know what Ruari's doing, but you honestly believe that if you just follow all her precious little rules and manners and regulations, you'll fit right into proper society. The only thing you'll ever fit into is the dockside trade, Sophie. You're no different from me. You've never been ashore, you've never learned the rules, and you'll never be able to carry it off, no matter how much Cristine tries to change you."

"Thank you for the kind words of encouragement. I love being likened to a wharf rat."

"We are who we are, Sophie. I've found a way to use what I am, and all you're interested in is changing what you are. It won't work; changes never do, not even when they're instituted by someone like Cristine Halladay."

Sophie forced herself to relax her hands, even though the impulse to deck her sister was still almost overwhelming.

"I don't know why you don't like her. She's never said anything about you other than that she'd rather not lead the same kind of life that you do."

"I have a suspicion that you've just taken everything that Cristine says and swallowed it in huge gulps without even thinking about whether it's good for you or reasonable or even right. She's so damned perfect that it's a wonder her dresses will fit over her wings!"

Sophie nodded. So Annabelle was jealous of Cristine. That made sense, considering the kind of friends that she had herself.

"Cristine has been kind enough to help me learn a lot more about how things are done on land. We knew everything about ship society, but nothing at all about living with other people. All she's done has been to show me what is important to the landlubbers. It's been quite an education."

"A prudish woman, far too interested in her own good. She's a nasty-minded, selfish bitch, and the faster you get rid of her, the better."

"She's my friend."

"She'll do you no good, Sophie. You need a friend like Josie."

"Oh, now we get to the wonderful Josie, who does everything for you, including leading you into a life of prostitution. Yes, I need that kind of friend. All my life I've wanted to be welcome in the houses that we used to sail by. Cristine would be welcome. Josie would not. Not one of your friends, or you either, would be welcome in any kind of respectable house,"

"We not only live in a respectable house; we run one."

"Cristine won't even go into the Painted Lady; she says it's not the place for a woman with a good reputation."

"That puts me in my place, doesn't it? I don't have a good reputation; I've got an honest one. I'm honest with the cards, I'm honest with the drinks—I don't water them by more than half—

and the men know it, and I'm honest with the men that I have as friends."

"You mean that you have sex with," Sophie said flatly.

"Yes, the men I have sex with. I'm honest about it, Sophie. I haven't lied to you."

"Cristine can't even bear to think about what you do, and neither can I."

"So she judges my life and you agree with her. You don't like my life; you don't like what I do for a living; you don't like my friends. What exactly do you like?"

"Damn it, that's not fair. When I try to get involved with the people that you know and like, I'm pushed away. I can't even get close enough to find out who is right, you or Cristine. 'No, I don't need to go shopping with you.' 'No, I really don't need to stop by the Painted Lady.' 'No, it isn't convenient right now.' You've said every one of these things to me. And you think I'm the only one that's being difficult? You act like you're afraid that if I come anywhere around your friends or your business, everyone will start being friends with me and leave you behind. You're jealous, did you know that? Jealous and petty and mean."

"I am not!" Annabelle was almost screaming. "The reason I don't want you around is because I'm sick to death of you. I want my own friends, my own lovers, and my own business. You can have your own—I don't care about that—but stay away from mine!"

"And you think I'm any less sick of you? Trying to grab Ruari because you're worried someone might not fall under your spell? Trying to keep me out of your life? Well, let's give it one hell of a good try, all right? Let's get out of each other's lives and stay out. I'm disgusted by what you've done with your life anyway. I can't imagine letting those men do that to you, over and over—it isn't power; it's something worse, something terribly dirty, and I don't like to be around dirt."

Annabelle was stunned into silence for a moment. They'd

fought before, but never like this, never to where it sounded like they hated each other.

"Sophie, please listen—"

"No, I don't want to know. You only care about what keeps you satisfied, and what makes you feel good makes me feel sick with shame for you! I wish you weren't my sister. Your kind of satisfaction is sordid and nasty and it makes you the same."

Annabelle gasped and her hand went to her stomach. She looked for all the world as if Sophie had just punched her in the gut.

Sophie stopped, shocked at what she'd said. She wished she could have called the words back; she would have done anything to stop the ugly sounds the instant they left her mouth.

Annabelle stared at her sister. Her face went white and her eyes sparkled with either anger or tears; even she wasn't certain which. Nothing she could say to her sister could even approach the pain that Sophie had just inflicted on her. She and Sophie had had fights before, but they'd never said hurtful things to each other.

"I'm sorry. I didn't mean that."

"Yes, you did. You've fallen under Cristine's spell, and nothing will be the same between us until you've broken free of that woman."

"No, this isn't about Cristine and what she says or does. This is between you and me, and we're the only ones who can sort it out."

Annabelle stood up, and started for the door. Her face was drawn and tight, and she didn't even look at her sister.

Sophie reached out toward her sister. "Can't we discuss this?"

"I don't think so. I'm leaving and I'm not coming back, not for a long time."

"No—"

But the sound of Sophie's voice was cut off by the echo of

the door to the cabin slamming as Annabelle ran from the room and up the stairs to the deck.

Sophie tried to follow her sister, but she was still too weak from the fever to be able to rush up the steps and out onto the deck to convince Annabelle that she didn't mean what she'd said.

And the worst thing was, even if she could have followed her sister, she'd have been lying if she told her nothing mattered except being friends.

She collapsed back in bed and the tears began to flow down her cheeks. She tried to reach out, as she had all her life, to connect with Annabelle and tell her using their one special closeness that she was sorry.

She stiffened, startled.

There was nothing there.

Not a whisper. Not a feeling, nothing.

It was as if Annabelle had disappeared from the face of the earth. It was an even deeper blackness than it had been when Annabelle had been drugged and stolen from New Orleans. And it was different—there was a thread that let Sophie know that this time it was deliberate. Her sister had, for the first time in both of their lives, cut her completely out of her mind and refused to let her back in.

11

SOPHIE WAITED ALL NIGHT BEFORE SHE WAS certain that Annabelle was really gone. She had cut herself off, and there was no going back. Still, Sophie couldn't believe that Annabelle didn't even want to talk to her. They didn't have to be close, like they'd been before, but surely Annabelle couldn't mean to cut off all communication between them.

One entire day went by without any kind of communication from Annabelle. When Ruari came to visit, Sophie turned him away.

Occasionally she felt a tendril of thought from Annabelle, but nothing aimed toward her, nothing of the old connection that they'd always had. Worse, when she felt something, it was because Annabelle was discussing Sophie with other people.

It was like a slap in the face to know that Annabelle would talk to others about their personal problems. They'd always cloaked their relationship in privacy, because they were so much closer than most sisters.

For the first time in her life, Sophie felt as if Annabelle had broken a trust between them, and the ache that she felt was so strong that she could do nothing except sit in the cabin and stare into the darkness.

The next day Sophie asked Cristine to find out what was happening at the Painted Lady.

Dominic continued the steady pace of renovating the ship as the women talked. Their sentences were punctuated by the steady blows of his hammer.

"No, I've told you before, it's not the kind of place that a proper woman would enter," Cristine said, repressing a shudder at the very thought.

"But I need to know that she's all right. What if she's hurt? What if that's why she didn't come back to patch things up last night?" Sophie knew it wasn't true, but she'd like to have at least some confirmation that Annabelle was at least as miserable as she was.

"I'm sorry, there's no way I can help you. I will not demean myself by even walking past such an establishment with the intention of looking inside. I have people deliver my pasties there, but I never go inside myself as a matter of principle."

Cristine put her hand on Sophie's arm, squeezing to emphasize her words. "You need to realize that while she is your sister, she's not involved in a business that you should even be near. You said that you wanted to learn something about proper society. The way to make a start in proper society is to stop associating with people like the women in the Painted Lady and patronize only establishments where women are treated as the fragile creatures in need of protection that we are."

"Fragile creatures?"

Sophie bit back anything else she might have said, but she might have included pointing out how Cristine was making her own way, working harder than many men and totally without the protection of any male creature. In fact, when Cristine had needed male help, the only help she'd been offered had been a forced marriage just to allow her to live at the Presidio. Neither she nor Cristine qualified as fragile bedewed blooms.

Sophie's thoughts must have shown on her face, because Cristine rushed to explain.

"Even if we aren't quite the delicate flowers that we aspire to be, that doesn't mean we should forget all breeding and upbringing and allow ourselves to become the type of woman that your sister has fallen to."

Sophie drew back, moving her arm from under Cristine's hand. Damn it, she was beginning to see what Annabelle had meant when she said that Cristine wasn't a good influence on her. "But I need your help, the same as you needed my help when you wanted to stay here." Sophie said it so low that she didn't think anyone else could have heard her.

Dominic, however, laid down his hammer and stepped between the two women. He stared down at Cristine.

"Give me the pasties for her sister; I'll deliver them and find out how her sister is doing, if you're so proper that you can't even help out a friend when she asks you to. I need to find out if anyone has seen Nellie, anyway. I'll take care of both errands at once."

"It's not a question of helping a friend. I'm trying to help her become something more than she's been," Cristine said, drawing herself up and glaring at Dominic, ignoring the fact that he was almost two feet taller than she was.

"Something more than what? I think she's fine the way she is, and I don't think anyone needs your kind of meddling," Dominic said, his voice dangerously low.

"You would, considering your background," Cristine said and turned away.

Dominic's hands clenched and Sophie knew that if Cristine had been a man, she would have been flattened against the far rail or dumped into the sea. As it was, Dominic turned and stalked away, carrying the cloth-covered trays of pasties down the plank and out into the bustle of San Francisco.

Later in the day, he brought back his report to Sophie.

"There is good news about Annabelle, but she is not a happy

woman. She's dealing her games and meeting her men friends and carrying on like nothing ever happened. But the entire establishment has been thrown into a frenzy because Josie disappeared. She was there last night, she talked with your sister after she came in from seeing you, but sometime in the night she was spirited away by someone."

"She probably just found—" Sophie was appalled to think what had almost come out of her mouth to describe what Josie had found that would lure her away from the Painted Lady.

"No, it wasn't what you think. There was blood in the room, and one of the women remembers hearing a scream quite early this morning."

"And Annabelle is worried about Josie?"

Dominic gave her a strange look. "Yes, she is worried about the disappearance. After all, Josie is her best friend."

"I used to be her best friend," Sophie said softly, so softly that Dominic couldn't hear her.

Dominic continued. "I met Ruari McKay at the Painted Lady and he was asking after you. I told him that you were fine, but I don't think he believed me. He said he'd try to see you later."

Sophie turned toward the railing and stared out at sea. She had been so naive when she came here and only wanted gold to make herself happy.

"As long as I know that Annabelle is alive and well, we'll manage to work it out eventually," Sophie said with a lot more confidence than she felt.

She spent another horrible night lying awake, wondering what she was going to do if Annabelle didn't relent.

"Why doesn't it get any better? I thought that people were supposed to be able to survive a death in the family, or a tragedy that cut one person off from another? Why is this almost killing me?" she whispered in the darkness as she reached out once more for her sister and found nothing.

It was like having part of herself cut off, and it felt like the bleeding wouldn't ever stop. There was no healing; there was only raw pain and grief at her own stupidity and at Annabelle's callous disregard of their closeness.

The grief overwhelmed her and she wanted nothing more than to sit down and cry, but she couldn't even do that. Crying made her jaw and head ache, and she couldn't stand any more physical pain.

Instead of crying, she stayed in bed. The kittens lay beside her, and occasionally one of them would venture up toward her face to see if he could help her by giving her little kitten licks, but nothing worked. Finally, in the small hours of the morning, she would lie back, exhausted, and drift off into dreams of being reunited with Annabelle.

On the third day she awoke to the sound of someone pounding on her door. She could hear Cristine's voice rising in exasperation.

"I'm telling you, you cannot go in there; that is a private cabin and you haven't been invited and it wouldn't be proper even if you had been!"

Suddenly the door was flung open and Ruari strode into the room. The kittens arched their backs and fluffed their tails and then scurried to the back of the bed as he approached.

He looked at the cats and smiled. "Enough of that, you ungrateful wretches! Next time see if I bring you anything nice to eat!" He plopped another basket containing more eggs, a tin of milk, and some meat for the kittens and a huge box of Mexican sweets for Sophie down on the bed. Then he turned to Sophie.

"All right, that's quite enough of staying in bed and feeling sorry for yourself. What do you think you're going to do, sit down here until you rot away with the mold and fog? Don't be silly." Ruari took Sophie's arm and pulled her out of bed. He ignored her frantic effort to pull her bedclothes around her to shield herself from his gaze.

"What do you think you're doing? Who said you could come in here?" she demanded, trying to wrench her arm free of his grip. "I'm just fine; now leave me alone! And for your information, Annabelle is perfectly capable of searching for Josie on her own. She doesn't want me around her friends anyway."

"You are not fine; you are wallowing in self-pity and for no reason at all. I'm sorry you had a fight with your sister, but it's time to get up and go on with your life and let things work themselves out without you burying yourself down here in a hole.

"Look at you. You haven't combed your hair in a week, the kittens look like they're the only ones who've been eating regularly, and not to put too fine a point on the quill pen, my dear, but you stink."

"Get out of here!" Sophie shrieked.

Ruari nodded approvingly. "Good. You're still capable of anger. Then you're not too far gone. Feed the kittens, get dressed, and come up on the deck. We've got business to talk about. And eat one of those candies; it'll give you strength. Look at you, letting yourself get into this condition!" Ruari shook his head in exasperation. "Annabelle isn't pining for want of having you around, so you certainly shouldn't give her the right to make you miserable when she's not suffering."

"I don't like candies." That was a lie, probably the biggest lie that Sophie could ever have thought of. The one thing that she loved above all else was sweets.

"You love candies. Annabelle told me. The lady who makes them is a friend of mine, and I've never tasted anything better than her candied squash," he said, smiling his perfect smile. "I'd never have thought that most of the things she makes sweets of would be good, but I've enjoyed candied goat's milk, squash, and even cactus. If you'd like, I'll bring you more after you've finished this."

Ruari opened the tin and held it out invitingly toward her.

Sophie wanted to stay furious with him. He'd just been horrible to her, and no man should be forgiven for telling a woman that she smelled. But sweets had always been her downfall, and the spicy scent of the candied squash filled the room, begging her to taste just one.

"Thank you." The words barely made it past her teeth, but they did make it into the room.

"You're welcome. Now, you have a couple of pieces of candy, get dressed and come up on deck, and we'll have a nice breakfast at one of the hotels around the square. I think some hot coffee and cinnamon buns would do wonders for your temper." He handed the box to her, turned, and walked out of the room before she could tell him what she thought of his orders and his plan for the morning.

She gripped the box with full intent of throwing it at him, but the sweet smell stopped her before she could ruin a perfectly wonderful gift.

Ruari looked over his shoulder and smiled. "I knew you couldn't throw it at me. Try the orange ones first; they're the best." He disappeared up the stairs.

Sophie looked at the squares of deep orange and swallowed. She'd been up all night, her stomach was in open rebellion because she hadn't eaten anything in almost forty-eight hours, and she knew she had to take a taste of this or Ruari would be bitterly disappointed in her. She didn't like him too much, she still didn't trust him, but she had a perverse fear of making someone think that she wasn't quite civilized. A civilized person would eat and smile and say, "Thank you," so that was what she would do whether she liked it or not.

She picked up one of the squares, nibbled off a small piece of candy, expecting it to taste horrible, and then smiled as the sweet pumpkin taste filled her mouth. She'd always liked pumpkin but never had a chance to eat much of it. This was delightful! Even her stomach agreed, quieting to a murmur of hunger from the full-throated roar.

"This is wonderful!" she said and took another, larger bite.

In a matter of minutes she'd eaten three pieces of candy and for the first time in a week felt like she could face the world outside. She ran her hand through her hair and grimaced. Ruari was right. She needed to clean herself up.

Wrapping herself in a robe, she bobbed her head through the hatch at the top of the stairs.

"This will take a little bit longer than a couple of minutes. And, Cristine, I'll need your help in warming water on those stoves. It won't slow you down, since you're only cooking in the oven. We've got barrels of water, heat enough for a bath, and have Dominic bring it down." Sophie saw the mutinous look on Cristine's face and ignored it. She was getting a free ride; she could help out when asked. Sophie had decided right then that the next time she asked Cristine for help and didn't get it, Cristine was going to be walking the streets of San Francisco looking for another place to cook her pasties.

It took almost half an hour and a full barrel of water before Sophie felt clean enough to get dressed. It wasn't even her being so dirty, despite Ruari's remark about her stinking, that made her take such a long, leisurely bath. She'd long since discovered that when she had the luxury of a bath, she could sit in the steaming water, the waves gently lapping around her, and think through the great problems of her life and sometimes actually solve them.

By the time the water had cooled and her body's lobster-red color had subsided to a gentle pink, she'd decided that if she couldn't solve the problems with Annabelle, then she'd have to go on alone. She'd do what she needed to start a new life apart from her sister.

It was hard, it was painful, but it was the only way to go forward after the break that she'd caused, until she could heal that break sometime in the future.

Sophie appeared on deck, her copper hair shining, her skin scrubbed and fresh, and looking for all the world like a proper lady in her wool skirt and coat that Cristine had sewn for her during the voyage to San Francisco.

"Thank you, the candy and the lecture were both exactly

what I needed, but I still won't help Annabelle with anything that has to do with Josie," Sophie said.

"We'll see," Ruari replied, smiling at her.

Sophie didn't think she'd ever seen such an expanse of perfect teeth. The only problem was they weren't as pretty as they had been when he boarded the ship that first time. He was beginning to lose his seaman's tan, and the teeth didn't look quite as startlingly white against his skin.

"Shall we go? I'm sure there's a table waiting for us at the Palace, and we can talk about everything while we eat." He held out his arm and Sophie took it, feeling for all the world like the proper lady that Cristine kept telling her she ought to be.

They'd finished the meal before Ruari broached the subject that he'd come to discuss.

"Remember the ship I offered to sell you? I wanted to give you the first chance at the ship. I just didn't know whether you still wanted to deal with me now that Annabelle is no longer a part of the deal."

Sophie took another sip of the tea and sat back in the chair. "I'm still interested. It's still a good idea, and I want to get on with my life whether Annabelle is a part of it or not. However, before we do anything more I'd like to visit the *Mary Kathleen* and see whether she's worth more than a thousand dollars," Sophie said.

"You mean you're interested in buying her yourself, without your sister's help?" Ruari was clearly surprised. "I didn't think that you'd be able to do anything on your own." It was obvious that he was curious about where she'd get eleven hundred dollars, but she had no intention of satisfying his curiosity. The money was there; that was all he needed to know.

"I've had another offer since I talked to you and your sister."

"How much and who from?" Sophie asked. She felt a thread of irritation. Was this what the sweets and treacly words had been about—a chance to raise the price on her before she even saw the ship? Suddenly all her good feelings toward Ruari

McKay evaporated as if they'd never been. She'd been right the first time—he was a pirate.

"Let me tell you about the offer," Ruari said hastily when he saw Sophie stiffen with anger. "I won the ship in a card game at the Painted Lady. I wasn't even sure that the man who lost her had the right to put her up for his debts, but I took a chance. I asked around and no one else came forward to claim her, so I assume that everything is fine, that I actually own her and can sell her. But not more than twenty-four hours after I won that game, I had a man offer me ten thousand dollars and a share of the profits if I would gather a crew, empty whatever is left of the cargo, and leave for China in the next five days."

Sophie felt her heart sink. It had been a nice idea, all that cargo and a good ship, too, but there was no way she could afford to deplete all of her gold reserves just to match that kind of outrageous price. There would be other ships in the harbor; all she had to do was wait for a better deal.

"Then I'd suggest that you take that offer. Didn't you say that you wanted to get out on the ocean again and that you were tired of being on land, especially in a place like San Francisco? This is the chance that you've been waiting for to make another fortune, isn't it?"

"I did. But there's something strange about the offer. Something just doesn't quite ring right, and I'm not going to accept until I'm sure that everything about the offer is shipshape. I think the man is trying to secure business for someone else, and if what I suspect is correct, it is for a person I have no wish to associate with. Besides, if he's really serious about outfitting a ship and sending it off to China, we could always use the *Flying Angel.* She's more than enough ship to cross the Pacific."

"Who was the offer from?"

"A man whom I believe to be in league with Thomas Fry."

The name was enough to make Sophie grit her teeth until her jaw started to ache.

Ruari saw her jaw suddenly tense. "Oh, don't do that; it will make your face hurt again. Don't worry; I'm not selling to him. I'll find another ship, something just as good, for Fry to buy, or he can use the *Flying Angel* and we can proceed with the bargaining from there about the trip to China.

"I offered the *Mary Kathleen* to you, and you shall have it for eleven hundred dollars if you wish."

"Why?"

"Why what?" Ruari looked at her blankly.

"Why do you want to do that for me, and why do you want to lose nine thousand dollars?"

Ruari blushed. It was so unexpected that all Sophie could do was stare.

"I'd rather not explain it."

"You'd better, because right now I don't trust you."

Ruari leaned over and covered her small hand with his larger suntanned hand. "I am offering you the deal because I am trying to court you and the only way I can even get your attention, short of giving you another three kittens, is to help you obtain the ship that you want and that I own."

"Court me?" Sophie's face was white and her voice a mere whisper.

"Yes, of course. You mean you have been completely oblivious to—? Oh, my dear." Ruari didn't know what to say.

"Oh, no! You can't mean it."

"Please, don't say no yet," Ruari pleaded. "Let me work with you on the *Mary Kathleen*. Let me show you that I'm not a pirate, that I want to be fair with you. If nothing else, take the ship as an apology that I wasn't able to convince you I meant no harm when I boarded the *Salud Y Amor* that night while you were drifting free."

"I had no idea," Sophie said and meant every word. She began to relax. She hadn't been wrong. Ruari McKay hadn't been coming around the ship because he felt worry for her, like her sister had said. It made her feel better just to know that she hadn't misread his intentions so badly after all.

Maybe she would work with him. He was very handsome, he was nice, and he liked her. It wasn't a bad start. "I'd like to inspect the *Mary Kathleen.* When can we go have a look at her?"

Ruari's smile lit the room. "Are you really up to inspecting a ship? I know I dragged you out of the cabin because otherwise you'd have rotted in there, but you still haven't completely recovered from the beating."

"Almost all of the bruises have healed. I am perfectly capable of looking at a ship." She didn't need to add that it felt like her ribs were on fire and that she still didn't dare take too deep a breath for fear of letting out a most unladylike yelp in public.

"If you are sure, we can go right now. There's a rowboat down by the *Flying Angel* that we can use. If you buy the *Mary Kathleen,* we can lower her rowboat and tie it up beside the *Salud Y Amor* and you'll be able to come and go from the ship as you wish."

Sophie was glad that she'd never been prone to seasickness. The ride out to the *Mary Kathleen* was rough, the seas heavy from the wind that rushed in from the west, bringing the threat of rain. But it was only a threat; it hadn't rained in San Francisco for months and the city's hills were constantly awash with dust swept up by the unrelenting winds.

The ship was worth the ride. She was everything that Ruari had promised. The *Mary Kathleen* had been the pride of someone's yard. Some nautical architect had spent endless hours designing the fastest hull line, and Sophie's practiced eye saw immediately that the drag and deadrise had been reduced to a minimum. She looked like she was ready to fly at the least opportunity. Lift the *Mary Kathleen's* anchor, set her sails, and she'd have been flying past the Farallons in an instant. Even the carved sea sprite on the bow looked self-satisfied. It would be a shame if this proud lady never made it out to sea again.

The *Salud Y Amor* was a nice ship, but nothing like the *Mary Kathleen.*

The climb up the rope ladder was harder than Sophie had expected. Her arms ached with every foot that she gained, and by the time she reached the railing and pulled herself onto the deck, her side hurt so much that she was gasping in pain.

Ruari watched as she stood quietly for a few moments, trying to look as if everything were just fine. Her color was dead white, and every inhalation was guarded as she tried not to breathe so deeply that her lungs expanded against the broken ribs.

"If you need help, please just ask," he said quietly. He wasn't going to force his attention on her, but he wanted her to know that he was aware that she hurt.

Sophie smiled at him, but it was forced.

"There now, shall we go belowdecks?" Ruari asked when it looked like she could breathe again without almost crying with each intake of air.

Sophie nodded. She didn't trust herself to talk just yet. She looked around the ship, walking toward the bow and inspecting the layout of the deck.

"She's beautiful," Sophie finally said, running her hands over the fine wood and beautiful brass. "Look how the poor thing needs to be scrubbed. You can see how nicely they used to take care of her, all shipshape and Bristol fashion. Just a few weeks and look what happens in the salt air." Sophie scrubbed at one patch of brass, bringing one square inch back to a shine. The wooden deck had been allowed to pockmark with droplets of sea salt instead of being kept to a shiny surface by oil and plenty of scrubbing, and she frowned, wishing that the captain had taken the time to give everything one last polish of heavy oil and wax just to keep things from rotting in the cold salt air.

Ruari was warmed by her obvious love for good workmanship. It was rare to find a woman who appreciated what went into a ship like this.

"I suppose it wouldn't hurt the deck too much to put in deck lights. We'd need some kind of illumination belowdecks if I actually moved men in here."

Sophie had always loved the deck lights that had been put into one of her uncle's ships. The lights looked like upside-down glass pyramids with the flat bottoms laid even with the deck and the pointed ends of the pyramids pointing down below the deck. It was amazing how much natural light that one square foot of glass allowed into the cabins.

"I even know where you could buy a couple of the lights for almost nothing. Ask me when we get back to shore, and I'll take you to the marine repair ship where I saw them, if everyone hasn't already left for the goldfields. Actually, it wouldn't be bad if they did leave; then we could pick the lights up for nothing."

"Free sounds good," Sophie said, staring at the deck and planning to bring the ship back to her former glory with a little elbow grease and spit polish once the ship was her own. If they converted this ship to bunks, it would be with sleeping areas that could be ripped out at a moment's notice, if and when the ship finally had a chance to go to sea once again.

She made her way over to the hatch that had been closed over the stairs leading down to the lower areas and pulled at the cast-iron ring that served as a handle, but she couldn't budge it, no matter how hard she pulled. She sat back, biting her lip in frustration. Her hands were shaking and she was covered with sweat.

"Would you mind if I got that?"

She nodded and his fine muscles rippled as he gave the hatch one heave that pulled it free.

"It would have done that for me if I'd tried one more time," she said hastily, but both of them knew that she couldn't have tried one more time.

She lit a tin can candle that had been set to one side of the hatch and descended into the belowdecks area. It was dusty and smelled of old fish and human sweat and almost-fresh wood. It was clean, almost preternaturally clean after a long sea voyage.

The captain, she was willing to bet, had been a slave driver to his men, insisting that everything be shipshape and Bristol fashion, even if it meant working long, hard hours before the captain was satisfied. She'd been with captains like that, and they were the easiest of all men to work for. A sailor always knew exactly what he was to be doing and how to do it and what would happen to him if the captain wasn't satisfied.

But this made the captain's desertion of the ship even stranger. Usually men like that would rather go down with the ships than abandon them to the elements. Still, gold fever did strange things to men's brains, enticing them to leave behind everything they held dear for the chance to muck around in cold water for the glint of five dollars' worth of metal in the bottom of a pan.

Something niggled at her brain as she walked around, climbing over the timbers that framed the ship and checking out the various sections. She was used to the mustiness and salt odor that accompanied most ships, but this one had a smell of something else that she couldn't put her finger on. She could sense it, just as she could tell that something was wrong, but she couldn't figure out what it was. Overlaying it all was a sound, nothing that Ruari would have heard, of course, but the sound of unhappy people. It left a buzz in the ship that was slow to dissipate after the people who caused it left.

She still couldn't discover what made her so uncomfortable or what had made the people so unhappy, so she shrugged and climbed into the next hold.

It was filled with bottles and casks and square ceramic holders. The odor was indescribable, a cross between a flower garden and something dark and heavy that made her nose and throat sting like old smoke.

"What on earth?" she asked, running her fingers over several of the wooden casks. They were sealed with wood first and then what looked like thick candle wax and finally with leather tightened across the top, lapped over the side, and tied in place with rope.

The ceramic canisters' lids were held by more wax, but the

odor of the contents still seeped into the air.

She wished she could read Chinese as well as speak it; then she would have known what all this was. She had a sneaking suspicion that Dr. Mao might be interested in this cargo. It smelled like some of the stuff he had in his apothecary. She made a note to see him tomorrow and ask for his help. If he wanted the cargo, she could have her thousand-dollar investment back in her pocket before sundown. It sounded like a wonderful plan.

"No one wants this cargo?" she asked.

"No, it's yours to do with as you wish. Someone in the heathen Chinatown will be interested, I'm sure, but no one in the rest of San Francisco gives a fig for all of this nonsense."

Sophie bristled at the characterization of Chinatown, then realized that she might have felt the same way if she hadn't been practically raised with Tsao Liu and a couple of other Chinese who had taught her the languages and the ways of their country. She'd cut Ruari some slack this time, but the next time he made a comment like that he was going to be educated as to her sensibilities on the subject of the Chinese.

She went on with her explorations, stepping into the galley. Everything had been left just as the cook walked away from it; the flour, sugar, and tea were still in containers held in place with cords. The kettle still had water in the bottom, though it was slimy and smelled awful. She had an odd feeling, as if she shouldn't go any further or she might find something terrible. Like Nellie's body. Where *had* that woman gone? Sophie shook off the feeling and continued the exploration.

She ran her hand over the tiny black stove that had served to cook all the meals for the men. A little stove black would work wonders for the spots of rust that were beginning to appear on the surface.

The woodwork in the ship was as fine as any she'd seen in a long time. She'd shipped on buckets that could barely hold water and the newest and best out of Baltimore, and this was as good as the best she'd ridden on. A ship this good deserved to end up as something more than a floating hotel that would eventually disintegrate and sink to the bottom of the bay.

It wasn't until she poked around into the farthest holds that she realized just what a treasure she'd found left behind in the ship.

There was flour and salt beef and candles and bolts of muslin that had been left behind as the sailors ran for the goldfields. In another hold, hammocks swung in the draft as she opened the hatch. If the men who wanted to rent space weren't too particular, the hammocks could be used for sleepers. This ship, she decided, could easily be ready to sleep men in a matter of two or three days.

She stood in the main hold and looked around her.

There was something wrong.

Something didn't match, but she didn't have a clue as to what it was that had caught her attention.

Damn, she thought, as she reached out for Annabelle, only to be met with the solid wall of silence. She needed her sister. She needed to talk to her and see if she could unravel the puzzle that the ship presented.

She'd have to do it on her own. The realization made her droop with tiredness.

Ruari lowered the *Mary Kathleen*'s rowboat, tied his own little rowboat to the back, and towed it back to the dock.

"Thank you for your time, for the sweets, and for rowing me over to the ship. If you'll come early in the morning, I'll have the money ready for you and the *Mary Kathleen* will be mine," Sophie said.

"At eight, then?" Ruari asked.

"That's fine." She turned and walked up the plank to the *Salud Y Amor* and down to the cabin. Cristine was gone somewhere, Dominic was nowhere to be found, and she was too tired to talk to anyone anyway. She'd never expected to be this weak after almost two weeks of recuperation. She grabbed another piece of candy while she changed into the last clean sleeping shirt that she owned.

She fell face first onto the bunk and slept, the kittens curled on her back.

In her dreams she heard someone calling her. Someone needed her help and she couldn't find them in the darkness. And she had the oddest feeling that she didn't want to find whoever was calling her.

12

SOPHIE WOKE UP AND STARED AT THE CEILing of the small cabin.

Who wanted her help? She had a very vivid memory of having been summoned to help a woman in need, but she couldn't see the face or hear a name. Of course it might have been Nellie—she'd been gone almost a week—but then it could also have been Josie. And if it was Josie, the woman could die and rot in hell for all she cared.

She petted the kittens and tried to recapture more of the dream, but it moved steadily away from her. Finally she thrust the puzzle aside. She'd find out soon enough what her dreams were trying to tell her; she always did.

Instead she concentrated on the *Mary Kathleen.*

She knew what was wrong with the ship. She'd have to go back and make another tour of it, but she'd awakened that morning with a detailed plan of the *Mary Kathleen* in her mind and at long last she could identify what was wrong with it. The main hold was just about eight feet narrower than it should have been, all the way along one side of the ship.

It wasn't until she'd gone to sleep that her mind had put

together all the pieces of what she'd seen and felt while she was on board the *Mary Kathleen*. Now she had a pretty good idea of why the captain hadn't worried about abandoning his ship and cargo. If what she suspected was right, he'd already cleared most of his profits as soon as the ship landed, just as soon as the main cargo of Chinese women had been unloaded, taken into the city, and sold to the waiting men.

She'd have to have Dominic come with her to check the contents of the cargo if Dr. Mao didn't want it. She hoped that he could read the Chinese script and tell her what she had in those casks and bottles. At the same time, she'd ask him about that strange little space where women might have spent the entire voyage to San Francisco.

She'd talk to him when she went up onto the deck.

She considered dressing in her one good outfit, but her side hurt after the exertion from the day before and she wasn't sure she could take the weight of the rather tightly fitted coat against her skin. Besides, she might be going into some rough neighborhoods. Instead, she dressed in her old pants, a loose cotton shirt, and the heavy Irish knit woolen sweater that had served to keep her warm all throughout her convalescence after the beating. The last thing she did was stuff her glorious red hair under a cap so that she wasn't obviously female. The sweater helped to create the illusion of a slight male figure. If it had been warm summer, she'd never have been able to get away with the disguise. Cold and windy weather made it much easier to hide and disguise herself. And disguise it was, because she intended to talk to Dr. Mao, and it was easier to find him if everyone thought she was a boy.

"Sophie, what are we going to do with the other three stoves? We've got to get them out of the hold before I can do any more of the renovation." Dominic leaned his hips against the railing, and once again Sophie was reminded of just how big the man was. The railing was almost breast-height for her, which was why she only came to a little above Dominic's belt buckle when she stood next to him.

"Three more stoves?" she asked faintly. She had been certain they'd used all of them with Cristine's enterprise. At least that was what she remembered, but she'd noticed that since the beating, parts of her memory weren't quite what they used to be.

"I've tried selling the black beasts; no one is interested—they're too heavy to pack up to the goldfields and everyone here who needs a big stove already has one," Dominic said. "I even talked to your sister last night, and she just laughed. There isn't a market for them."

She ignored the mention of her sister. If Annabelle didn't want to talk to her, she didn't want to talk about her sister.

"Why can't we put them somewhere on the deck?"

"Would you like to tell me where?" Dominic asked. "Shall we put one to one side of the hatch and every time you come up from belowdecks you can fry yourself? Or shall we move the privy and do without that small modicum of civilization?"

"All right, I'll think of something. Give me a little time, though. I'm just beginning to recover from the last disaster," Sophie moaned.

"I know, but since you've got plans for this ship, there's no way around telling you that we have a problem, short of having the stoves lifted out of the holds and thrown over the side of the boat and then telling you what we've done." Dominic grinned, knowing what her reaction would be to wanton waste of anything. He knew that Sophie would have hooked the stoves to chains and used them as fancy anchors rather than see them jettisoned completely.

"No! I'll find a way to use them. I'm getting another ship, so maybe we could install several of the stoves there and let the men do some of their own cooking?" she asked hopefully.

"That isn't a bad idea. You could make a certain percentage of profits if you brought in the basics, like flour, lard, eggs, that kind of thing, and had someone run a small store out of the ship. But that supposes that you could find someone who would be interested in that kind of activity. Chances are if you found him, you'd end up with him deserting everything within a month to go back out and hunt for gold. I'm telling you, Sophie, it's crazy out there. I've heard about gold fever, but I've never seen it in action before. The lure of that metal is quite impressive."

Sophie looked at Dominic curiously. "Why aren't you out there with them? Why hasn't the gold fever hit you like it does all the other men around here? Someone your size could surely be digging up all kinds of gold much faster than the puny little men I see all over the place," Sophie asked. "Every morning I wake up and think that this has to be the day you leave to go up to Murphys or Columbia or Sonora, but you're always here. Don't you have any itch at all to find out what's up there in the mountains?"

Dominic shrugged. "Of course I do. But you helped me when I needed a place to stay, and I promised my skills as a carpenter in payment."

"I wouldn't hold you to that. You could go if you wanted," Sophie objected. She didn't like anyone to be bound to her by some imagined debt.

"He won't leave for the same reason that I won't leave. You've been a good friend to us and we'd like to return the favor." Cristine joined them. She'd just extracted the last of the morning's pasties from the oven and was ready to take them down to the various places that were using her cooking as the mainstay of their meals. A number of runners for other establishments like the Painted Lady had already come aboard and picked up their morning orders.

Sophie managed to keep from saying what she thought, which was that Cristine was staying around because it was easy for her to cook for her various clients aboard the *Salud Y Amor*. If she actually struck out on her own and had to look for a place to cook, buy the stoves and all the ingredients, and then do the work, too, she'd go broke in a couple of weeks. Cristine wasn't staying for love of anyone except herself.

"He's also probably worried about you and he stays because of that. Mr. Tibeau has impressed me as being that kind of person," Cristine went on. It was as close as she'd ever come to acknowledging that Dominic might be a person with real feelings.

"Worried about me? Whatever for? I've healed just fine," Sophie said in amazement.

"Yes, you've managed to come back very nicely from that beating. But, Sophie, what are you going to do the next time Fry comes after you? What if he finds you alone someplace and you can't fight him off and Dominic's not there to throw him overboard? Haven't you given that any thought? If he came after you once, he'll do it again. And this time he'll kill you, and that's what Dominic is afraid of. He feels obligated to keep you safe."

Sophie was shaking her head. "Dominic isn't obligated to do anything for me. I can take care of myself. And I certainly am not going to turn tail and run just because I got beaten up. I can't leave. I've got to make money here despite the risks. I could hardly go to the goldfields and rent out space on a ship, now could I? This is all I have and this is what I will use to earn my fortune."

"You don't have to stay here. You could do something else, anything else. Look, I'll even come to the fields with you and we'll find some way to help you get rich there. But if you stay here, one of us is going to find you dead in a puddle of blood and there'll be no Dr. Mao to save you with his heathen miracles."

Sophie didn't even bother to explain that Dr. Mao had been educated in the best medical schools and there was nothing heathen about his form of healing.

"I can't leave. I've bought another ship. I'm finally making some money; I can't just up and wander away." Then there was her sister. Even if they weren't talking at the moment, she didn't want to leave Annabelle. She was sure her sister would finally come back to her senses and then everything would be just fine between them. "I promise that if anything else happens, I'll seriously consider going to the goldfields. But for right now, I've got to get to Dr. Mao and ask him if he wants whatever is down in that cargo hold, so we can get it cleared out and you and Dominic can come and look at my new treasure. We'll worry about Fry later."

"You're going to Chinatown?" Dominic asked.

Sophie nodded.

"I'll walk with you. We can talk about the goldfields on the way. I may actually be going soon, once the ships are renovated and I can leave."

"I knew the lure of gold would finally catch you!" Sophie said triumphantly.

"No, it's not gold that I want. I have searched everywhere for some sign of my mother and found nothing. There are a few people who say they met a French-speaking Chinese woman here, but no one can tell me where she went or even how long she was here. Two people have said that they think she went up to Sonora. It's possible I suppose; she might have decided the mountains were safer than San Francisco. I'll just have to follow her there."

Sophie was just about to tell him that she doubted that his mother was in the mountains and then closed her mouth. What would she tell him, that she just felt that the woman was still in the city and that he should believe her even though she had no proof? They weren't that close as friends yet. They'd worked side by side until the beating, they'd talked and planned and laughed together, but it still wasn't the kind of friendship where she could tell him that she had these little insights and premonitions and have him listen to her instead of deciding that she was crazy.

However, she could ask for his help.

"The ship that I'm going to be buying has a cargo of Chinese merchandise. It looks like it's mostly dried stuff, herbs, that kind of thing. I'm giving Dr. Mao first choice, but if he doesn't want it, could you help me sell it?"

"I'd be glad to, but there isn't much market for those goods. If Dr. Mao offers anything, take it," Dominic advised.

"I'll keep that in mind."

"You're going to the doctor's dressed like that?" He was clearly scandalized by the idea of her going out in men's clothing.

"For heaven's sake, you're beginning to sound like Cristine, with all her rules about what a proper lady does. What would you prefer, that I go as a white woman with a Chinese man for an escort and we get beaten along the way for trespassing on someone's ideas of right and wrong? Or would you rather I go into Chinatown as a white woman alone and we see whether I manage to come out of there free and alive?"

"I don't think that would be wise. I've been hearing rumors that don't make me feel particularly sanguine about your chances of safety there."

"Then just ignore the clothes, all right? I'm sure no one will object, because they'll never know that I'm not a young boy," Sophie said. She was beginning to remember why she did almost everything alone. She hated to have to justify her actions to anyone.

Dominic strode on ahead of her to clear the way of people who might want to impede her progress for whatever reason. There'd been accounts of all kinds of cutthroats on the streets lately, and while women weren't usually in danger, he didn't want to take that chance with Sophie, even if no one knew she was a woman unless the wind pushed the heavy sweater flat against her breasts.

No, he thought suddenly, that wasn't the way he wanted his thoughts to go. He was all too aware of what was underneath those clothes. Any thoughts of any kind of alliance were doomed before they started, and he had to remember that. It was all right to frequent the Painted Lady once in a while and to see her sister when she was available, but Sophie was not at all like her sister.

Sophie was glad for his help, but it was obvious that Dominic hadn't quite caught on to the fact that they were vastly different sizes. He approached the one sidewalk in the entire city that she always avoided because it was too tall for her to step up onto without crawling as if there were nothing wrong with it. For him, there wasn't anything difficult about stepping slightly higher than normal and continuing on his way. For Sophie, however, it was an almost insurmountable obstacle, one that she almost always went around when she had the chance.

She was small. Worse than that, her legs were short and the sidewalk was meant for mammoth-size men.

She was sunk. There wasn't any graceful way to get up onto the flat wooden part of the sidewalk short of getting down on her hands and knees like a child and pulling herself up. She considered running along the side of the walk and catching up with him that way, but there were horses all over the place and piles of wet-looking stuff that she didn't even want to contemplate stepping into.

She'd have to ask for help.

"Dominic!" she called.

Dominic had taken two steps when he realized that she wasn't following him. He turned just as she called for help. He immediately saw what the problem was and pulled her up onto the sidewalk with one mighty tug. She was glad to see that no one in the crowds around them took it as anything other than one man helping another over an obstacle. She was glad to know that she hadn't been spotted as an impostor quite yet.

The familiar scents of vinegar and onions, ginger and garlic made her stop and sniff and look for the source of the odors.

"Oh, I haven't had any of that since Tsao Liu made that rice gruel for breakfast every day back on the *Sea Sprite.* I hated it the first time and loved it every time since then. It's best with that clear red-hot sauce," Sophie said, pointing to the bowls of thin rice soup laced with green onions and smoked pork that had been set out on the sidewalk for sale to passersby.

She wished she'd remembered to bring money with her; she could have bought a couple of bowls of the gruel.

She got thumped from behind and almost fell to the ground, but again Dominic was right there to catch her. He pulled her back onto her feet almost before she knew that she was going down. She whirled, ready to do battle with whoever had hit her between the shoulder blades. There was no one behind her, no one in the crowd who even met her eyes, yet someone had hit her on purpose for slowing the flow of traffic.

Either that, or he'd hit her because she was with Dominic. She didn't like that possibility at all. Did the trouble between the races extend to two men, one white and one Chinese, being friends?

"I have money, if you'd like some," Dominic offered, obviously delighted that she liked one of the dishes that most Westerners turned their noses up at before even tasting it.

Sophie hesitated just a moment before shaking her head. "No, we'd better get on to Dr. Mao's and get that concluded. But I'll take you up on the offer some other time when we're down here together."

"Do you even know where exactly you're going?" Dominic asked after they'd walked the length of one of the streets and turned twice into streets that dead-ended into a dirty little circles. "Or do you intend to wander around Chinatown waiting for divine inspiration to hit to bring you back to Dr. Mao's?"

"Look; you don't have to stay with me. I'll find it just fine on my own eventually. You do have other work to do here, don't you?" she asked tartly. "Would you rather just go on your way and I'll go on mine and we'll meet back at the ship?"

"I don't think so," he said slowly, weighing the way people were looking at him. Part of the attention was due to his size—it always was—but there was something else in some of those gazes. Something that meant that not everyone was fooled by her disguise. "I think I'll stay with you until we get to the doctor's."

"If you're sure, then let's go," she said ungracefully.

"You're welcome," he said blandly.

Sophie didn't answer as she started up one of the mountains that masqueraded as streets. She was almost certain that the office she'd seen through Annabelle's eyes was up this way. One street up and to the right, she decided, that was where she would find Dr. Mao. Now all she had to do was get there, straight up what looked like an unclimbable street.

By the middle of the block her lungs were ready to burst and she cursed the heavy shoes that felt like blocks of wood on her feet. She was sweating and if she'd had a decent shirt underneath the sweater, she'd have stripped down to the cotton, even though a sharp wind pushed against her as it rushed in from the bay and up the streets.

She'd never walked up a hill so steep. How did all these Chinese men manage to pass her without even breathing hard? She wasn't amused by the steady stream of small men in blue coats and pants and black shoes who made their way around her as if she were standing still.

Maybe it was those little black sandals that they wore. Maybe they made the hill easier to negotiate. She'd feel a lot better if some of the men were panting, she decided.

She took another two steps and felt a stitch in her side when she tried to breathe. The pain reached around to her front and ended in a knot at her breastbone. She tried to take another breath but couldn't. She lurched toward the side of the building and held onto the rough wood and waited for the spasm to pass. She made sure to have her back to the wood; she wasn't fond of people trying to beat her up from behind.

"Maybe this wasn't the best idea I've ever had," she said, pressing her hand against her side. It hurt bad enough that she wavered. She closed her eyes, willing the pain to go away. She had to find Dr. Mao.

She wished with all her might that someone would come along and whisk her away, lifting her to the top of the hill so she didn't have to struggle upward. Damn San Francisco anyway, with its crazy geography. Why couldn't the natives have gone a few miles in either direction and found some flat land to develop? She hated to have Dominic see her like this; she much preferred when her acquaintances thought of her as invulnerable, too strong to be hurt.

"How about if I carry you?" Dominic said, almost reading her mind. "You're still not completely recovered from that bastard's beating."

"I don't think it would be a good idea," Sophie said when she could talk without the effort costing her pain.

"Why not?"

"Hasn't it occurred to you that there aren't that many seven-foot-tall Chinese around? You've been here enough that they already know you. Go ahead and start carrying a man around in your arms and they're going to wonder just what kind of man you are."

"All right, we'll stand here and talk until you feel better."

She waited for a few seconds and then trudged on, all the while wishing that Dominic weren't around to see that she was still weak. If people knew she was weak, they'd try to find a way to take advantage of her. It had always been that way before, no reason it should be any different now.

A sweetish odor wafted out from one of the side alleys. She'd smelled that before in Shanghai when she'd had a chance to wander around the docks. It came as no shock to her that the languors of opium had been imported to the New World.

"No! Don't look directly into the room. The man who owns it would just as soon kill you as talk to you," Dominic warned, pulling her along so that she didn't even slow her pace.

She looked sideways, careful never to peer directly into the dark caverns where the men lay on rough wooden pallets one above the other and inhaled the smoke that was more important to them than life. This bunch would be dead in a matter of months and new men would take their places and no one would even miss them.

Finally she reached the top of the hill and turned right, looking for the brick steps and the grand arch of cast iron that she'd seen in her fevered dreams when Annabelle went searching for medicine for her.

Two blocks farther, she was beginning to wonder if her sense of direction had failed her completely when she realized she'd almost walked right past the iron leading into Dr. Mao's courtyard. She leaned toward the garden, inhaling the rich smell of the flowers that bloomed even in the cold San Francisco air.

"Come in, please; I was expecting you." Dr. Mao materialized at her side as he ushered her into the garden. She was surprised to find that the garden's imposing black wrought-iron gates weren't locked. She was even more surprised that Dr. Mao wasn't fooled by her disguise.

"Would you like to come in also?" the doctor asked Dominic.

"No, thank you. Now that Sophie's safely here, I'm going to go on about my business. I just wanted to make sure that her first trip away from the ship wasn't too much for her," Dominic said. "You will see that she gets home safely? She shouldn't be allowed to walk through Chinatown alone."

"Of course, I'll get her back to the ship once we're done," Dr. Mao said. He looked from Dominic to Sophie and back again, making up his mind about their relationship. "Don't worry about her for even a minute. She'll be protected as long as she's with me."

Sophie accepted a cup of steaming herbal tea with a pleasant orange taste from the woman who appeared out of the shadows of the house at the back of the garden and then silently disappeared again. Sophie tried to make eye contact with the woman, but she was like a shimmer, a ghost; she slipped in and out of Sophie's line of vision barely registering. Sophie was baffled by the lack of psychic substance for the woman; she was used to picking up at least some kind of noise from everyone she came in contact with, but this woman was utterly still. Either she was the calmest person that Sophie had ever met or over the years this woman had raised truly formidable barriers within her own mind to keep out intrusions.

Interesting, Sophie thought, and then moved on to talking with Dr. Mao.

"There are some containers on the ship I've bought that I think you might be interested in."

"Why would I be interested in them?" Dr. Mao asked. "Here, take off that sweater; I'd like to see how those ribs are healing. You were awfully pale when you came in here, and I know what a toll that street can take when you walk it in even the best condition."

"You want me to disrobe in the middle of Chinatown with nothing between me and that gate?" She was scandalized at the thought. "I thought you doctors had little dolls for me to show you where it hurt!"

"That's Chinese doctors. I'm an English doctor and I will not assume that you are doing fine until I've checked everything out myself."

"Not in the middle of the garden," Sophie insisted, still scandalized at the thought.

"You may step into that room, but I really would like to take a look at those ribs. You seem to have remarkable powers of recovery. The last time I saw you, you were almost in a coma from the beating, yet the bruises on your face and neck have all but disappeared."

Sophie sighed and nodded. She knew when a doctor wasn't going to let her out of his clutches. They were persistent enough to get their way almost every time, and that went for any kind of doctor, anywhere.

Sophie went behind the ornate screen and took off the sweater. She had on a cotton top that was ripped and stained from work on the ship and that never should see the light of day except when she was hammering nails and cutting wood. If she'd known that she was going to have to strip, she'd have worn something more presentable.

Dr. Mao, however, wasn't in the least bit interested in what she'd worn.

He probed the ribs, pushing in until she cried out and then nodding in satisfaction. "If it takes that much pressure to get a response, then you've all but healed. I'd love to say that it was the herbs and lotions that I prescribed, but I doubt that they did much more than your own strong constitution did by itself. I'm well satisfied with your progress."

He sat down in one of the white wicker chairs that were set amid the bright flowers of the garden, sipping the tea that had been magically replenished while he checked her. "Now that your physical condition has been ascertained, please tell me about this cargo."

"I don't know much about it. I opened one small ceramic jar and it had deep yellow powder inside. I smelled it and it sure smells like some of the stuff that goes into curry. I ate a lot of it when I was allowed to work with one of the cooks from India, and he called it saffron. If it's saffron, it's worth a fortune. If it's not saffron, it still smelled good enough to be used on any dish that I'd care to eat. Another container had a thick brown gooey mass inside that smelled an awful lot like some of the fish stock that is cooked around here. You know the kind, almost a paste that can be used in almost everything. Whatever it is, I think you'd be able to sell it a lot easier than I would, because it's definitely not something that most Westerners would relish. Why don't you come and look at it and then we can agree on a price if you're interested? The reason I came to you first was that you helped me when I needed it. That and the fact that I can't read Chinese, so I have no idea what the cargo consists of, and I have to hope that you will not try and cheat me as much as someone like Fry might."

"I hope your trust isn't misplaced. How big a jar of saffron?" Dr. Mao asked.

Sophie's hands sketched a container five inches on each side.

Dr. Mao betrayed his interest by a slight widening of his eyes.

Sophie already knew that it might be worth several thousand dollars, and she expected Dr. Mao knew the same thing.

"Shall we go and see it?" she asked.

"That would be an excellent idea. Lisa, I am going out. If patients come, ask them to wait," he instructed the woman who was still in the shadows and still silent.

Sophie strained to hear the name again. Surely it couldn't have been Lisa, as she'd heard. It had to be some Chinese name that simply sounded like the Western name.

This time the walk down to the wharves was a simple task—they were heading downhill instead of up and Sophie was able to match strides with Dr. Mao, so that they arrived at the dock in almost record time.

Neither of them noticed that the man who had been following Sophie occasionally ever since she'd landed in San Francisco was back on the job, only this time there was a second person following the first man.

Sophie led Dr. Mao to the *Mary Kathleen*'s rowboat, which Ruari had brought to shore and left tied up. Within a few minutes they were climbing up onto the *Mary Kathleen.*

Sophie let him lift the hatch for her and then preceded him down the stairs to the herbs and spices, and he spent a few minutes poking amid the various jars and containers, moving them, reading the signs, opening a few here and there.

Rich spicy smells filled the air. Sophie particularly liked the sweet notes added by the cask of what seemed to be vanilla beans soaking in alcohol.

Dr. Mao started poking around the hold, opening containers and casks, unwinding the rope that sealed some of the jars, and breaking the seal on one container of oil that smelled like the most potent mustard ever made.

He stopped for a few moments, investigating one small blue

and white jar that, as far as Sophie could tell, was filled with black sludge.

"I'll take everything for ten thousand dollars."

Sophie bit her lip to keep from betraying herself. She wanted to whoop, to dance, to shout. She was going to make ten thousand and she'd still have the ship? Of course she'd take ten thousand—unless she'd underestimated the value of the cargo and she could get more by jobbing it herself?

Dr. Mao misread her hesitation. "The most I can offer is twelve thousand dollars."

Sophie felt the adrenaline surge through her. There was something in the cargo that the good doctor really wanted. Why not ask for more and see what happened? Maybe there was something really worthwhile here that she shouldn't be in such a hurry to sell—but where else would she find someone to buy it? "How about fifteen thousand, I get to keep the cask of vanilla beans, and you can offload the rest immediately?"

"Done," the doctor said with such amazing alacrity that Sophie was left feeling that she might have cheated herself. If only she'd thought to ask for twenty thousand, what a difference that five thousand would make for her. Maybe she should have trusted more in her own ability to sell the goods directly to whoever wanted them.

But she hadn't and there was no chance to change her mind. They'd already made the deal.

"I'll stay here; I've got some measuring to do. You can come back with the money and take your merchandise today," Sophie said. She didn't want him to get the idea that he could do to her what Fry had done, though she had no doubt that the doctor was much more trustworthy than Fry had ever been. This time she intended to have money in her hand before she gave up even one small bottle of the cargo.

"Give me an hour and I'll be back. Will gold dust be acceptable?"

"I'd prefer coins," Sophie said. It wasn't that she needed

coins, but she'd already learned to ask for them if they were available.

"Two thousand dollars in coins is all that I have, if that is acceptable," the doctor said.

"That will be fine."

True to his words, the doctor was back within an hour, bringing with him four hefty men to carry out the cargo to the boats that he'd hired to take everything to the waiting wagons.

The gold was already sewn into gray chamois bags the size of her middle finger.

"Please, weigh them when you have a chance. If there is any lack of gold, I will certainly make it right, though I trust Lisa to have weighed everything correctly. She is far better at such things than I am, which is why she's so invaluable to the apothecary," Dr. Mao said as he handed Sophie the bags and the one flat bamboo container of coins.

Sophie wished that she had a scale on board, but even if she had one of the devices, she doubted that she could have been accurate enough to know whether Dr. Mao had actually brought all of the gold or not. She wished that Annabelle had been on the ship; she could have hurried back to the Painted Lady and weighed it for her. Or she could simply have lifted it. Annabelle was as accurate as any scale when it came to gold.

Within an hour and a half, Sophie was fifteen thousand dollars richer and the happy owner of a ship that had already paid for itself many times over. She put the heavy bags into the safe along with the other gold coins and sat down to plan what she could do with the money.

"Did the doctor help you out?" Dominic asked as he climbed up the gangplank, slowly dragging his weight as if it were an anchor that he couldn't quite lift.

"Indeed he did, far more than I expected," Sophie said. She didn't want to tell him how much money she'd made or what with.

"If this deal with the doctor includes money and you want to buy something worthwhile, why don't you go down to the end of the dock and find a man named Mifflin who's selling a twenty-foot-wide strip of waterfront property. All he wants is twenty thousand, and you could build your own dock and put your ships there." He meant it as a joke, but Sophie surprised him by quizzing him on the investment.

"How many others do you think are going to want to buy it?" she asked.

"I don't know. I just heard him say he needed the money a few minutes ago, when I was talking with him. I don't think he's even mentioned it to anyone else."

"Get him, bring him here, and tell him it's sold. I want that property!"

Dominic didn't move. Instead he laughed at her. "That was good; you almost had me believing that you wanted me to go back down to the docks and actually buy a piece of San Francisco waterfront."

Sophie forgot how tired she was; she forgot everything except the need to have that piece of land before anyone else found out about it. It would be her first real acquisition of something that couldn't be lost. Boats could sink or burn, sisters could abandon her, but land was forever, especially land in a boomtown like San Francisco. And it would be even better than what Annabelle had, because it would be hers alone, not shared with a bunch of women.

"I mean it. If you can't go down and bring him back before he talks to anyone else, then at least tell me what the man looks like and I'll find him myself."

Dominic straightened slowly. He peered down at Sophie, looking for all the world as if he'd never seen her before, which in truth he hadn't. He'd never expected such a tiny package to have such big ambitions. He'd heard her say that she wanted all the gold in California. He hadn't dreamed that she actually meant it.

13

MIFFLIN AT THE HOBNAIL CHANDLERY, ONE block down and one block to the right," Sophie repeated to herself. She'd tried to pry some kind of physical description of the man out of Dominic, but she had the distinct feeling, from the way he described the man as white, with brown hair and some color eyes and not very tall, that Dominic tended not to notice what people looked like except in extreme circumstances.

He'd almost insisted on coming with her, but she'd managed to slip off the ship while Dominic was in the privy. If she was going to buy land, she wanted to do it privately.

She was very glad that she hadn't changed from her work clothes. She could still pass as a boy as she slipped into the crowd and hurried toward the chandlery.

She stopped for a moment, careful to check behind her so she didn't get trampled by some thoughtless men. She wished she could shake the feeling of trouble that seemed to be following her around. She had no idea why it had suddenly appeared, full-fledged, as she stepped down onto the solid land from the *Salud Y Amor*, but there it was.

"Damn, what's wrong?" she whispered, looking around her.

She hated the feeling. Her stomach had a knot in it the size of a bedknob. Her hands were sweaty, and just beyond consciousness there was a flicker of some impending disaster that she couldn't quite bring into focus yet.

"I'm still not over the beating; that's what it is. I'm just not well and that's causing these strange feelings." But she knew better. She'd had this kind of feeling two days before Annabelle had been kidnapped from the bunk beside her own bunk. She'd had the same feeling the day that they'd been shipped off to her uncle's place in Baltimore. If she was truthful about it, she'd had the same kind of feelings the day of the fight with Annabelle.

Sophie always knew that terrible things were about to happen, and no matter how hard she'd tried, she'd never been able to change anything. She'd always thought that if she was going to be cursed with this kind of sight, at least it should have been the useful kind, something that she could act on and change the future instead of the helpless feeling that came from knowing something bad was ahead and heading straight for it without being able to stop.

"Miss Sophie?" She heard a lugubrious voice from behind her and turned in surprise. Few people ever recognized her when she was in her little disguises.

"Yes?" she said, turning with her hand on her knife until she realized it was the ever-genteel Mr. Abernathy.

"My dear, you shouldn't be out and about in this area, not even in that getup," he said, sniffing slightly to show his disapproval.

"How nice to see you again, Mr. Abernathy," Sophie said, trying to be gracious and all the while wondering how she could get rid of the man so she could find Mr. Mifflin and pay him the money for the land and have that piece of real estate all to herself without alerting a thousand other investors that prime real estate was up for grabs.

On the other hand, she was glad to see Mr. Abernathy for another reason.

"Tell me, is my sister well?" she asked. She never would have ventured a question about Annabelle if it hadn't been for that damned feeling of doom. If it had to do with her sister, she wanted to know it.

"She is well, though she has had a bout with the chill lately. But the business prospers and I have always had the feeling that if there is gold flowing into her pockets and staying there, then Miss Annabelle is happy. Although she would be much happier if Josie had come back to the Painted Lady. There still is no sign of her."

"She'll survive," Sophie murmured, happy that her sister wasn't in the midst of a serious crisis. But that still didn't solve the puzzle of what was giving her such a feeling of doom.

"My dear, you must let me take you wherever you are going." He offered her his arm as if she were dressed in the finest of gowns and jewels instead of men's clothing. The gesture collected a fair number of curious stares of several of the men around them.

"No, sir, I'm just fine and if you'll excuse me, I have to be on my way," Sophie said. She hated to cut him short, especially since he'd set her mind at ease about her sister, but if she had him beside her she'd never have a chance to barter for the land. She scooted ahead, blending into the crowd around her before he had a chance to say anything more.

He caught up with her. His long legs could take one stride to her two, and he made full use of their extension against her steps.

"Who might you be looking for? Perhaps I can help you?" He pointedly ignored her rudeness.

"I'm looking for Mr. Mifflin," she said. She knew when to accept defeat. Mr. Abernathy was even more persistent than she was. "The only trouble is, I don't know what he looks like or anything about him, except that Dominic saw him a few minutes ago in the chandlery shop."

"Roger Mifflin? Well, by all that's saintly, there he goes

right now!" Mr. Abernathy said, and he was off like a shot.

Sophie would never have guessed that such ungainly legs could have covered ground as fast as they did. Dandelion hair flying, Mr. Abernathy caught up with a man and pulled him to one side, motioning for Sophie to join them.

"Mr. Mifflin, may I present Miss Sophie, Annabelle's sister, though you could hardly tell it from the outfit that she's wearing. I believe that she has some business with you."

"Miss? Business? Am I aware of it?" the older man asked as he looked at what was apparently a young boy standing in front of him.

"I believe Dominic spoke to you?" Sophie was in agony. She didn't want to say anything more for fear Abernathy would jump in and offer more money than she could bid for the land.

"Dominic—oh, the Chinese gentleman. Yes, of course. I told him twenty thousand. Is that acceptable to you?"

"Is that your absolute lowest price?" Sophie hedged. She was rather beginning to enjoy haggling. It had already brought her an extra five thousand dollars on the goods on the ship. Maybe a few shrewd questions would bring him down in price. At least it was worth giving a try.

"Twenty thousand is more than equitable," Mifflin said. He raised his eyebrows in disbelief when she seemed to hesitate. "What were you thinking of offering?"

"I had considered fifteen thousand." The most he could do was yell at her and tell her not to be a fool.

"Fifteen thousand in coins, perhaps, but even that isn't important anymore. I'm leaving. I have no more need for coins than I do gold dust; they'll both sell equally well back in the States, and that's where I'm going as soon as this is concluded."

"Fifteen thousand in dust?" Sophie ventured.

"Are we talking about your waterfront property here?" Abernathy asked suddenly.

"Oh, shit," Sophie said under her breath. She'd known it was a mistake to let the man come anywhere near the deal. Damn it, why did Abernathy have to stay round where he wasn't wanted? He was going to ruin everything.

"We are," Mifflin said shortly.

"Then fifteen thousand should be more than enough for the purchase. That strip of land is barely wide enough for the most slender of ships. It is never going to grow in width, and you are already hemmed in on both sides," Abernathy said blandly. "In fact, I might actually suggest that this is not the land that she wants to buy."

Sophie considered kicking him.

Abernathy, unaware that his shins were in dire danger, continued. "Will you sell to the lady at that price if she delivers the gold to you by tomorrow morning? Surely you'd have the paper ready by then, right?"

Mifflin hesitated. "What you say is true, it isn't very wide, but it's waterfront, and that's worth a fair amount of gold these days."

"Not more than fifteen thousand. And if you hesitate, then I shall be forced to tell Miss Sophie to leave your bargain behind and hunt for something better."

Sophie's foot fairly itched to connect with Abernathy's bony legs, but she held back, watching in fascination as she saw how Abernathy had become a wealthy man.

"Fifteen thousand? No, I won't settle for that. I think that twenty thousand would be easy to get if I asked around. I have no doubt, Abernathy, that if you can't talk the lady into twenty thousand, you'll come up with it yourself."

Sophie's lips thinned. Here she'd thought Abernathy was helping her and all he was trying to do was offer a price that was ridiculously low so she lost the land and he could move in. She'd been right; he was out to protect his own ass.

"I need the money by Wednesday; that leaves me a day and a half to find out if there are any other takers."

"And if there aren't?"

"Then I'll consider the fifteen thousand."

"You'd better consider it right now, because if we leave here without a contract on your property, I will immediately take Miss Sophie over to the Gold Coast. I have good information about James Colwell selling his property. It is already improved and I believe that this afternoon in the store he was discussing a price of twenty-five thousand. That is so much better a deal that I would even be willing to partner Miss Sophie on that property, if she so desires and is in need of the cash."

Abernathy laced his thin hands in front of him, waiting to see the impact of his counteroffer.

Sophie began to smile. The old fox, he really knew how to do business. She wished she had more time to learn from him; it would be fascinating.

"If you'd like to partner me, I'd be delighted," she said, taking up the cue.

"Well, let's not get hasty here," Mifflin said. "I didn't say I was turning you down."

Mifflin pursed his lips as he thought about the offer.

"You have the gold available right now?"

"I do."

"Then I'll sell. I've got the deed with me. You deliver the gold and we'll have a deal." Mifflin smiled at both of them.

"Shall we repair to the *Salud Y Amor?*" Sophie asked.

"May I come with you, then?" Abernathy actually looked as if he expected to be told he couldn't come with her.

"Of course, Mr. Abernathy. I wouldn't think of excluding you," Sophie said and meant every word. She was delighted to have Abernathy at her side while she concluded the negotiations.

14

SOPHIE WOKE EARLY THE NEXT MORNING. IT was still dark outside and for a moment she thought it was still night, but she could hear the sounds of men up and about on the wharves and guessed the time at about four or four-thirty.

"Damn, I thought I could sleep late just this once," she muttered. But the years of training of being up early on shipboard still hadn't been broken. Besides, the kittens were already up and pacing, anticipating their breakfast early.

She sat up and felt something crinkle in her hand. She was holding onto something.

She was clutching a piece of paper. She lit the bedside candle and stared at the piece of paper.

She owned land. Land in San Francisco. She had a place to dock her boat and a piece of land where she could put up a small warehouse for the things that she was going to need to keep the ships running smoothly. She was on her way to being a success and she hadn't even needed her sister's help to do it.

"Yes, I like being a landowner," she said and laughed. She'd have to tell Annabelle, since they'd always joked that the first thing they wanted to do when they broke away from their uncle was find a way to become totally independent. Annabelle had found it with the Painted Lady, and now Sophie was going to find independence for herself with land and the ships.

Suddenly the reality hit her. She wasn't going to tell Annabelle, because Annabelle wasn't talking to her. Annabelle had cut off communications with her. Annabelle was behaving like a person that she didn't know.

The pull of talking to her sister, the sister that she'd known and loved for all those years, was almost too much to bear. She wanted the old Annabelle back so they could at least be friends again. She was tired of grieving for someone who wasn't even dead.

"Well, it wouldn't hurt to walk past the place and just happen to see if she sees me, would it?" Sophie said to herself. Of course it wouldn't hurt. Maybe if Annabelle saw her they could begin to patch things up. She'd love to boast to Annabelle about the trades she'd pulled off that left her with a second ship and a piece of land. Annabelle would have to be impressed. She liked a good deal as well as anyone else, and she'd laugh over Abernathy's way with bargaining.

Sophie put her hand against the rough planking of the cabin to steady herself. She was suddenly dizzy with wanting to talk to her sister. She'd been lonely when she was working her way down the isthmus and across to San Francisco, but she'd never had to deal with the kind of complete emptiness that filled her now.

She wanted Annabelle back and she didn't know how she was going to accomplish a healing between the two of them, but she had to try.

"For right now, I'll just go past the Painted Lady and look in. She doesn't have to see me, but if she does, then we'll talk. I know she wouldn't turn me away on her own doorstep," Sophie whispered.

It was the best plan she could come up with.

She dressed hurriedly in her old pants and top and started

up the stairs. At the last minute she grabbed the captain's sweater. It was almost certainly colder abovedecks than it was in the sheltered hold of the ship, she decided, and it was none too warm belowdecks.

"Up so soon?" Cristine called out as Sophie came abovedecks, ready to leave for the Painted Lady. A brisk wind-driven fog was washing across the deck, but Cristine was wearing only a light cotton dress as she worked. Cristine had found out that the sides of the ship, the tarp over most of the cooking area, and the heat from the stoves conspired to make it almost tropically warm around the deck where she worked. She pushed back the strands of golden curls that insisted on breaking loose from her tidy French braid. Her cheeks were pink again, a nice change from the way she'd looked when they first landed in San Francisco, when her complexion was white with shock, fatigue, and worry.

Suddenly a figure materialized, tall, dark, thin, at the back of the ship, the fog swirling around him and obscuring his face.

"Who the hell is that?" she asked.

"Mr. Abernathy. He's been coming very early in the morning to get loads of the pasties."

"Good morning. I trust that our transaction last night left you feeling satisfied?" His dandelion hair still swirled around his head, but for the first time that Sophie had ever seen, there was an actual smile, just a tinge of a smile, but one nevertheless, playing around the edges of his lips.

"Indeed it did. I am more than grateful for your help," Sophie said. She could see Cristine turning to look at them, her expression both curious and censorious.

"I am glad to be of service. May I ask if you are going to see your sister this morning?"

Cristine sniffed. "No, she is not. She and her sister are not speaking. I thought you knew that," Cristine said, determined to keep Sophie away from any of the temptations that might be put in front of her at the Painted Lady. She was still determined to make Sophie over into a proper lady.

"I do believe I will be seeing my sister, if she has time to talk today, though I have no real hope that she will," Sophie said, staring coolly at Cristine. Cristine's mouth pursed into a thin line, and Sophie was struck by how unattractive the expression made her.

Abernathy sighed and shook his head. "My dear, I believe that this estrangement has gone on long enough. If you will accompany me to my establishment this morning and stay out of sight until the grand unveiling, I believe you will have a chance to talk with your sister and right the wrongs that you have done each other."

"Unveiling?"

"Yes. You know how much I admire artists. If you remember, I said that your sister was unparalleled at her specialty of trompe l'oeil painting. Those murals are worth thousands of dollars. She could make her living painting them and instead she—" He couldn't even bring himself to voice what she did.

"The paintings that she did on the outside of the Painted Lady are worth money? They aren't just pretty?"

"Exactly. I have wanted a painting by your sister since I first saw the canvas that she decorated. I was able to hire her to finish one wall of my emporium. It seems that the little disaster with you several weeks ago left her feeling quite unhappy. Painting makes her feel better, so she gave in to my pleas and filled one wall with her art. The painting will be unveiled today, and I believe that it is a masterpiece that will be preserved for generations to come."

"My sister did a painting? Of course I'll be there! What time?" It made her feel good to know that her sister hadn't been able to walk away from her without looking back. If Annabelle was upset, she painted. It was what she'd always done, and some things never changed.

Annabelle's passion had been painting, ever since they were small children. When they were confined on ship, she'd made use of anything she could find to draw, paint, design, and otherwise make beautiful any place that they lived. The rough pine ship's cabin had been a bower; the hallway had been touched with tiny designs and pictures. In particular Sophie remembered one painting of a cat sitting at the head of the stairs cleaning its paws, a neatly severed rat's head at the cat's feet. They'd laughed about it, as if the drawing of a feline could actually have an effect on the rat population of the ship. The funny thing was, once Annabelle did that drawing, no rats ventured near their bunks again.

"Twelve noon. We will be serving refreshments. Cristine's pasties as well as some fine sweets from a French baker who just arrived a few weeks ago. It will be a true celebration, and I will press my suit to have your sister take up her art again. I'd be happy to sponsor her among my friends. San Francisco isn't always going to be a town of dirt and confusion and grossness. It will become a beautiful city one of these days, and I'd like to have Annabelle be a part of that sea change from monster to beauty."

Unstated was his desire to have her stop doing what she was doing to make money now, because painting was a more honorable profession than whoring. Sophie could have told him that it wouldn't happen. As she'd found out, Annabelle liked her new business and wasn't about to change.

"I'd like to see her painting, too, but I don't think she will change."

"We can only hope."

Cristine broke into the conversation. "Here, both of you, try one of these pasties. I've just worked out a new recipe using some of the curry that Jacques recommended. I have been trying new spices as they become available, and I think you'll like this." She handed each of them a still warm pasty. "Jacques must be quite a cook if he can give you new recipes as good as this. I can hardly wait to meet this mystery man," Sophie said.

Sophie bit into hers and then another one and sighed happily. Whatever else Cristine was, she was a fine cook. "This is the best you've ever made. What's in the curry?"

"Just a touch of cinnamon, coriander, cumin, and red pepper. It shouldn't taste as good as it does, but it really is quite delightful."

Sophie looked over at Abernathy and could tell what he was going to say before he even gave voice to his own opinion.

"My dear, I prefer your plain creations." He laid down the partially eaten pasty and retreated to the back of the ship to wait for his own order to be cooked so he could take it for the celebration that afternoon.

"You can't make everyone like something new," Sophie said, shrugging. "I like it; it's something that I'd go out of my way to buy."

Cristine glowed with the praise as she handed over the half-eaten pasty. "Here, take this down to the kittens; they might enjoy eating it, since Mr. Abernathy obviously didn't," she said. "Of course if Nellie were around we wouldn't have any problem with leftovers, would we?"

"That's not nice," Sophie chided her, but she laughed all the same. "Where do you suppose that woman disappeared to? She's been missing for ages and no one knows anything about it. I wonder if both she and Josie went someplace without telling Annabelle."

"I can't imagine where she'd go, unless she fell into a vat of food and hasn't eaten her way to the top yet."

"That's not very nice."

"No, but it is accurate, don't you think? But I do wonder where she's gotten to, because a woman with that dead white skin and blond hair is rather difficult to miss."

"I'm sure we'll all find out what happened to her in time, but for right now, I'd better be on my way."

"You know, I never did find out why you're up so early this morning," Cristine said.

"I'm going to do some measurements and then come back and plan a building and a wharf," Sophie said. "Then I'm going to attend Mr. Abernathy's party. It will work out; I'm positive it will. Two sisters who are as close as we are shouldn't be apart, no matter what has happened between us.

"Look what I bought last night from Mr. Mifflin. Maybe this will help bring Annabelle back, if I have something she can use."

She showed Cristine the deed to the land, the paper carefully straightened from the crumples that had happened when she held it all night. "We've finally got a place to dock; you'll be able to sell right from the ship instead of having to ferry things across part of the bay. I'll be able to rent out the rooms on the ships so much easier than I could ever do right now. Things are just going to go right for me."

She had to find a safe place for her papers, some hidey-hole away from the ship so that no matter what, she could come back and reclaim what was hers. Maybe Abernathy had a place where she could stow her things for later retrieval.

"I'm going to need your help."

"Ask away; I'll give it if I can. You know that I owe you the world for setting me up and giving me something to do once that miserable man at the Presidio ruined my chances of a widow's pension there."

Sophie blinked. It was the first time that Cristine had actually acknowledged the help that she'd been given in starting her business.

"I did nothing except give you the chance, and of course it was a good thing that you didn't mind working on a ship, since that's all we have available," Sophie said, and it was true. Cristine's steady small payments of part of the profits had been most welcome.

"Mind the ship? It's clean, I'm safe, and I like being rocked to sleep," Cristine said.

"Good. Because I'm going to ask you take care of the ship and everything on it if something goes wrong. I'll leave the ownership papers to the ships and the land with Mr. Abernathy, and I'll make provisions to make certain that you are well compensated should your visions be true. And if not, I'll still pay you for helping out and, most important, taking care of the kittens."

"Of course I'll take care of them, and the ships, too. I wouldn't think of not helping you. But why do you think anything will go wrong?"

"I don't. I just like to be safe," Sophie said.

Sophie relaxed. There, that was one problem out of the way. She hurried belowdecks, gathered up the papers, stuffed her pockets with as much gold as she could carry, and petted the kittens good-bye, rubbing their ears for good luck before she set them down on the floor beside the milk and egg mixture that they liked so much. She wiped away one lone tear. She hated to leave them, but there wasn't any other way to make certain that they were safe.

It was silly, she thought as she hurried down the beach to her own little parcel of San Francisco land. She shouldn't be carrying those papers with her; it was tempting fate. She hesitated for a few moments, then decided that she'd just take a look at the land and then walk over to Mr. Abernathy's store and give him the papers to hold for her.

She found the land that she'd only seen in the dark last night and stared at the strip of beach that formed an alleyway between two ships that had been hauled up onto the beach and were being used for gambling saloons and whorehouses. The gambling places were nothing like the Painted Lady; these were places where men entered and were never seen alive again. She looked up and sighed. She could have hoped for better neighbors, but she'd have to make do with what she had.

She measured and remeasured, trying every possible way she could to find a way to bring her ship closer to shore. The only possible solution would be to buy wood to build a pier that would extend past her unsavory neighbors. The problem was lumber. There was no wood to be had in San Francisco at prices that she could afford. She might even have to ask Abernathy if he could help her, since he'd done such a good job defending her rights with Mifflin. If anyone could find reasonably priced material to build piers, it would be Abernathy.

The papers crinkled in her pockets, reminding her that she still wasn't completely safe. Besides, it certainly wouldn't hurt to be at Abernathy's before the unveiling. She could find an inconspicuous place at the back and wait for a good time to approach Annabelle.

Oh, I should have watched the time and gone back to dress in my skirt and coat, Sophie wailed inwardly as she realized that all she'd managed to do that morning was get wet, cold, and dirty. She was going to look like a ragamuffin asking for food when she appeared at Abernathy's shop. Nevertheless, it would have to do.

She hurried up the street toward the emporium. She could feel Annabelle's aura meshing again with her own, even though Annabelle fought it with every bit of her being.

"She's got to talk to me; that's all there is to it. I can force her to settle the differences; I'm sure of it," Sophie exulted. She'd tell Annabelle she was sorry for the fight, and they'd go back to being as close as they ever were.

She ignored the warning flashes from Annabelle that it wasn't going to be quite that easy.

She turned a corner abruptly and caught sight of a furtive movement to the side of her, almost like someone trying to stay out of her line of vision. She turned completely around, but there was no sign of anyone who looked suspicious.

She took another few steps and then whirled around, hoping to catch someone.

A man had just stepped out of a doorway. He looked familiar; she was sure she'd seen that dirty red shirt and those denim pants that bagged at the knees and seat before.

She realized that she'd seen this same man before, standing

inside Fry's store while she tried to bargain about the cargo on the *Salud Y Amor.* He'd followed her until she'd been stopped by Mr. Abernathy.

How very odd, she thought and then pushed it from her mind. What was she going to say to Annabelle? How was she going to heal the rift that she'd caused? That was much more important than anything else that might be going on around her right now.

She had almost reached the intersection—she could see the store ahead of her—when she heard an agonized scream from an animal. It sounded like one of the kittens in pain.

Nothing in the world could have enticed her into that alleyway except a cat in danger. She rushed into the darkness, ready to do battle to save the animal, and walked straight into an ambush.

"Got you, bitch!"

Someone grabbed her from behind.

"Now, get that damned cat away from my face before she kills me. Put her in that hamper right now," a man's gruff voice ordered.

"What the hell!" Sophie tried to fight, but there was no way she could dislodge the arms that pinioned her. "Let me go, you idiots! Whoever it is you want, I'm not it. Please, just give me the cat and I'll leave you alone." She struggled against the arms that held her, trying to find some point where the person who held her was just a little careless.

There wasn't another sound from the animal, and even as she struggled, her heart sank. Had they already killed it? Were these the kind of madmen who tortured animals for enjoyment? When the man had said, "Put her in that hamper," Annabelle hoped he hadn't meant after breaking the cat's neck.

Her heart was racing with fear, but she tried to keep from panicking. If she could break free, she could grab the cat and run toward the end of the alleyway and be out of their sight in a matter of seconds. There was a quick babble of voices and muttered orders. She tried to scream, kick the side of the building, anything that would attract someone who could help her.

"Help! Let me go!" she shrieked. Someone had to hear her. Someone had to rescue her. She started to scream again until whoever it was holding her stuffed a filthy old rag into her mouth. She tried to take a breath and gagged and almost passed out. She pulled against the hands that held her, trying to force them to release her, but she couldn't break the grip.

She tried to twist in their hold to see who had grabbed her, but the darkness between the two buildings masked the identity of her abductors.

She was forced along the dark alley to a hidden door. If she hadn't been watching, she'd never have seen the section of wood slide aside, opening into an even darker hole in the wall.

She tried to scream again, but the rag made it impossible. She couldn't even breathe and she began to see flecks of gold in front of her eyes as the air was inexorably cut off.

She stumbled as she was forced down the stairs that she couldn't even see. Her ankles twisted under her, and her foot landed squarely between her captor's foot and the wall, tripping him. She fought to regain her balance as he plummeted the two steps to the bottom of the stairway.

"Damn you, bitch, don't you try and trip me again like that or I'll knock you cold and you'll be carried where we're going!"

Even though she couldn't see him, she flinched from the anger in his voice.

"Down this tunnel, and don't you try any funny stuff. I know all about you, and you're not going to get away from me, not even with your fancy tricks."

Another door opened in front of her and she was shoved into a dank, musty little room piled high with all kinds of miners' supplies. The walls were dirt and the air was cool and stale. They were underground again, but she didn't have a clue where she was. If they'd gone no more than a couple of steps to either side of where she was captured and just headed downward below the street, then she should be just about at Fry's store. She was so terror-stricken that her heart was threatening to jump out of her throat with every beat, but she tried to keep details clear in her head. Her location was most important. If she managed to break free she had to know which way to run to get away from this monster.

The room was barely illuminated, but she could see clearly enough to see that neither of the men held a cat. *Good,* she thought. Then the only person she had to rescue was herself.

She tried to spit out the dirty rag, but all that did was get the disgusting cotton threads caught in her teeth.

"Come on, we've got a long way to go, and I'm not being paid to dawdle," the man said, pulling aside a couple of trunks and some rope to reveal another exit from the room.

She was half-pushed, half-carried down stairs, into some kind of subterranean tunnel that extended in the distance, then turned off into other corridors. It was wet and smelled of old sea-water. She shuddered as she heard rats scuttling in the distance. Just a few feet into the corridor, they stopped, and she heard a heavy iron door bang behind her, cutting off the retreat that she'd hoped she could use to flee from these men.

There was a dim light in the hallway, but not enough to really see what was happening. A shadow moved out from the wall, and if she hadn't been gagged, she would have screamed.

"I got her; now you take over. She's already tried to dump me on the stairs, so watch out, hear?"

The man who had been holding her thrust her toward the shadow, and for one glorious moment, she was free.

Then her hands were caught behind her and she felt silken bonds wrapped around her wrists. No matter how hard she tried, she couldn't loosen the ties.

"Find Jui and have him take the cat up to the room. She is still well, is she not?"

"Yeah. She screamed right on cue when I tried to pet her.

Sounded like I was killing her and I couldn't even lay a finger on the beast."

"She does not like you. You are too rough," the woman said. She turned toward Sophie.

"Please, you will come with me and not try to run?" The voice was soft, insistent, and female. Sophie had heard it before, she was certain, but the only face that came to mind was clearly impossible. What would the woman from Dr. Mao's be doing down here guiding her toward God only knew what?

Sophie's heart leaped. Maybe, just maybe, she'd be able to get away from the woman. When she'd seen her at Dr. Mao's the woman hadn't been anything impressive. Sophie cataloged what she'd seen—older, rather frail-looking, her hands, she remembered distinctly, were soft and plump. No, this woman wasn't any match for her. The first chance she had, she was going to be off and away down the corridors, and they could try to find her after she'd long since disappeared.

"I will search you," the woman said. "Please stand quietly. I would not like to hurt you."

Sophie tensed. This might be the chance. If the woman leaned over to search her, she was going to get a knee in the face and Sophie would be gone. Down there, toward the light, and always bearing to the left instead of the right—someone had told her most people turned right; she'd do the opposite. She was ready to sprint the instant she had the chance.

"Do not even think of running," the woman said softly. "I would hate to damage you," she added, punctuating the remark with a small movement of her hand. Her fingers connected with Sophie's arm at the elbow. Sophie gasped and crumpled as pure anguish shot through her. It wasn't hard pressure, but it was exquisitely painful.

The woman proceeded to search her while Sophie was still trying to clear her head from the dizzying effects of the fingers to the nerves in her arm. She didn't even have the energy to protest when the woman discovered and removed the knife that was always strapped to Sophie's waist. Twice now she'd failed to keep control of a situation by using the knife, both times because she'd been caught by surprise. She was going to have to start watching what was happening around her more carefully if she managed to come out of this alive. It would be nice to be able to use the knife once in a while to save herself in a bad situation.

There was a quick babble of orders and she tensed. Someone else had slipped up beside Dr. Mao's woman.

"Bring her through the door and stand on the opposite side. She'll try to run, and I don't want her to get too far."

Sophie listened to the Chinese, trying desperately not to show that she understood every word of it. The man was right—if she got a chance, she was going to be going so far, so fast, that he'd never catch her.

The door opened, light flooded out, and she was ushered into a room that seemed to be all lacquered black and red, with gold writing everywhere. The smell of incense was strong enough to make her eyes water. It was obvious that the room, which was still underground, hadn't had an infusion of fresh air in months, maybe years. She wondered that any of the men could stand the stink without choking.

A small man sat on a black lacquered chair with red cushions. He held an orange cat that could have been the twin of the smaller kitten at home, except that this was a full-grown animal. She was regally beautiful.

"We are glad to welcome you to our humble meeting place." The Chinese man motioned for the bonds and gag to be removed, and suddenly Sophie was free again.

She drew in a huge breath preparatory to letting out the mother of all shrieks, sufficient to bring the devil to her aid, when the man waved his hand at her.

"You may scream if you wish, but even if someone hears you, no one would dare come to your aid. Better to save your energy to answer my questions."

Sophie closed her mouth and regarded him thoughtfully.

"Ah, so very smart of you," he said.

"No, I don't think I'll scream. I think I'll just refuse to talk to you until I am in a safe place and with no one else around except you and me. I want to see sunlight and a street in front of me before I answer any of your questions."

It was worth a try, even though she didn't expect him to give in. Even if it didn't work, though, it would show him that she wasn't totally cowed by him.

"I do not think that you are in any position to bargain, young lady," the man said, his face grave. His hand strayed to the cat, and he petted her ears.

"I'm in more of a position to bargain than you think. I'm just going to stand here and contemplate my surroundings, which are very interesting." She looked around the room and then smiled at the cat. The cat closed her eyes slowly and settled down on the cushion.

There was a rush of Chinese from behind Sophie, and she heard words she didn't like, like "torture," "fingernails," "fire," and "stripping the skin from her breasts and genitals." She kept her expression pleasant, not betraying by even a flicker of an eyelid that she understood what was being discussed. As she looked around, she assessed her chances of being able to make it past the door at the far end of the underground room. If she could make it out into a street of any sort, she'd be safe, at least for a few minutes, enough time to disappear.

"No, I'll have the answer within a few minutes. She is only a white woman. She will be no trouble." The man speaking was clearly contemptuous of Sophie. "First we will seem to comply with her request. Then we torture her if she does not cooperate."

She was taken through two tunnels at right angles to each other and then up a set of stairs to a room that might have come out of the best palaces in China and was a complete contrast to the stuffy little room she'd left behind. There was gold and yellow everywhere, rich brocades and tapestries and carved ivory that was worth a king's ransom.

The man carried the cat, carefully keeping her away from the men that made her growl and hiss every time she saw them.

"Will you sit?" Sophie was offered a chair with delicately carved legs and a pretty yellow silk cushion on the seat. It looked too fragile to support even a bird's weight, much less her own. The entire room seemed to be lined with yellow silk, until it looked like the place was flooded with sunshine.

She stood.

"I'm sorry; perhaps my English isn't as clear as I thought?" The man gestured politely toward the chair.

"The English is fine. I'm still not free and I'm not talking," she said.

The man sighed. "This is the best I am able to do under the circumstances." He set the cat on the ground.

"Then you'll get no answers from me until there is no one near me."

"That is sad. It could be very painful for you." There was the veiled threat.

"And if you hurt me, I still won't talk to you, but then you'll have the blood to clean up. I'll try to spatter on the silk; it should make a pretty fine mess."

"Blood? Torture? Have I said anything about such things? For shame, I would never think of treating you in such a manner." The man smiled at her, but there wasn't a lick of warmth in his whole face.

"I'm sure you wouldn't," Sophie said, backtracking as best she could. Damn, she didn't want him to know that she'd understood. The cat helped her along by ambling over to her and then reaching up and scratching her claws along Sophie's trousers. The claws were exquisite agony, digging into her flesh with each rhythmic flex of the pads. However, her own kittens had been doing the same exercise, with a few added fillips like climbing up and launching themselves off her, for the past few weeks. She was completely inured to the pain from the claws.

The Chinese man raised his eyebrows. This was not a cat that took well to strangers. In fact, she had been known to launch herself into a death attack if one of his men came within two feet of her. "Perhaps you are something more than I thought," he said in Chinese. He stared at her for a few seconds and then seemed to change tactics.

"Would there be any difficulty with discussing a problem that is of mutual interest to each of us?" he asked as the cat finished sharpening her claws and began to wind her way between Sophie's legs.

"I have no problems that need to be discussed with you."

The man shook his head gently, smiling for all the world as if he were a simple kindly old Chinese uncle. Sophie was not taken in by the seemingly amiable character.

"I believe that you may have information about a cargo that was carried in with the *Mary Kathleen.*"

Sophie bit back the impulse to ask him if he happened to be talking about a cargo other than the Chinese women that had been unloaded from the ship.

"The *Mary Kathleen?*"

"Indeed." The man nodded once, slowly. His eyes never left her face.

"I don't know anything about a cargo; there was very little left aboard the ship when I bought her. If you've got a complaint, I think you should talk to the captain about it. I bought the ship from another man, not from the captain himself."

"We realize that. That is the only reason you are alive. The captain tried to play a game with too many people and he lost. The captain is not alive."

The words chilled her. It was all so matter-of-fact, the disappearance of the captain, his death. The message was clear. She could, with very little provocation, be next.

"What do you want from me?"

"I'd like a chance to unload the cargo that is mine from the *Mary Kathleen* before you begin work on the ship."

That was not what Sophie wanted to hear. She thought about the piece of paper that she had stuffed in her pocket, representing the money that she used to have. But what was she going to tell this man about the cargo that had long since disappeared from the *Mary Kathleen*?

She didn't know what kinds of shadowy intrigues were going on in Chinatown, particularly since Dr. Mao's woman had been there to take her as a captive to this man. Were they working together? Was this a kind of extortion plot—get the cargo, pay money for the cargo, and then steal the money back? Was Dr. Mao at the root of all her problems?

What the hell was she going to do? If she told them where the cargo was and Dr. Mao wasn't part of their little gang, they'd go to his apothecary and take whatever it was that was so important to them, and she didn't like the odds of him surviving the visit.

She liked Dr. Mao. She wasn't ready to believe that he was trying to double-cross her, so that left her with no way to tell the truth about the bottles and casks that she'd already sold.

She could always give back the money if she sold the land.

The idea was ludicrous. She needed that land and she'd sold the cargo in good faith. She'd had no idea that anyone else had contracted for it ahead of time.

She'd have to find another way out of the problem.

She opted to lie.

"I don't have the cargo. When I bought the ship, there was nothing aboard. The cargo holds were almost completely empty. Some of the things in the cargo, such as flour, salt, meat, preserved and tinned foods, will be used when I open the ship as a boardinghouse. There were a number of spices that my friend, a lady who cooks pasties for sale, will also use. I don't believe that you would drag me in here because of flour and meat, so there must have been some other cargo that I don't know about."

She met the man's gaze straight on, hoping that her green eyes were as innocent as they needed to be to fool him.

"No, we are not interested in flour and meat. If there was nothing else, we will, of course, have to kill the man who sold you the ship."

"What?" Dammit, she hated surprises.

"Certainly. I know that the captain did not dispose of the cargo. He told me it was still on the ship right before he died. Therefore, the man who sold it to you must have taken it. He will either deliver it to me or be killed."

"But there was nothing on the ship when I went there!" she said, trying to think of a way to save Ruari. She didn't want him to get killed over something like this. And she particularly didn't want these gentlemen coming back into her life if Ruari managed to convince them that the cargo had been intact when she bought the ship.

Damn! She was well and truly caught.

"Then someone, sometime, removed it from the ship and I expect that Mr. McKay knew about it. He will clear up any of the enigmas of the missing cargo."

She had to get them away from that line of reasoning, and then maybe she could think of a way to save Ruari's skin.

"What's so important about the cargo, anyway?" Sophie demanded, trying furiously to think of a way out of this mess. "And how come you're so sure that the captain you killed didn't have something to do with the unloading of the ship?"

"He might well have. When I hired him I didn't think that the captain was stupid enough to try to work for me as well as for another man. Particularly when the other man was already a partner of sorts in the shipping venture."

"But what was the cargo that you're so worried about?"

"Opium."

Sophie's eyes widened. So that was what was in those jars.

"The captain made a deal. He would bring back my cargo. In addition, he would bring back the opium for another man.

This is not an acceptable way to deal with me. When things did not go as anticipated and there was no money to pay the captain for his cash outlay, he tried to find someone else to buy the opium. If he had come to me, we might have been able to work out some deal, but he did not choose to do that. Instead, the captain 'lost' the ship to Mr. McKay while he tried his hands at the gold mines."

The Chinese man stopped and smiled at her; it looked even more like the smile of a shark. "The captain never made it to his gold mine. There are some deep caves in the area, caves that are well known to the Chinese who are working in the gold country. His body will probably never be found. It's a shame; he could have had whatever his luck brought him up there, if only he hadn't been double-crossed by his second partner."

Opium.

That explained it all. The cargo wasn't worth just ten or fifteen thousand dollars. It was worth several hundred thousand, at the very least. And Dr. Mao must have known what he was buying. She'd seen that look of interest when he opened several of the pots. A thick, black, sticky substance, of course she'd heard it all before, she'd just never put it together with what had been on the *Mary Kathleen*, but Dr. Mao would have known immediately.

Damn.

Even worse, she'd been played for a fool while she thought she was getting a wonderful bargain. Mao must have laughed at her innocence when he got home with all that opium after he paid a fraction of the worth of it. No wonder he'd been so fast about delivering the money and unloading the cargo.

A perfectly brilliant idea began to take form.

"Would you allow me to look aboard the *Mary Kathleen*, just to make certain that you have not overlooked something?" the gentleman asked.

"Of course."

There was nothing there; she was certain of it. Nothing that would tie her or Ruari to the missing cargo. "You may look, but now that you have been so kind as to explain what you were looking for, I believe that I know the final destination of your cargo."

The older man leaned forward. "And will you share that destination with us?"

"Yes. I noted a number of pots and casks that looked as if they contained various Chinese cooking oils and herbs. I contacted the only person I know of who might be able to make use of them, and he took them."

"And that man was?"

"Mr. Thomas Fry."

The Chinese man stared at her. He didn't betray what he thought by so much as the flicker of an eyelash.

She stood, her hands tense at her sides, wondering if he was going to buy it. If he did, she might be rid of the man who had cheated her and beaten her. As far as she was concerned, any pain that the Chinese might mete out to Fry was well deserved. Even better, she didn't have to sully her own hands with his blood.

The Chinese man nodded to the people behind her. By the time she turned, they had left the room.

"I would still like to check the cargo."

"That is acceptable." Sophie would have agreed to serving him dinner there if only he took the bait about Thomas Fry and killed the man for her.

"Shall we go then, so this will not take any more of our precious time?"

Sophie hesitated. As much as she would have liked to conclude this strange business, she didn't want to miss Annabelle's party. "No. Not right now. I have business of my own to conclude. If you wish to meet me at the ship in an hour or so, that's fine. But I'm not going to allow you to dictate what I'm going to do right now. If you're so interested in the ship, post someone to watch and see that nothing is taken off. But don't try and bully me into leaving with you right now."

"Do not make me angry," the man said, and it was clear he meant every word.

"Don't make me angry. You've only dealt with Chinese women, haven't you? You've never had to deal with an American one. I might be more of a surprise than you'd think."

"That is not entirely without interest to me. However, I have no time for another woman at this point." He was rubbing the cat's head again.

"Return my knife and I'll be on my way and I'll meet you in an hour at the dock."

"I'll return the knife when we meet," he said. He turned and issued an order in Chinese to the man standing behind Sophie.

"Bring the blond one. We will get rid of her. No one would ever buy her in China, too much trouble, too much cost."

"But we will lose money if we don't have her to sell. She is promised."

"We will use one of the other women or we will find another blond one. Get rid of this disaster before we set sail and take another one, because we must leave tonight. We will use the same ship as the last time, despite this woman thinking that she owns it. She will not be available to complain."

Sophie listened intently. He was going to ship women back to China tonight, using the *Mary Kathleen* and that hold that she'd found hidden behind what looked like a solid bulkhead?

Like hell he would!

The man turned back to Sophie. "There is one more thing that you can do for me." He lifted one finger and the door opened again and a bedraggled blond woman was pushed into the room.

"Nellie!"

"I'm hungry!" Nellie announced petulantly. She looked at the table set with various sweets and dim sum and advanced on it, ignoring the old Chinese man and the other people around her.

"Get her out of here, please!" the man ordered. "I will overlook almost everything if you will simply remove her and make sure that she never comes back under my roof."

For the first time, Sophie saw a crack in the smooth facade of the man's face.

Nellie ate five pink sugared candies in succession and picked up a couple of shrimp rounds, popping them into her mouth and swallowing them almost whole. If she'd been a small snake, Sophie thought, she probably could have swallowed a chicken without any trouble at all.

"Remove her now," the man ordered Sophie.

Sophie didn't wait for a second invitation. She grabbed Nellie by the hand and then wished she hadn't, because the woman's hand was still sticky. Nellie took another two rolls before she headed for the door.

Sophie looked longingly at the cat and then decided that it was probably better to leave her behind with the Chinese man than to grab her and take her along. He might forgive anything else, but not a catnapping, not the way he petted the cat and fed her tiny pieces of the same shrimp rolls that Nellie was enjoying.

Sophie was in agony, trying to pull Nellie along and still make good her escape. She kept expecting at any moment to be caught and stuffed back down in that underground tunnel, but nothing happened. She ran outside leaving the door slightly open. She stopped for a moment to get her bearings.

Nellie bumped into her. The other two rolls had disappeared, and she was licking her fingers.

There was no way that the man inside the room could know that Sophie was listening as hard as she ever had in her life to hear what the man would say now that she was out of the room. She had to know what his plans were for her, though she suspected the worst.

"Follow her. When she is out of our territory and cannot be connected to our tong, take her into one of the tunnels and kill her. Dispose of the body in the sea on the rocks where the sea lions and sharks will take care of any nasty little problems with bone and flesh. Get rid of the other one before she devours all of San Francisco. Then we're going to kill Ruari McKay and Thomas Fry. That should keep our secrets safe from the others."

15

OH, SHIT," SOPHIE WHISPERED AS SHE HEARD the death sentence. Suddenly it felt like every gun in San Francisco was aimed at the exact middle of her back. She could feel the silken rope tightening in a stranglehold around her neck. Her shoulder blades tightened against an imaginary assault from one of the wickedly sharp Chinese knives that could carve her into tiny pieces just like one of those lovely brown Peking ducks that hung in the butcher's windows.

Nellie was completely oblivious to the threat. Instead, she headed for one of the vendor's stands where she could eat her way through buns and steaming rice bowls.

"Nellie, get ready to run!" Sophie said urgently. There wasn't any time to explain; all she could do was hope that the woman would listen to her.

"Run where?"

"Away from here. They want to kill us."

It was all the explanation she had time to give Nellie.

Sophie turned, hunting desperately for some kind of escape, anything that would give her a chance to elude her pursuers. Even if they weren't running after her shouting, she had no doubt that even at that moment there was a silent stalker pacing her every step, waiting for the right moment to kill her.

Nellie believed her. Already they were half-walking, half-running through the street, pushing past the Chinese who stood in their way as they headed straight down toward the non-Chinese section of the city. Even at a run, Nellie didn't neglect her stomach. Almost magically, a duck appeared in her hands, and Sophie heard the shrill screams of a vendor who discovered that he'd just had a fowl ripped from his display without the exchange of money.

"What's the big hurry? They're not going to come after us. They wanted to be rid of us just as much as we wanted to get out of there. Come on; this is hurting me. Slow down!" Nellie whined.

"The hell they're not going to come after us. You know when we walked out the door and I hesitated on the steps? I heard that sweet old man giving orders to kill us and feed us to the sea lions. So stop eating and start running before we get a knife in the back, all right?"

Instead, Nellie slowed even further. "No, I won't run. We're splitting up. Anyway, it's harder to keep track of two people, so let's give them a hard time. I'm heading back to the Painted Lady. I'll meet you there if you manage to survive."

And with that Nellie disappeared into the crowd.

It should have been easy to see her blond head amid all the Chinese, but Nellie seemed to have an uncanny ability to transport herself away from trouble and near food.

Sophie shrugged. If Nellie thought splitting up would help, maybe she was right. There was also the ungracious hope in the back of Sophie's mind that the killers would follow Nellie and not her.

"And I'm not standing here one second longer. I'm not about to die for opium!" she said, ignoring the people around her who were looking at her as if she were crazy. They moved away from her, leaving her a clear space that made it possible for her to thread through and into another crowd, hopefully losing whoever was pursuing her.

She heard a scream of outrage in the distance and smiled. She'd be willing to bet that hungry Nellie had struck again. Nellie would survive. Now all she had to do was concentrate on her own survival.

First things first. She stopped for just a second to get her bearings. She was deep inside Chinatown, but she could see a glint of gray bay water from the left side of the street. She had to get out of Chinatown fast, get back into her own section of town, where she knew at least some of the places to hide. Once she was there she was at least momentarily safe. While she was still within the Chinese part of the city, she was completely vulnerable. She'd heard tales about people venturing into the wrong district at the wrong time and disappearing forever. She'd rather that didn't happen to her.

Get out of Chinatown. Then make a run for it. She didn't know where "it" was yet, but she'd think of that on the way.

She felt a light brush on her arm, and the touch startled her into bolting down the hill. She was sure that she was letting out a long ululating scream until she took another breath and realized the whistling scream in her ears was the sound of her breath trying to force its way through her throat, which was constricted with terror. She dodged through the crowd, knocking one little man into an unforgiving wall. Angry curses followed her down, interrupted by an: "Oof" as someone hit the man again.

Someone was running almost as fast as she was, and they both knew that she had a couple of blocks to go before a Chinese man would be stopped and summarily strung up for chasing a white woman.

"Please, please, let me reach Montgomery," she whispered as she ran. She couldn't have said anything out loud if her life had depended on it. She drew in short whistling breaths as she tried to force her feet to run even faster, her legs to jump farther with each stride.

It was agonizing, like a bad dream where her legs moved, but she stayed in the same spot.

Suddenly a knife stabbed her, plunging deep into her side. She grabbed at her waist, expecting to find blood, but there was nothing. Still she ran as the pain burned through her. She tried to breathe in, and another stabbing pain shot through her. She would have laughed if she hadn't been in such pain—it wasn't an attack; it was a muscle knotting in her side.

A stitch, that's all it is. I can manage a stitch in my side, she thought grimly. The crowd was thinning; the boundary between the Chinese and white section loomed ahead of her. She was almost safe, or at least safer than she had been in the middle of Chinatown.

She rounded a corner and shot across the dusty street, her feet dancing across the wood, stones, and general debris that made footing chancy at best. A dray driver cursed her equally fluently in Chinese and English as she bulleted across the street in front of him, startling the horses and making him pull up short to keep from flattening her. The sun was barely halfway up the sky, but she felt like she'd lived a hundred years between her first few carefree moments that morning when she was still exulting in owning land and now, when she was almost certain not to live to enjoy the fruits of her good deal.

One block, that was all she had to go before she was at least in safer territory. She could hear someone coming closer and closer to her, almost on her heels and well within stabbing range. She didn't dare turn around to make certain, because if she slowed down, the last thing she'd see would be her killer's face.

She sprinted as a space opened ahead of her, a clear area where she could run straight into Montgomery Street and then make a sharp turn toward the Painted Lady and safety. Once she was in the middle of the morning crowd, whoever was following her would at least have to slow down.

Someone else saw the opening, too.

"Catch her!" the shout went up behind her in Chinese. Someone grabbed her arm and she yanked loose, ripping her shirt free from the grasping hands. A man stuck out his foot to trip her. She leaped high in the air, aiming her feet at his midsection and pushing off as hard as she could as he toppled backward, a stunned look on his face. The man's mouth opened, but no sound came out; she'd knocked the breath out of him.

The maneuver gained her a few extra feet of space against anyone else pursuing her.

She made a desperate lunge and burst into the middle of the morning crowds that thronged the streets.

The crowd closed around her, and for a moment she felt safe. She slowed to a walk, constrained by the crowd around her.

If she could get to Dennison's Exchange, the Painted Lady would be within reach. She could hide there for an hour or two and get Annabelle to help her plan her escape before the men found her and murdered her.

Hell of a Christmas present, someone trying to kill me, she thought as she saw an opening and rushed down the street. Her side still ached, she was certain that she'd ripped off a good portion of her heels when she started running in boots that were never meant for high speeds, and her arm ached where she'd ripped it loose from whoever had tried to grab her as she ran past.

She had just reached the corner of the mercantile when she realized that her feet were bleeding. She looked down and saw red streaks at her ankles from the blood pooling in the shoes. She touched the blood, wincing at the sight, even though the pain hadn't hit yet. There was an eerie sound as she bent down, a whoosh of something going right past her ear, and then there were shouts and screams and curses ringing from the men around her.

"Damn! Damn! Damn!" she wailed, as the crowd bolted around her. She tried to get up, but she couldn't push herself upright with men jostling her every time she tried to get a foothold.

"Get down! Some damn fool is shooting!"

Her first thought was that she was already down, and then she realized what the man had yelled.

She whipped around, looking back into the crowd to see who had fired the gun. There was no one. And even if there had been a chance to see who had taken a shot at her, the person was completely hidden in the panicked crowd.

Then, for just a second, she caught sight of a Chinese woman at the edge of the crowd, the same woman who had led her to the yellow satin room. She was stuffing something metallic into the front of her dress.

"No—I don't believe it," Sophie breathed; then she brightened. "And if it was you, I hope that hot gun burns your tits off, you miserable bitch!"

Then, before she could even catch her breath, the one shout that could terrorize an entire city rang out.

"FIRE!"

Someone grabbed her and set up her upright and rushed on, while other men running the opposite way almost knocked her off her feet again.

"Fire!"

"Fire! Look at Dennison's—it's going for sure!"

She turned around just in time to see a puff of smoke from the second floor of the exchange. It looked so innocent, nothing more than a little bit of white cloud against the darkness of the morning sky. Underneath the white there was a deadly yellow light, and then the entire top of the building burst into flames. The white-painted canvas that had acted as a ceiling burned to ashes in a matter of seconds, and the flames raced up the beams supporting the roof and down the frail sticks of wood covered with tar paper. It popped and burned furiously. Within seconds, the fire spread to other buildings around Dennison's.

There were storage buildings at the back of the lot, and the men began to shout as they saw the flames licking up the side of the lean-to.

"Powder, stored powder!"

Some of the men had purchased powder for their guns there; they'd seen it measured out of the small wooden casks; they knew the explosive possibilities that lay waiting in that frail structure.

The entire crowd of several hundred men surged away from Dennison's, almost trampling Sophie in the rush. There were a splatter of small explosions, then one powerful enough to knock the men closest to the exchange flat on the ground. She turned just in time to see the roof lift off the lean-to and go sailing through the air trailing flames behind it. The wood landed a few feet away, starting a fire in one of the businesses that backed Dennison's.

The building next to Dennison's went up in billowing flames and then another one, all within the blink of an eye. A breathy roar from the flames almost drowned out the sound of the panicked men. The fire lit up the morning sky with the blaze. From somewhere farther away she could hear the clang of the fire alarms going off. While she looked, another building disappeared in smoke and turned to ash in a matter of seconds. Glowing embers littered the ground where restaurants, hotels, and mercantiles had stood a few minutes earlier.

Sophie gasped and then started coughing as the acrid smoke bit into her lungs. The coughing broke the fire-induced paralysis that had held her prisoner.

The Painted Lady—nothing's going to stop this fire before it gets there and Annabelle will be asleep; she'll never know what's coming!

Sophie knew only too well that once Annabelle went to sleep nothing short of the crack of doom would ever wake her up. She'd sleep until her sleep was finished, even if it was finally over in eternity.

Sophie hugged the walls to get through the crowds.

"Move out of my way, you buggerly bastards," she growled, pushing with all her might against the mass of humanity that streamed into the square. "Are you all daft, running toward a fire instead of away? Do you think you can blow it out with your collective breath?" she screamed as she fought her way through them, pushing and kicking her way toward the saloon.

The winds from the bay began to kick up, just as they had every day at dawn for months, carrying the smoke and crackle of the fire toward her. Horses whinnied and fought, trying to turn away from the fire while men cursed and pulled them forward, trying to save anything that they could reach from the deadly advance of the inferno.

A fire company finally emerged from the crowd, pulling a cart with a pump bolted to a wooden frame. It was the city's only hope of fighting the fire, and Sophie could have told them that there wasn't a chance that the little drizzle of water they could pump out of the underground cisterns would have any effect on the fire that raged behind her.

She turned the corner and sighed in relief even as she ran toward the canvas structure. The Painted Lady was intact, at least for the moment.

She dove through the door and started yelling, amazed that no one had responded to the noise outside.

"What's wrong?" She heard two other women responding to her shouts, but her sister's distinctive throaty voice wasn't one of them.

Nellie straggled out of a room, looking for all the world like she'd been there all night. She was still in the dirty dress that she'd had on at the Chinese place. For once, however, she didn't have anything in her hands to stuff into her mouth.

For the life of her, Sophie couldn't figure out how Nellie had managed to get to the Painted Lady before her and why she wasn't eating.

"Fire!" she yelled. "Everything's burning just one block up from here. Get out now! If it heads this way, you're going to be lucky to save your hides. Move it! The fire won't wait!"

The women began to look out the doors at the glow that showed even through the canvas.

"Don't just stand there bug-eyed staring at the fire; run for your life! Everyone head to my boat; we'll be safe there!"

She bounded up the stairs and began trying doors to find Annabelle. She startled one woman with two men, another man asleep alone in a pink frothy bedroom, then finally her sister.

Her sister wasn't alone. The man who was in bed with her had his face to the wall and was still snoring, even through the incredible din.

Annabelle, as usual, rested peacefully, her face the face of an angel without a care, her long red hair tangled around her head and one strand laced through the man's fingers.

"God damn it, move your bloody ass!" Sophie shrieked. "Can't you hear, there's a fire out there and it's heading straight down the street!"

Annabelle turned over and buried her head in the lacy pillow cover. "Go away," she mumbled, her usual morning salute to anyone who tried to wake her.

"Fire?" the man said, his voice blurred with sleep. Then, as the word "fire" penetrated the sleep fog and the acrid smell of the smoke began to drift in the room, he sat up, awake, his eyes staring into the hallway where there was already a haze.

"Ruari McKay, as I live and breathe!" Sophie said, amazed at the man who occupied her sister's bed. Even more amazing was the expanse of what he showed when he stood up, completely oblivious to his complete nudity.

Her sister in bed with Ruari McKay?

It was amazing how much that hurt.

"Oh no, please, Sophie, I didn't—I wouldn't. I just slept here because I had too much to drink." He blushed all the way down to his navel and then back up again.

"We'll talk about it later. I needed to find you. Ruari, you're going to have to get the hell out of here. Preferably a long way out of here, because there are some little men with very big knives who are looking for a chance to carve you and me both into shark bait."

"What the hell are you talking about?"

Sophie heard more fire bells, and the breathing of the fire came closer. "Do you mind if I tell you a little later?"

Sophie nodded toward the front of the Painted Lady, which was beginning to glow an ominous red as the fire rushed closer.

"What?" Annabelle finally turned over and opened her eyes. Her hair was in wild disarray, her robe open to an indecent level in front.

Sophie knew that she was about to ruin her last chance of making up with Annabelle, at least until her sister had a chance to stop and reflect on the reasons for what Sophie was about to do.

She took two steps forward, slapped her sister as hard as she could across the right cheek, and then retreated at a most undignified pace as Annabelle lunged out of the bed, her fingers in talons, her eyes glittering with fury at the assault.

She was, however, completely and fully awake.

"Grab what you want to save and get out—there's a fire coming and nothing is going to stop it."

At the same moment Sophie inhaled and almost choked on the acrid smoke that began to swirl around her.

"Annabelle, you'd better not wait to get anything; just get out of here while you're still alive!"

Annabelle didn't listen. She could smell the smoke as well as Sophie could, but she had a stubborn streak that would have choked a mule.

"I've got to get my gold; it's the only thing I can't live without!" She scrabbled under the bed and began to haul out bags of gold dust.

"Here, take this. I'll settle up with you later for the slap." She handed two hefty bags to Sophie. "Ruari, you take this, but if you leave with it instead of giving it back to me, I'll hunt you down and take away something you prize a hell of a lot more than mere money," Annabelle said, looking toward his nakedness.

Ruari blanched. "Fine, yes, but let's get out of here now, all right?"

Annabelle staggered under the weight of the last couple of bags and then managed to start down the stairs. In the instant between her hesitation at the landing at the top of the stairs and the first floor, the Painted Lady's canvas front disappeared in flames.

The fire reached the sawdust on the floor and the sawdust exploded into a dancing carpet of flames.

"Get back up here; we'll jump out the back window!" Ruari ordered. The fire was above them now; the scenes that Annabelle had painted on the canvas ceilings were gone in an instant.

Sophie felt the heat lick at her hands. Her ankles burned; her eyebrows began to singe and crinkle. She inhaled and then couldn't breathe again as the fire seared the air around her.

She pushed forward, heading blindly toward Annabelle's old room.

"No, damn it, this way!" Ruari grabbed her and hauled her along through the flames to the back of the building.

"Jump!" he ordered Annabelle and heaved her over the side of the windowsill. She screamed as she fell, and landed on the stones below still cursing him.

"You next!" He threw Sophie forward and she tumbled out

the window toward the street. She reached outward to block her fall and crashed to the ground. She was certain she heard bones break as her feet hit the ground. Almost immediately she heard Ruari yell as he leaped out of the window. He tried to aim his body to the right of the sisters, but Sophie saw him plummeting directly toward her.

Sophie tried to move, but she couldn't make her legs respond and she couldn't catch her breath to scream for help.

Ruari stood up, rubbing his backside where the flames had connected with a few stray patches of his bare skin. He brushed himself off and helped Annabelle to her feet. Annabelle gave a cry of despair as she lurched forward. "My knee! I can't walk; it hurts too much."

Flying brands from the fire began to rain down on them as the first tiny flames began to eat through the flimsy wood and the rest of the wall caught and began to crumble.

Sophie pushed herself up, intending to stand up until she felt the pain lance through her feet and up her legs. She'd done some damage when she hit.

"Ruari, you have to help me," Sophie pleaded.

"I can't take both of you. What am I going to do?"

"Ruari, listen to me; there are people out there waiting to kill you. You have to save me and we'll make a run for the coast, where they can't reach us." Sophie tried to stand up, then fell back, moaning as firebrands burned their way through her ankles.

Ruari hesitated for a moment. The building was burning furiously, they were still in danger, and he could only rescue one woman.

His choice was made for him as Annabelle lurched forward into his arms and collapsed, making him hold onto her. The smoke swirled around them as the facade crumbled. "Wait there. I'll be back—I promise I will—just wait for a moment!"

"You bastard, don't leave me! I'll let them kill you!" Sophie panicked and began to pull herself forward, desperately trying to inch away from the fire that rained down around her.

"I'm coming back!" Ruari shouted through the smoke. "I'll save you, love."

Whatever he did, it wouldn't be fast enough, Sophie knew. She looked up in time to see the remains of the flaming building collapsing in slow motion toward her.

16

SOPHIE CLOSED HER EYES AND PREPARED TO die.

Her last thought was that she'd always been afraid of fire and now she was going to die because of it.

It wasn't fair.

Suddenly she was snatched up and carried beyond the burning building.

"You get yourself into the damnedest scrapes, don't you?" Dominic asked as he cleared the smoke and they could both breathe again.

"What? Where did you come from?" She coughed and tried to ask more questions, but somewhere along the line she'd taken a mouthful of superheated air and her throat didn't want to cooperate.

"Ruari sent me. He yelled out something about meeting him on the *Flying Angel,*" Dominic said. "Now shut up; I've got to get us out of here without any more damage."

Sophie opened her mouth to protest being told to shut up and then decided he was right. They were in danger here, much more that Dominic had any idea. Besides, she was concentrating too much on trying to keep from screaming as her ankles jostled with the movement. She was absolutely positive she could feel bone scraping against bone. She tried to hang on and not make a sound while Dominic carried her, right up until someone hit her feet.

"You bastard!" she moaned, trying to pull her knees up.

Dominic stepped into an alleyway out of the general panic. "What hurts?" he demanded. Until then he thought she'd just been bruised and dazed by the jump out of the window that he'd witnessed as he passed by the back of the Painted Lady.

"My ankles," Sophie sobbed. The tears were making streaks through the soot on her face and her hair was no longer bright red, but red and black where the fire had touched it before she jumped.

He loosened the shoes, looking up just in time to see her clenching her teeth so hard he was sure they'd crumble on the spot from the pressure. Her face was white from the effort to keep from screaming, but she wasn't going to let a sound escape her.

He looked at the ankles and winced. They were terribly swollen and already blackened from bruising. He pushed into the flesh, trying to see if he could feel any of the bones that might be broken. There was no sign of bone poking through the skin, and he didn't feel any movement underneath his fingers. In fact, he thought, taking another look at the damage, he suspected that she hadn't actually broken anything; she'd just sprained it with the fall. He'd seen breaks and bones and all the other damage that people could do to themselves, and this didn't look that terrible.

"I'll have to splint this; that's the only way I'm going to be able to get you back to the ship. I'd hate for this to be broken and do more damage while I'm trying to rescue you." He looked around for something to use to immobilize her leg, but for the first time in the history of San Francisco, the alleyway wasn't littered by pieces of board, trash, and other debris.

Dominic, however, wasn't one to be deterred by a clean alley. He merely stood up, reached onto the top of the building, and pulled off one of the shipping crate slats that had been carefully nailed in place to work as shingles. He salvaged four of the slats, pulled a couple of pieces of twine out of his pocket, and proceeded to immobilize her ankles as best he could.

"I think we can continue on to the ship, if we're careful. It's going to hurt, but I've done the best I can for the pain, unless you'd rather go straight to Dr. Mao's to see if he can help you?"

Sophie laughed shakily. "I don't think Dr. Mao could help me right now, not with the trouble I'm in."

"Trouble? Again?"

Sophie nodded. "I'll tell you all about it once we're safe aboard the ship."

"Then let's get going. If I can find a carriage or a wagon or something, I'll hire it on the spot to get you back to the ship. Otherwise, you'll just have to hang on."

Sophie nodded. Anything was better than having her feet dangle loose, and the splints were already giving her blessed relief from the pain of bone moving on bone.

It took only ten minutes to negotiate the rest of the distance to the ship. Dominic grabbed the skiff from the ship and rowed them out to the *Flying Angel*, where Ruari and Annabelle were waiting. Annabelle had tea brewing and Ruari had whiskey for the men.

Ruari rushed to her side and carried her gently over to a chair that had been placed on the deck. "Darling, Sophie, my dear, I was coming back; I promise you I was. Nothing is as it seems!"

"It doesn't matter," Sophie said tiredly, turning to watch the devastation that was roaring through San Francisco. "Nothing matters anymore."

They'd been on board the ship for several minutes when Ruari spotted Nellie frantically signaling for help in getting out to the ship.

"I'll go get her," Dominic said, and did so in a remarkably short time. Nellie, however, was the only one of the Painted Lady women who had actually showed up and asked to come aboard.

"Where do you think the others are? Did they all get out?" Annabelle asked worriedly. "I thought sure they'd come here."

"I'm sure they're fine. They've got places to go, friends that they can stay with," Nellie said.

Annabelle hobbled over to the rail and stared out toward the fire. "I hope that Josie is all right. I wish I knew if she was still alive," she said into the wind. No one heard her.

Sophie was not surprised to see that her sister could walk. She'd thought there was something just a bit too theatrical about her throwing herself into Ruari's arms.

Sophie only wished that her own ankles could heal as fast as her sister's knee had. She hurt so bad that she couldn't even stand up. She'd removed the splints and checked for broken bones herself and found nothing, so she didn't bother to put the pieces of wood back in place. She'd heal faster without them, she decided.

Healing. that was something that she'd started out the day expecting to find with her sister. Now she was going to end it with a rift so great that it would never be healed.

Over and over, the painful memory of her sister and Ruari disappearing into the smoke and leaving her behind to die in the flames came back to haunt her. Annabelle's disregard for her sister's safety hurt more than any physical damage Sophie had as a result of the fire. She had thought, before the fire, that she could apologize for her hurtful words and they should have been able to heal the breach. But Annabelle had abandoned her to die and nothing would ever make that all right.

"How could you?" she whispered as she looked at her sister. "How could you wish me dead?" But if Annabelle heard her, she didn't answer as she stared out at the fire that was ravaging San Francisco.

"Look. They might have stopped it at Field's; there's a change in the color of the smoke. Doesn't it look like there aren't as many flames?" Dominic said, scanning the downtown area for signs that the fire would be stopped before all of San Francisco burned.

"It doesn't really matter, does it? It's too late for the Painted Lady," Annabelle said. "And for all we know, it's too late for Abernathy's, too. All that work on the painting and it's probably gone up in flames along with everything else." Her voice was quiet, tired.

"Damn near along with me," Sophie said. "Dominic, give me some of that whiskey. I need it for the pain."

Annabelle turned and looked at her sister sharply. Sophie never drank anything, not since they'd both finished off a bottle of rum in a little less than four hours and damn near died from the hangovers the next day.

Dominic handed Sophie a tumbler filled with whiskey, and she lifted it in a mock salute to her sister before she took a couple of gulps of the deadly brew. She stared at Annabelle, still unable to believe what her sister had done.

"Look; the fire's taking off again, coming down toward the shore. I thought they had it out," Dominic announced, pointing toward the flames that had suddenly begun to leap skyward again.

They could still hear the roar of the crowd, the shouts and screams as the fire took off in another direction. Wagons milled around the shore, as if the water would somehow protect them, even though the buildings were built almost to the waterline, meeting the line of ships that had been beached, and everything so close that water wouldn't give any protection unless the teams and wagons were hip-deep in the ocean when the fire approached.

Smaller ships were putting out to sea, and with every launch Sophie worried that the Chinese who were after her were going to find her on the *Flying Angel.* She kept scanning the harbor, watching for movement on the *Salud Y Amor* or the *Mary Kathleen.* Those were the two where she expected to see trouble first. Then, just as she expected, lights appeared on her ship.

"Look at the *Salud Y Amor,*" Sophie said. Wavering lights illuminated the furled sails and deck as people moved about the ship. Even if Cristine had invited everyone she knew to come sit out the fire on board the ship, there shouldn't have been that many people.

As abruptly as the lights and figures had appeared, they disappeared. If they'd stayed, she might not have worried; it might have been Cristine aboard the ship. With the lights' disappearance, she was almost certain that someone had searched the *Salud Y Amor.*

"Dominic, Ruari, I have to get over to the *Salud Y Amor.* As soon as I'm back, we have to leave just as soon as we can raise the anchor of the *Flying Angel.*"

"Why do you need to go to the *Salud Y Amor*? You can barely walk," Ruari objected.

"What the hell are you talking about, leave?" Annabelle interrupted, shocked. "I was just burned out. I've got to get back there and rebuild before someone else jumps my claim. Don't you dare raise any sails while I'm still on board."

"I think you'd better reconsider that," Sophie said. She sipped the whiskey, reveling in the raw burn down her throat. It felt good, soothing almost, to cauterize the pain from the superheated air that she'd breathed. It also gave her something to do while she tried to calm her nerves.

"Give me one reason to reconsider!" Annabelle challenged her.

"Because if you or Ruari go back to the Painted Lady there's a good chance you'll be dead before sunset," Sophie said. "You might not care what happens to me, you might even have thought it was all right to let me burn to death while you escaped, but I'm trying to be a good sister; I'm trying to keep you alive."

"I didn't leave you to die!"

"The hell you didn't. You and Ruari ran as far and as fast as you could and you never looked back. If Dominic hadn't shown up, I'd have died and you wouldn't have cared." The whiskey was loosening her tongue, she decided, but maybe that wasn't a terrible thing to have happen.

"I'd have cared," Annabelle said. "But there's no way to prove it to you. And I'm not going to stay on board a ship and sail away into the sunset because you're being overly dramatic."

"I don't think that it's overly dramatic to say that someone was chasing me, shot at me, and started the fire instead of killing me. That *is* what happened, you know."

"Who'd be shooting at you?" Ruari asked.

"The same people who'd like to see you dead," Sophie told him. "Let me tell you all about my day in Chinatown, and then maybe you'll see that I'm not just making things up." She explained the trip to the yellow silk room and the discussions of the cargo that couldn't be returned because she didn't have it any longer.

"But I left that cargo on the ship. I wasn't sure who owned the stuff, but I damn well knew that it'd have to be returned to the rightful owner before long. That was opium in those jars, and whoever wanted it brought in from China wasn't going to walk away and leave it all behind. Why didn't you just tell them where you stored it and let them take care of it? If you'd done that, all of these problems could have been avoided."

"Because I don't have it anymore and I didn't know that it was opium because you didn't see fit to tell me what was in the cargo."

"I thought you knew! What the hell did you do with it?" He grabbed her, his fingers biting into her shoulders. "You didn't just offload it and leave it somewhere, did you?"

Sophie wished she could manage to come up with a better answer, but the truth was going to have to do.

"Of course I didn't dump it. I sold it. And I couldn't very well tell them that, now could I, when Dr. Mao was the one who bought it? I'm not sure how they'd treat him, but I have a feeling it wouldn't be pleasant. I didn't know it was opium, but he did. So I lied about what happened to it."

Ruari looked at her, his expression one of absolute disbelief and doom. "Don't tell me. Let me guess. You told them that it wasn't on the ship when you took it over."

Sophie shrugged. "Not exactly. I had a choice. I could either tell them that you took it with you before you sold me the *Mary Kathleen,* but that wouldn't have been fair, particularly since that miserable excuse for a man said there was a question about where you got the right to sell this ship. So I said that I'd sold the cargo to Thomas Fry."

Ruari sat down abruptly on the cargo hatch. "And then what did they do?"

"Nothing much. They brought Nellie into the room and told me that we could both go. What they didn't count on was my being able to hear and understand the man inside when he gave orders to have us both killed because we knew about the opium. You, too, because for some reason you seem to have stepped on their toes for taking over the *Mary Kathleen.* And of course they have probably already taken care of Fry."

"They still wanted to kill you and me even when you shifted all the blame and told them about Fry?" Ruari's face had gone dead white. "Shit."

"I know, I thought they'd back off, but that man is out for blood and I don't think he cares whose blood it is. I thought they'd leave me alone once I told them Fry had it, but this guy obviously thinks that the only safe woman is a dead one."

"My God, woman, do you have even the slightest idea what they do to people who might have taken something they want? Or even people who look at them cross-eyed on the street? You haven't been here long enough to remember the poor soul who lurched out of Chinatown and into Murphy's Saloon with only half his skin still attached. You could see the muscles where the skin used to be. He wasn't even bleeding too much; they'd done a good clean job of skinning him just like a rabbit. He didn't survive very long. He was lucky. I'm damned attached to my skin, and I'd suppose that you'd like to hold onto yours for a few more days, too."

Ruari abruptly let loose of her shoulders. "What the hell am I going to do now?" he asked softly, of no one in particular.

"I don't know. If you don't want to sail out of here until things get a little cooler, then maybe you'd rather go to Chinatown and try and reason with Mr. Yellow Silk Room," Sophie suggested.

"And will you be sure and rescue my stinking body from the surf after they've decided that I need to die just to show people that they can't play around with the tongs? These guys will kill at the rumor of wrongdoing. Nothing has to be proved; they just like to make points by murdering anyone who might think of getting out of line."

"I kind of figured that it might be a little more serious when he said to kill us. It doesn't look like these guys want to be reasonable. So the only solution that I can think of is for all of us to leave. Go for a nice long sail, go up the coast, anywhere other than around San Francisco, until we figure out a way to take care of the Chinese before they take care of us."

"What do you mean, leave and then try and sneak back into the city and hope no one spots us? Oh, that's brilliant; it really is," Ruari said.

Sophie shrugged. "Don't get nasty. If you've got a better idea, I'd like to hear it, short of heading back to the States and never setting foot in California again."

"You've never impressed me as a particularly stupid woman, but the idea that they'll leave us alone once they calm down makes me wonder about you. We can leave, but we'll never be able to come back. Never. It'll *have* to be the States or we head up to Siberia and go into Mother Russia, and I don't like being cold."

"How about if we just leave when I get back from the *Salud Y Amor* and then we'll figure something out once we're on the high seas? I don't know how you feel about it, but just sitting here within easy reach of the shore is making me damned nervous," Sophie said.

"And why do you want to go back to the *Salud Y Amor*? Doesn't it occur to you that they might have left someone there just waiting for you to show up?"

Sophie was silent for a moment. "No, I never thought of that. But I have to get there. I have to rescue the kittens. I can't just leave them on the ship."

"Won't that woman take care of them?" Annabelle asked, not even trusting herself to say Cristine's name.

"I guess she would, if she stays on the ship and no one scares her away. She's always bringing them leftover meat and milk, so they won't be neglected," Sophie said doubtfully. "But it isn't the same. They're my kittens; I want them. They're like my babies!"

"You can't get them; you can't even walk. And if what you're saying is true, I'm not sure I want to take the risk of going back to the *Salud Y Amor* or staying around here too long. Maybe you're right, we should just hoist anchor and leave," Ruari said. As long as they were within rowboat distance of San Francisco they weren't even marginally safe.

"I'll hoist the anchor, you set the sails, and we'll be on our way," Dominic said.

"Stop right there, mister. What about me?" Annabelle demanded. "I'm not going with you; I've got to get the Painted Lady rebuilt. I can't just walk away from my land or someone will jump the claim and I'll lose all my money. I can't leave."

"And what about me?" Nellie said. I don't want to go anywhere. I just want to get back home to the Painted Lady just as soon as we're back in business. I didn't like the ocean to begin with, and I don't want to go back out in the middle of winter with all the storms coming in from the west." She was twisting her hair around her finger as she talked and looked for all the world like a worried twelve-year-old. "Besides, I'm hungry. I want to get back to the kitchen so I can cook something. Ugh, I never want to see anything resembling Chinese food again!"

"Nellie, I don't think you want to go back to San Francisco, at least not right now. They did say that you should be killed, too."

"That silly man couldn't possibly mean it. I didn't do anything to him; he's got no reason to kill me. Except . . . ," Nellie said, hesitating.

"Except what?" Dominic asked.

"Well, I kind of wonder what they're going to do with Josie and Serena and Maggie and Gertrude. You know, they were being held in the same place that I was. I couldn't even find it again, but it's somewhere under Chinatown in one of the tunnels."

Annabelle spun around and stared at Nellie as if she couldn't believe her ears. "What the hell are you talking about? Josie and the others were with you? Do you mean you know where Josie is and you didn't mention it until now?" Annabelle took a threatening step forward.

"But you never gave me a chance to tell you! Yes, Josie is down there, and so are a couple of others," Nellie whined.

"So that's what they were talking about. I kept thinking I was being melodramatic, you know, the way you always accused me of making too much out of nothing when we were younger?" Sophie turned to Annabelle. "But I guess I really did understand what the man said."

"Tell me all about it," Annabelle ordered. Her face was thunder dark, and Sophie knew that expression. Her sister had decided that she'd done something horrible and she'd never be forgiven for it.

Frankly, Sophie decided she was getting damned tired of Annabelle always being angry with her. She had a couple of unforgivable things of her own to hold against Annabelle.

"Right before they brought Nellie in, the man in the yellow chair said something about having to move the women out tonight. He said they'd need another blond woman and that they were going to use the *Mary Kathleen* to ship the women back to China. Now, I'm pretty sure he wasn't talking about Chinese women because he smuggled them in on the *Mary Kathleen* in the first place. And once you showed up, I knew exactly what kind of women he was talking about. It's a nice way to make sure that you have two profitable trips instead of just one-way."

"Did you know Josie was there?" Annabelle's voice was deadly quiet.

"I suspected as much."

"My best friend disappears from the face of the earth, I'm crazy with worry about her, and you know where she is and don't say a word?" Annabelle's voice was still quiet.

"How could I tell you before this? I don't know if you remember, but you were busy with other things, including leaving me behind in the fire."

"You should have told me."

"You should have rescued me."

The sisters stared at each other, separated by a gulf that was far deeper than the ocean that they rode on.

17

SOPHIE DECIDED THE BEST IDEA WOULD BE to ignore Annabelle, since it didn't look like there was any chance of settling their differences soon. She pointedly turned her back on her sister.

"Nellie, I think I'd like to hear a little more about how you managed to end up in Chinatown."

"Actually, it was because I didn't believe you," Nellie said.

"Me? What did I have to do with it?" Sophie asked, amazed. She didn't remember anything that would have caused Nellie to be captured and taken into Chinatown.

"Remember when you crawled out of bed and came to the stairs to warn me to be careful just before I left the *Salud Y Amor*?"

Sophie grimaced. "I sure do. That hurt, but I had to tell you about the dream I had just had. It was weird, one of those dreams that's absolutely lifelike, none of the dream quality about it. That's when I know they're going to come true, or at least they usually do."

"Well, you were absolutely right; it did come true. It was like someone was waiting for me, knowing where I was going to be so they could grab me off the street. I never had a chance. They just grabbed me, took me down into a cellar and then through all kinds of tunnels until I ended up in a cell underneath the streets. It was damp and smelly and there wasn't a thing to eat."

Sophie nodded. "That's how it was for me this morning; it was like someone was waiting there to get me." She remembered the sound of the cat crying. Nothing could have caught her attention other than the sound of the animal, and someone had to have known that. Just as Nellie said, it was almost as if someone knew where she was going to be and was waiting to grab her.

For the first time that she could remember, Sophie saw Nellie lose her bounce. The eyes that always glittered with the promise of some devilment looked haunted, the color drained from her face, and she clasped her hands. "I wish I didn't have to talk about it, though. I hated it down there."

"Why? What happened?"

"You know all those tales that we keep hearing about women disappearing and never being found? Well, it's true. These men have pens down there, nothing but dirt and water and not even enough room to stand upright in. That's where they kept me. They kept giving me some kind of drug. I still don't know what it was except that it gave me an awful headache. I tried not to drink the tea that they put the medicine in, but they wouldn't feed me unless I drank the tea first."

"And then what did they do to you?" Sophie almost didn't want to hear. She knew what Nellie did for a living, but she had the feeling that even if Nellie treated sex as a matter of business, she could still feel violated if someone forced her.

Nellie clasped her hands tight enough that the knuckles were completely white. Her voice dropped to a whisper that Sophie and the others had to fight to hear. "They undressed me and let men come in and look at me. It was like a slave auction, and I was going to be the slave. They put their fingers everywhere, and I saw one man playing with himself as he did it; it was great fun for him." She shuddered at the memory. "I don't understand

Chinese, but I think they were taking bids on me. At least they didn't rape me, not the way you think of rape, anyhow."

"Were they going to keep you here in California?" Sophie asked.

Nellie shook her head. "No. Just as you suspected, they were going to take me to China and sell me. I have a feeling my natural life wasn't going to be too long, or too natural, for that matter." She rubbed at her eyes. "I feel really strange. Very disconnected." She hesitated for another few moments, and then her eyes widened in surprise. "I think I'm going to—" She managed to race to the edge of the ship before she started vomiting everything that she'd eaten in the last couple of hours. The retching went on and on, until she collapsed on the deck moaning.

"Opium. It looks like an overdose," Dominic said worriedly. "I'll see if I can't get her something to ease the pain when I bring in supplies. Cocaine is good for this, especially when it's put into a nice sweet drink."

"I'll watch her. You go ahead with whatever you need to do," Sophie offered. It wasn't like she could actually help the other woman, but at least she could talk her through the worst of the pain.

"Wait a minute. I've got a couple of questions," Annabelle said. "For instance, you said there were other women with you, and you saw Josie was down there, going through this? Maggie and Serena, too?"

Nellie nodded.

Annabelle was looking thoughtfully at Nellie. "Someone is taking the women from the Painted Lady and selling them into slavery? Does that sound like something our friend Fry could cook up?" She was talking directly to Sophie.

"He could."

"Not only could he; I'm beginning to think that he's done a lot more damage than we gave him credit for. He was already crazy, and I'm afraid that I might have just driven him a little crazier by making him empty his building and move out of the store by raising the rent far beyond what he could pay."

"I don't think this is just retaliation against you or me. I think he's been doing this for a while and he just decided to enlarge the business a little by taking women from the Painted Lady along with a couple of his other captives. He can't do it too often, though, or someone would notice."

"We've noticed and we're going to do something to stop him permanently," Annabelle said grimly. "I wonder who else has been snatched and we don't even know about it. I remember one other woman who used to work with us, Elvira, who just up and left one day. At least we thought she'd left. . . ." Annabelle's eyes narrowed thoughtfully. "The man that she'd become very friendly with was a certain Mr. Fry. It makes sense—Fry is working with the Chinese to get these women. And for some reason, he's out to strip the Painted Lady of every woman who has ever worked there. He's trying to drive me out of business, the son of a bitch, and I'm going to stop him before he does it."

Sophie considered what her sister had said. The more she thought about it, the less she liked it. It made her back itch, just where she'd thought she was going to get shot while she was running through Chinatown.

"You do realize that we could be in even more danger than I thought?" Sophie said. "I said the person who got the opium was Fry and that miserable excuse of a man in the yellow chair never blinked. He knows Fry didn't have anything to do with it because he's already working with Fry on other deals, and that's why he's coming after us. No wonder he wants me dead!"

"Don't forget me. He wants me dead, too," Ruari said. He stared at Annabelle and his expression wasn't friendly and it wasn't the look of a lover. "Tell me, Annabelle, were you ever going to mention this connection with Fry or were you going to keep it to yourself?"

"I'm telling you now. I wasn't sure before this, but when Nellie tells me that two other women from the Painted Lady are down there with Josie, then it's pretty obvious that Fry thinks he can drive me out of business by stealing my friends. It won't work, even if I have to go in after them myself."

"You wouldn't be that stupid!" Ruari said, echoing Sophie's sentiments exactly.

"I don't think it's stupid. Now, if you don't mind, I'm leaving."

"I thought you weren't going to be stupid," Ruari shot back.

Annabelle gave him a withering look and turned her back on him.

"I'll go with you. I have to get to the *Salud Y Amor,*" Sophie said.

Ruari stared at the sisters, shaking his head slowly.

"So you're both completely crazy, is that it? Neither of you is capable of understanding just how serious this is? You can't go to Chinatown, Annabelle; they'll kill you on sight because you look like your sister and no one is going to ask who you are before they slit your throat or garrote you. And you, Sophie, I love those cats, too, but they're going to have to take care of themselves for a while. You can't go back there no matter how serious it is. Now can we get out of here?"

"But . . ." Sophie started to object and then swallowed the words. Her heart ached, her eyes were bleary with tears, but she knew that Ruari was right. She couldn't risk walking into a trap just because she wanted to make sure her kittens were safe.

"Well, you can stay here on board if you want, but I'm leaving. You may have left Josie and the others there, but I'm not going to abandon them. If you want to run out on us, that's fine, but I'm going to save my friends," Annabelle said.

"You can't be that stupid," Sophie said, not believing that her sister would put herself in mortal danger for a friend when she wouldn't do it for her own sister. That hurt even worse than anything else Annabelle had said or done. "What are you going to do, search Chinatown tunnel by tunnel, until someone traps you and kills you? You'll do this for a friend, but you left me to die? I can't believe that you've changed this much."

Annabelle didn't even bother to answer her. She just headed for the side of the ship, letting herself down to the skiff. At the last moment Dominic launched himself over the side of the ship and took over the oars.

"Now what the hell are we going to do?" Ruari asked.

Sophie watched Annabelle leave. Her sister didn't even wave to her, and the awful silence was still there between them. The way she felt at the moment, she didn't care if she ever saw Annabelle again, and if she never heard that peculiar communication between them again, it wouldn't matter one bit to her.

"Great. One possible crew member leaves and it's a sure bet that she's not going to survive more than a couple of hours and we're left sitting here where anyone can come and get us." His voice was rising to a frustrated roar. "What the hell are we going to do? You might have tried to sail with only three people on board, but I'm not willing to end up dashed to pieces on the shores somewhere. We don't dare raise anchor!"

Sophie shrugged and tried to stand up, wincing at the pain in her ankles. She hastily sat back down. She could walk if she had to, but at the moment a seat facing the city and the fires was much preferred to trying to stand on what still felt like two broken ankles. "We don't dare sit here. Could we make it out past the Farallons and drop anchor and wait until we figure out what we're going to do?"

"I don't want to leave San Francisco!" Nellie cried. "Let me off this damned boat! I don't want to go anywhere!" She headed for the railing, though what she was going to do once she got there was unclear. She made it as far as the ladder, took one look over the side, and started throwing up again. It was several minutes before she could even talk again.

"I've got a great idea," Ruari said in a soothing voice more fitted to a child than an adult, once Nellie's spasms had subsided. "Why don't you go down into the galley and the storerooms and check how much food we've got? Once you've looked at everything, you come back and tell me how far we can get without bringing aboard more supplies, because I sure as hell don't want to be the one to go into the city and hope I get back out before someone takes a pot shot at me. We'll have to make do with what we've got until we can take on supplies somewhere else, supposing I've got the gold to buy the supplies," Ruari said.

"I'd rather you didn't go ashore either. I don't want to be left here alone," Sophie said. She wouldn't even begin to acknowledge to herself or to Ruari that she was beginning to take an interest in him and that she'd rather not have him hurt.

Sophie felt the weight of the gold that she'd brought with her that morning. They'd have gold, if they managed to live that long.

"Food?" Nellie whimpered. "I don't think I could stand the sight of food."

"Get down there and do what I asked. This isn't a request; it's an order," Ruari said, ignoring Nellie's greenish color and the rapid gulps that said she wasn't quite finished with the day's upheavals.

Sophie had been silent, watching the harbor. She was watching, in particular, a skiff that seemed to be hovering behind one of the ships, watching the *Flying Angel.* She didn't like the look of it, because the people should have been turned toward the fire, watching the destruction of San Francisco, instead of watching Ruari's ship.

"Ruari, come here," she said quietly. He didn't seem to hear her; he was standing looking out at the ocean, wrapped in his own worries.

The skiff moved, and Sophie grabbed Ruari's arm, shaking him to bring him back to here and now. She pointed out at the rowboat.

"I think now would be a great time to find out whether we're good enough sailors to take this out of the harbor," she said. "Right now," she added.

"Oh, God," Ruari said in despair as he saw the skiff advancing on them. He began hauling up the anchor. Sophie didn't even ask if he needed help; she began to pull on the windlass, using every ounce of her skinny little body to pull the weight of the anchor from the bay's bottom.

"They're still heading this way," she said, when she could spare an instant to look over her shoulder. The anchor was up, though it still wasn't reeled all the way in, as it was supposed to be. Free of the bottom would have to do in this emergency; they didn't have time for anything else, and even getting the anchor free was taking longer than they had to spare. All they could do was hope that they didn't rip it loose somewhere on the way out to the open sea and lose a fairly good-size chunk out of the bottom of the *Flying Angel.*

With every turn of the winch, Sophie prayed that the people who were after them wouldn't catch them. She had pretty good eyesight and she was almost certain that she could identify at least one of the men from the yellow silk room.

"Please, please hurry," she whispered and pulled again, happy to see another couple inches of heavy, thick chain wind onto the spool. Fear, she decided, must be making her stronger than usual, since taking up an anchor could be the work for several strong men.

"Hurry," she heard Ruari whisper, and realized that he was as terrified as she was. Somehow it helped to know that he wasn't taking this lightly.

The skiff was still heading toward them, gaining on them with every passing second. The ship and passengers were close enough now to recognize another person bearing down on them. The woman who had shot at her was sitting in the bow of the boat, waiting. Sophie wondered if her eyes were playing tricks on her or whether she really could see the glint of the gun in the woman's lap.

"Just another few inches. I'm not going to do more than just get the anchor clear of the mud so we can sail without ripping anything vital," Ruari said. Sophie gave a mighty tug, and the inches that Ruari asked for lay on the coil, shining with salt water.

"The sails." Ruari cast a worried glance toward the skiff. They couldn't be more than a hundred feet away, almost within range of the woman's gun, if that was what she had in her lap.

"We're not going to make it," Ruari said, but he never stopped working, not even for a second. He began to unfurl the smaller sails that could be set fast. Just one sail picking up the breeze would give them enough power to move toward the bay. They wouldn't be fast, but they'd definitely be faster than the skiff's rowers. Smaller sails allowed them the control that would take them out of the harbor without crashing into other ships because they were going too fast or couldn't control their course out to the open seas.

Sophie moved to help him. She'd set sails often enough to know what had to be done.

"We don't have time to snub it, just loose the hitches and pull like hell," Ruari said as he did just that. The skiff was within fifty feet of them as the halyards were placed and Sophie began to belay the lines, making the S-shaped hitch hold the canvas in place as she had done a thousand times.

Twenty feet away, the people in the skiff were shouting at them, and it didn't sound friendly. A shot rang out and Sophie ducked, even though she knew that the woman couldn't possibly get the elevation that she needed to clear the ship and actually hit someone on deck with a bullet.

"Move, sweetie; come on, *Angel*, move, please?" Ruari said, praying that the ship would catch the winds that were sweeping through the bay.

An inch at first, the slightest motion of the ship in relation to the others around it, and they were on their way. Another inch and the anchor began to unwind again as the water pulled it downward. In their haste they hadn't set an iron bar through the links to hold it fast.

Sophie grabbed the bar and shoved it in between the links

that were still moving and let loose as fast as she could, but not fast enough to keep her palm from being burned as the iron fetched up against the sides of the reel with a loud clang.

"Stay there, you son of a bitch," she said in satisfaction, blowing on her palm to soothe the screeching nerves.

They were still moving, but it wasn't far enough fast enough.

The skiff bumped the side of the ship and one of the men launched himself toward the ladder that both of them had forgotten to haul onto the deck in their rush to haul up the anchor and set the sail.

"Damn! Damn! Damn!" Sophie launched herself toward the railing and caught the rope. She tried to whip the ladder outward, so whoever was climbing toward them would be forced to drop back to the ship.

It didn't work. She couldn't budge the rope; it was held tightly against the rail of the ship by the weight of the person climbing up.

She grabbed a knife and started sawing at the rope, knowing that it would take her longer than she had to cut through the salt-soaked hemp. Still, it gave the illusion of doing something useful.

"Wait; don't ruin the rope. I've got an idea," Ruari said suddenly.

She could hear Ruari behind her but didn't have time to turn around and see what he was doing. She heard a door open and then close and prayed that he knew what he was doing, walking around on deck instead of working the sails.

One side of the ladder was almost cut through when she stopped. The ladder sagged under the weight of whoever was still climbing toward her.

"No, we're not going to lose now. I'll cut your damned head off before I'll let you climb aboard." She dared a look over the side of the ship and was rewarded with the crack of a bullet aimed toward her head.

Still, whoever it was would have to stick his head up first, and she could skewer it with the point of her blade then, as long as he wasn't carrying a gun and got her first.

She heard a peculiar dragging sound behind her, wood on wood, and there was a sudden smell wafting across the deck.

"Move!" Ruari ordered her as he came up beside her.

"I can't. I've got to be ready to cut this guy's heart out!"

"Move, damn you, or you're going to get this dumped on your head!"

The odor finally penetrated and she stepped back, gagging.

Ruari set the bucket on the rail. A shot pierced the side of the wood bucket as it appeared over the edge of the ship. A leak began to ooze out the side of the bucket, bringing with it the most horrible stench Sophie had ever smelled. The ooze came closer to them, touching Ruari's hands.

"The hell with this," Ruari said and tipped the bucket downward, aiming as best he could toward whoever was climbing the ladder, as well as the people in the boat.

There was a moment of silence and then a satisfying plopping sound as the contents hit the people, followed almost immediately by the sound of the bucket racketing off the boat below them and then falling into the water as Ruari dumped it. He didn't even dare wipe his hands on his clothes; he'd never get the smell out if he did.

There was a moment of silence, followed by screams of outrage. The ladder suddenly went slack in Sophie's hands and a huge splash echoed from below. Sophie's eyes widened as she listened to the curses. There were several that she'd never heard before and that were admirable for their physical ingenuity and complexity.

Ruari and Sophie waited a moment and then looked over the railing to the scene below. The skiff was a few feet behind the *Flying Angel* and there were three people in the water, all of them trying desperately to get away from a spreading stain of dark brown. A bucket bobbed on the water, almost by the head of the woman who had shot at Sophie. The smell was incredible, even from the vantage point of the *Flying Angel*.

"Good thing I hadn't emptied that slops bucket for a while, isn't it?" Ruari said in satisfaction.

"Very good thing," Sophie agreed. "Now get away from me and go wash your hands in salt water. You are disgusting."

"I love you, too," Ruari said, laughing.

The *Flying Angel* began to pick up speed, leaving the threesome far behind. Sophie would have cheered, if she'd had the time, but there was too much work to be done.

Ruari dumped salt water from one of the other buckets over his hands, washing them until they didn't smell quite as bad as they had.

"Maybe vinegar, when you have a free moment," Sophie said, helping him move the sail slightly to pick up even more of the breeze.

"We're out," Ruari announced as they made the mouth of the bay, but he really didn't have to announce it. The ship was already rolling with the choppy open sea. The wind that had whipped the fire into a frenzy in San Francisco was threatening to sail them right back onto the shore if they weren't careful.

Ruari and Sophie worked together as if they'd been sailing as a team for years. By the time the sun began to go down, tinted orange with the smoke from the fire, they were past the Farallons and had found a safe harbor hidden in one of the small bays down the coast.

By the time they'd managed to extricate the rod that held the anchor in place and let the anchor settle into place, Sophie ached in every bone in her body. She knew the location of every muscle and bone where she hadn't quite healed yet. Her hands were raw and her feet were so sore that she didn't think she could take another step. But miraculously, until she sat down, her ankles did not bother her.

She looked down and gasped, finally understanding why her legs hadn't hurt.

"What's wrong?" Ruari said.

Sophie waved toward her ankles, which looked like she'd cut a ball in half and pasted the sections onto her legs, front and back.

"Oh, my God. Cold water? Seawater compresses? What do I do?" He took one of her feet in his hand and began to massage it. Gradually his hands moved more slowly, and the touch became almost sensuous.

Sophie lay back against the hatch, enjoying the feeling of someone soothing away her aches. For just a few moments, she could pretend that he really cared for her. Reluctantly she let him stop after a few minutes.

"We've got to get belowdecks and eat something and then set watches," he said.

Sophie groaned. "I know it's got to be done, but I'm so tired I don't think I can stay awake another minute."

"I'll take first watch then. You eat and go belowdecks. You can use my cabin; it's quite comfortable. I'll wake you up at midnight to stand your watch; then I'll be back on watch at eight."

"What about Nellie? She hasn't been doing anything except throwing up," Sophie objected. "Just because she had some opium doesn't mean she can get out of all the work, does it?"

"Do you trust her to stand watch?"

"She's got to be part of the team if we're going to come out of this alive. Besides, both of us had better be alive and well tomorrow when we decide what we're going to do about those people. You don't think they'll just forget us, do you?" Sophie asked.

Ruari snorted. "Don't be stupid. We've outmaneuvered them; we've dumped slops all over them; we've made their lives miserable. No, I don't think that they're going to just let us sail back into the bay and go on about our business. We're going to have to find a way to stop them or we're going to have to disappear off the face of the earth. Either way, it isn't going to be easy and it isn't going to be accomplished by talking nice to the guys with the sharp knives. Now all we have to do is run away and hide until we come up with a foolproof, absolutely unbreakable plan for coming back to San Francisco without getting killed."

18

SOPHIE SLEPT LIKE THE DEAD. DREAMS haunted her, but she was so sound asleep that even the worst one, of her sister being knocked on the head and bound and gagged and then taken to a ship, couldn't wake her up. She felt Annabelle's pain and then lost her as she lost consciousness. She moaned in her sleep, but she didn't awaken, even as the constant undertone that she and her sister both denied existed slowed and then stopped completely.

Ruari stumbled down the stairs and automatically turned into his own cabin. He didn't bother with carrying a candle; he knew every inch of the ship as intimately as most men know their wife's body.

He lay down on the bunk, groaning as he stretched out, still fully dressed, and was instantly asleep.

Sophie felt the warmth next to her and backed up to his body without realizing what she was doing. The comfort of Ruari's even, deep breathing and his heat made her fall even more sound asleep.

Ruari, for his part, put his arm over Sophie and pulled her close for her warmth. He'd spent a freezing night watching anxiously for trouble to come their way, even though they'd sailed out of the bay and into a sheltered cove farther down the coastline where they should be safe for a while. Still he dreamed of people coming after him and gunshots all around him.

When Ruari sank into his deep sleep, the skies were clear and calm. He wasn't worried about Nellie standing watch; he'd told her all she had to do was keep a watch out for anyone sailing near them and keep an eye on the weather. He didn't expect it to change, but he'd been a sailor long enough to know about how fast trouble could come up from the west.

It was calm enough that Nellie curled up with a blanket around her, staring at the stars and out to the horizon until her eyes began to play tricks on her, showing her ships where there weren't any and hearing sounds of people splashing toward them when it was really only waves. To clear her mind, she closed her eyes, and within seconds she went to sleep herself, despite a cup of warm tea and a few biscuits that she'd brought to keep her company. No one had realized just how tired Nellie would be after the opium started to leave her system. For a few moments before she fell completely asleep, she seemed to be looking out to sea without opening her eyes, until the hallucination passed and she began to snore softly.

No one saw the clouds that began to drift over the horizon, the first signs of the storm that would bring the first rain in months to San Francisco. The rain was desperately needed. For the first time since spring in San Francisco, the dust would be settled. The fire would be completely damped, and the cisterns would begin to fill up again with water.

No one heard the creaking of the mast as the wind swept over the rolled canvas and played ghostly tunes on the ropes that had been snubbed over the wooden pegs to hold everything tight in place. No one felt the anchor beginning to pull against the sandy bottom and begin to move with the waves that suddenly went from choppy to blowing swells of water that hit the sides of the ship, coming closer and closer to the railing. A dark squall line bore down toward the *Flying Angel* and rain began to fall in a curtain as the storm moved across the ocean toward the coast.

Suddenly Sophie snapped awake. She didn't even register that there was another person in bed with her. The only thing that mattered was the feel of the ship as it wallowed in the heavy seas. She heard the ropes singing and the sails snapping and the sound of the creaking timbers as the ship tried to stay afloat.

"Oh, shit," she said quietly. "We're in trouble."

"Wha—?" Ruari poked his head out from underneath the blanket, but Sophie was so worried that even then she didn't bother to yell about him sleeping with her.

"We're in trouble. Listen to the ship."

But she didn't need to say it; Ruari was already out of the bed and struggling into his heavy coat.

"I'll meet you up there," Sophie said.

"Wait. Take this; you'll need it." He chucked another heavy woolen coat at her and she slipped into it. It didn't matter that it was sizes too large; it would be the only thing between her and the freezing rain and wind in what promised to be a long night.

The sails snapped on the masts and a cold wind rushed past her as she hurried up on deck. The clouds were closing in on them, whipping the sea into a frenzy beneath her. She could feel the ship bucking against the anchor as the waves lifted the bow of the ship.

Nellie was fast asleep in a protected corner of the deck.

Sophie tried to wake her by shaking her, but Nellie didn't respond. Sophie swore at her, vivid curses that should have brought some kind of response from Nellie.

"Damn opium," Sophie said, finally realizing what was wrong. "I can't leave you out here on deck; you're going to wash right out to sea if I do." She slapped Nellie as hard as she could to wake her up.

Nellie screamed and jumped up, ready to fight.

"Don't bother. Just get down below and hang on," Sophie said grimly, raising her voice over the wind.

Nellie looked around, appalled at what she'd missed during her watch. "But everything was calm!" she wailed.

"That's why it's called standing watch, in case things change," Sophie snarled.

"I'm sorry!" Nellie fled below, clutching the blanket that she'd wrapped around her earlier.

Ruari had been moving around the deck, sizing up the situation and deciding what action they'd have to take. "We've got to raise that damned anchor again and head the ship into the wind. We won't be going anywhere, but it'll keep us from capsizing. If we don't, we're going over or we're going to end up on those rocks." Ruari waved toward the rough shoreline.

"I know. It's bad."

Together they raised the anchor again.

"Easier this time, when we're not in so much of a hurry," Sophie said, though they didn't raise it all the way as they should have.

"I think I prefer danger from people to danger from storms in a ship without a full crew," Ruari said. "Now let's get at least one sail up and get headed into the wind."

Sophie grabbed any handholds that she could find to take her back to the boom. She pulled at the sodden mass of rope, but her fingers slid off the tangles that had been woven when she tried to help raise one sail.

She was still fighting with the ropes when the squall hit. The wind drove particles of ice into her eyes, blinding her for precious seconds, while she tried to find a handhold and keep from being swept overboard. The ship screamed with the strain of the wind in the rigging and she could hear the sails crack and whine with the stress even on the mostly furled canvas. There was an ominous popping sound that she thought might be the boom's wood beginning to crack through, but she couldn't see clearly enough to make sure.

"Oh, damn," she gasped as her fingers fought to unhitch the rope and free the sail. She looked over at Ruari. He was still hanging onto the rope, trying to work it loose and fighting at the same time to keep a foothold on the deck.

If she didn't manage to get that canvas up, they'd be breathing water for the rest of eternity. No matter how bad the pain was from her feet, she had to ignore it and keep working.

The ship lurched and began to heel over again. The little sail was almost unfurled, but it wasn't enough to bring them out of danger immediately. The pressure of the waves took them over until they were almost touching water again. Another couple of feet and they'd be scooping the sea instead of air and the ship would capsize. The ropes dragged in the water and everything that hadn't been lashed down had been swept away.

"Come on; give me a hand here, darling!" Ruari yelled, his voice almost lost in the fury of the storm.

Sophie didn't have time to react to the endearment. *Probably what he calls every woman he almost dies with,* she thought as she put out one hand toward the boom. She had to cover three feet and then she'd be in a position to help raise the smallest sail that could take them back out to sea. The ship turned and lurched beneath her and she felt her footing give way as the deck abruptly dropped downward, leaving her hanging onto the flimsy rope handhold. She couldn't even see Ruari through the sleet that pelted her. For all she knew he might already have been washed overboard. The thought made her heart sink, a completely unexpected reaction considering that she still disliked the man. At least she thought she did.

She lunged forward toward the boom, hoping that she wouldn't fall directly into the foaming sea that waited below her. Her fingers grasped the sheet bend, and she felt the knot begin to untie beneath her hand. She scrabbled to hang on, her feet kicking for any kind of purchase on the wet deck. The ship was going to capsize and she was going to be trapped underneath. Then, miraculously, she felt the ship begin to ease back upward, sluicing the seawater over her.

"We've got it!" she screamed and hauled again on the ropes,

hitching them as the sail reached upward. The waves broached the ship again, battering it with a force that threatened to carry them down again toward the abyss of water, but the ship fought gamely, edging inch by inch into the wind.

"I'll beat you yet!" Sophie yelled at the winds and rain. Her entire body ached and her heart was beating so fast and hard that it began to skip beats from the strain, but there was a tense exhilaration to the fight that would keep her going until either the ship was safe or she was dead.

She never stopped hauling and tying and moving. She seemed to know exactly where Ruari would need her next. Gradually they began to win the battle, as the ship turned into the wind and the waves stopped battering the sides. Still the *Flying Angel* rode terribly high on the cresting waves and then plunged downward, the water and foam washing over the bow of the ship. It began to feel like they'd never come up again, but Ruari held on, pushing the ship to her limits.

"Get the wheel! Steer into the wind!" Ruari shouted. Sophie had begun to pull herself toward the stern of the ship when there was a sudden flash of light behind her, a thump, and the smashing sound of wood splintering. She jumped, convinced that the mainsail had somehow come loose and crashed to the deck.

There was a momentary silence and then another flash lit the sky and the hair on her arms stood up as something sizzled beside her.

"Lightning!"

Sophie stopped momentarily. The sound hadn't been the sail hitting the deck?

"Let go of the ropes!"

Before she could move, there was an almighty crash and the whole ship shuddered as fire swept over the sails and downward.

Lightning flashed down the mainmast and hit the deck, sizzling and popping rivets. The thunderbolt ran along the floor, searing the wood and making droplets of water on the rails dance, heading right toward Sophie.

Sophie snatched her hand back but not soon enough. Electricity hit her fingers and the shock knocked her backward off her feet. Her hair stood out from her head and the knife she'd picked up burned along her back, searing her skin where the blade turned instantly red-hot.

The world went silent. The ship still plunged downward, the rain still pounded on the deck, and light from the storm flickered and bounced through the sky, but she couldn't hear any of it. The only thing that she could hear was the ringing of a thousand bells. She tried to put her hands over her ears, but nothing would work right. Her arm wouldn't raise; her fingers seemed to be permanently frozen as she grasped the ropes.

As fast as it had appeared, the lightning disappeared, leaving a corona of light in Sophie's eyes.

Ruari was insulated from the shock by his rubber boots. When he realized that she could not move, he strode across the deck, grabbed her, and pulled her back toward the wheel, holding her in one arm and the wheel in the other.

Sophie lay against Ruari's body and thought for a moment how nice it would be not to have to move for a while.

She could see his mouth moving and it looked for all the world like he was telling her to stay with him, that he loved her, that he couldn't do without her, no matter how much she hated him.

No, that was silly; he wouldn't be saying things like that. He'd slept with her sister; he'd tried to steal her ship. He couldn't have fallen in love with her; it was impossible.

She certainly couldn't have fallen in love with him.

But his arms felt so good. The warmth felt so welcome.

"Come on, Sophie; you have to be all right. I'm not going to have followed you around San Francisco like a puppy dog for all this time and then lose you to some damned lightning!"

She could hear again!

As fast as it had come, the deafness left her and she couldn't believe what she was hearing. Her lipreading capabilities had been better than she thought, because he was still saying those silly things that she thought she'd understood.

"What do you mean, following me around?" she asked, as she extricated herself from his arms and then regretted having done so. He had been very warm and there had been a safe quality to his embrace that she hated to lose.

"You can hear me? You're talking. Oh, Sophie, I thought I'd lost you for good when that lightning hit. You've been as limp as a dishrag for at least half an hour now."

He leaned over and kissed her full on the lips, a hard kiss that asked everything of her.

She clung to him, not only for support but also because his kiss had turned her knees to jelly. Of course it was just the effect of the lightning, but still, she felt quite odd as she kissed him back, matching his every move.

"Oh, no, I can't," she moaned, but she knew, then and forever, that what she'd been trying to hide from herself was true. She'd fallen in love with him.

When he finally let her go she slumped against him and stared out to sea. She was surprised to see the beginning of the gray dawn ahead of them. She must have been unconscious or close enough to it as to not matter. Somehow Ruari had done the impossible. He'd managed to keep the ship heading straight into the wind and kept her from washing overboard.

"Thank you," she said, her voice still shaky after the lightning and the kiss. She wasn't sure which one had affected her more. "How did you manage to keep me from going over the rail? I'm not sure I'd have been able to do it for you."

"Or whether you'd have wanted to, right?" Ruari smiled down at her, but there wasn't a lot of humor in his face. Instead he looked like a little boy who wished he could have a toy but knew it was forever out of his reach.

"What?" she asked blankly.

Ruari was silent for a few moments as he wrestled with the

wheel. The storm was subsiding, but he still had to fight to keep the ship headed into the wind.

"I know how you feel about me. Your sister and I have tried to figure out a way to make you understand that I am not this hideous person that you seem to think that I am."

"I don't think . . . ," Sophie started to say and then stopped. She had thought something of the sort when she called him a pirate.

"And when it looked like you might finally listen to me, I thought I'd lost you to the storm." Ruari reached out and hugged her, surprising her with the fierceness of the gesture.

Sophie stood in the circle of his arm, balancing herself against the rocking of the waves, and tried to make sense of what she felt and what he was telling her.

With the lightening streaking down beyond them, the storm seemed to soften a little. The waves still smashed against the bow, but the *Flying Angel* didn't buck quite so hard. In a matter of minutes the squall had almost passed and the ship eased upward until Sophie stood on a reasonably flat deck once again. She was so tired that she didn't think she could walk another step, yet if they were ever going to get any rest, the damned anchor had to go down again and what was left of the sail had to be furled.

Finally it was done. The ship was secure, they were safe, and both of them were stumbling with exhaustion. Sophie took one step forward to check the bow of the ship and collapsed into a sodden pile.

"Sophie, come on; you have to get up. I'll help you down to your cabin, but I can't carry you!" He tried to lift her, but he only succeeded in helping her into a sitting position. He finally managed to wake her enough to have her put her arms around his shoulders.

Together they stumbled down the gangway, walked the few paces to his bed, and tumbled into the warmth of the blankets that they'd left hours before.

19

FOR THE SECOND TIME IN A DAY RUARI AND Sophie slept together, sharing body heat as they cupped against each other. Both of them roused enough during the calm morning hours to shed their sodden clothes and wrap themselves in blankets before climbing back into the small bed. When Ruari awakened enough to look at her, he thought she looked delectable, her red hair curled tightly around her face, her complexion pink from the cold and the wind.

No one, he decided, not even her sister, had ever looked as pretty as Sophie did right then.

Ruari had rested enough that his interest changed from platonic to carnal in a matter of minutes. He was still a young man and his body still had desires that it would have been wonderful to satisfy with Sophie.

His body responded first to the desire and then almost as quickly to the heat that washed over him as he cuddled up against Sophie. She was hot, not with a fever, but from her own internal warmth. It was a familiar warmth, though Ruari would never have told her so. Annabelle had been delightful to sleep with because the sisters both had the same body temperature, a glow that made sleeping with them a pleasure. He'd always tended to be cold, and his sister Samantha had joked with him that he'd need to marry a woman with fire in her blood or he'd never get warm in the winter. Sammy had knitted sweaters for him, double-knitted gloves, and even gone so far as to try to make his socks as warm as possible, but he'd still chilled.

"Sammy, you were right. I found the perfect woman," he whispered as he drifted off to sleep, tiredness overcoming lechery.

Ruari and Sophie woke at the same time, though they didn't know it.

Sophie had been so sound asleep that it took her several minutes to figure out where she was and what she was doing in bed with Ruari.

She should have objected. She could have climbed out of bed and slapped him for the presumption, but it was too comfortable cuddled against him. Then, as she awakened even more, she blushed a deep red that Ruari would never see as she realized just how close they really were. The blankets had shifted during the night and there was nothing between them. They were now skin to skin, and parts of Ruari's body that she'd never thought to be intimate with were pressed against her backside. She moved slightly and felt an immediate quivering response from Ruari.

To her horror, Sophie felt her own body betray her as her hips relaxed and her legs opened slightly. She wanted to put her hand back, between them, and explore all the nuances of that muscle that tantalized her. She was, in a word, in heat.

"Oh, no," she whispered. It couldn't be. She wanted to make love to a man and she didn't even know if she was in love with him.

"Oh, no," she whispered again, as she realized just what had happened over the past forty-eight hours. She'd started those hours by thinking that Ruari was nothing more than a greedy lowlife who would steal from her at a moment's notice. Then, as they jumped from one crisis to another, she had begun to work with him, until now. She knew him. She knew what he was thinking; they'd been able to work without words between them, at the height of the storm, because they could read each other's bodies and expressions, because they'd shared the same thoughts at the same time and acted upon them.

The fever pitch of the struggle against the storm had finally broken through the wall that Sophie had erected, and she discovered that she could be as close with Ruari as she had been with her sister. The communication was there even if she fought knowing that it was. She'd known from the moment she realized she wasn't that good at reading lips that she'd been hearing him the same way that she did with her sister. They didn't have to talk out loud; the ideas formed and were answered, just as they always had been with her sister.

Ruari had known what was happening; he'd called her darling. He'd told her he loved her.

Now what was she going to do?

Ruari's hand moved against her body, a seemingly sleep-driven movement that caused his hand to connect with her right breast. His fingers caressed her skin for a moment and then cupped the breast.

She should have slapped the hand away, but it felt so good. She was surprised to find that his skin was almost as soft as her own. For some reason she had expected any male's skin to be roughened and hard. She moved again, and again there was the response. By now Ruari was erect and tight against her buttocks, and she wondered for a moment what would happen if she turned over and opened her legs and let him have his way with her.

But only for a moment. First she had to deal with what he had done with her sister. She didn't like leavings and that was what Ruari was. Her sister's leavings.

There would never be a man as well suited to her. She knew how rare their type of communication was. She knew him now better than any other man she'd ever been near, and he worked as well with her as her sister did. She felt safe with him.

She was also almighty curious about what he had between his legs. She remembered now, with regret, Annabelle telling her that she shouldn't be so ready to censure her sexual escapades until she'd had a few of those encounters of her own. She was beginning to see the wisdom in her sister's advice.

She wanted him to make love to her, and leavings or not, there wasn't any reason that she shouldn't do so. She'd shucked off Cristine's new morals like she'd shuck the husk off a corn. They didn't fit her, never had and never would. She was going to fall in love with the wrong kind of man, and society and Cristine's morals be damned.

The dazzle in Sophie's eyes when she looked at him and the thumping heart when she thought about him were true indicators of love.

Ruari pulled her toward him, turning her so he could cup her face in his hands as he kissed her. It was a gentle kiss, starting with a mere brushing of their lips, but it quickly changed into a passionate, deep kiss that brought her gasping to complete wakefulness.

She should have told him no. She should have turned away from him. Instead, she reached down between them and finally, for the first time in her life, touched a man.

He jumped and his penis quivered at her touch. "Oh, God, are you sure?" he asked, his voice almost a whisper as she continued to caress him.

"Yes, I'm sure."

He thrust upward into her hand and she played with the soft tip, touching it in wonder and then letting her fingers drift down the shaft until she touched the hair at the base.

"Show me how to do what you want," she said.

It took a few moments before Ruari was able to tell her that she was doing just fine.

She explored him, hefting his testicles in her hands, surprised at how heavy they were.

"Careful, they're a little blue from no exercise lately," Ruari said.

She should have asked him what he meant, but she was having too much fun looking at the forbidden fruit.

Finally, when she couldn't stand the itching ache between her legs one more second, she opened herself to him.

There was one agonizing moment as he penetrated her, and then it was lost in the blur of new sensations. He was big, larger than she'd thought a man would be, but it didn't hurt for too long. Within seconds the feeling of fullness made her respond by pushing upward to meet him, loving the way that he filled her and gave her everything that she wanted.

She felt dazed, like riding a ship in the worst of storms, except that all this heaving and pushing felt wonderful. She wriggled beneath him, eliciting a groan of delight, and with each wiggle she felt something more and then more again, until finally the ecstasy that she'd known was waiting for her just beyond reach washed from the point between her legs outward, bending her backward, laying her open to him as she'd never opened to anyone before in her life.

When it was over, she lay back on the bed, still shamelessly spread before him as he rested on his elbows above her. The sun that shone in through the deck light showed Ruari's self-satisfied expression. She imagined that her own expression was dazed.

When he finally moved, she sat up on the side of the bed and pulled the covers around her. For all the warmth that they had just generated, the room itself was still quite cool.

Don't ask, she thought. *Don't ask*, she told herself again. *You'll ruin everything. It will hurt more than you can stand; it isn't worth the pain.*

So she asked.

"Tell me, how do I compare to my sister?"

Ruari stared at her, completely bollixed by the question. "What do you mean?"

"I mean when I spread my legs and let you put your penis there and make love to me, how did I compare to Annabelle? That should be pretty easy to answer, considering that you were in bed with her when I found you yesterday morning."

"I can't believe that you are asking me that." Ruari's voice was suddenly less warm that it had been.

"Why? Is it because she's so much better than I am? She's had more time, you know." Sophie's voice dropped to a whisper. She was surprised to find that her heart ached when she thought of him in bed with her sister and the pleasures that they must have shared. For some silly reason she wanted to be the best, the most wonderful partner that he'd ever had in bed, even though she knew that was impossible. "It's all right; you don't have to tell me. When we get back to San Francisco, you can go to her. I won't try to keep you."

"Thank you for being so generous, but has it ever occurred to you that you might want to ask me how I feel about this whole situation?" Ruari's voice was colder yet, and for the life of her Sophie couldn't understand what was making him so angry with her. She hadn't done anything; she was just trying to let him know that she didn't expect any special favors because she'd lost her virginity to him. He didn't have to keep on telling her that he loved her, if he didn't. She knew how men would say ridiculous things just to get into bed with a woman; there was no reason to think that Ruari was any different.

"How can you be so stupid?" he asked, and now his voice dripped ice.

"What? I am not stupid!"

"You are in matters of the heart."

"What do you mean?" She stared at him, afraid to let her heart take even a small leap with hope.

"I mean that I've been trying to make an impression on you

for weeks. I've tried to take care of you and stir up even a modicum of interest since I saw you as you came off the *Salud Y Amor* that first morning in San Francisco. You fool, I was gone the minute I saw you, that beautiful face framed by your lovely red hair, your lips ready for my kiss. When I saw those men stop you and actually touch you, I could have killed them. Hell, I tried to kill them, if you remember. And I tried to help you with Fry and you turned me down."

Ruari was standing now, completely oblivious to the state of his unclothed body.

Sophie was listening, but at the same time she was looking at his body and she couldn't quite wipe all the memory of the glorious time that they'd just spent together out of her mind.

She would have said something, but Ruari wouldn't let her break in.

"No matter what I've done, I haven't been able to break through that barrier of yours because you decided that I had done something wrong and there was no way to gain your trust. Now you've given me the greatest gift that you could have given and all you want to know is how you compare with your sister?" He stared at her with such an expression of hurt and anger that she'd have done anything to wipe it off his face.

"I'm sorry," Sophie whispered, but he didn't hear her. She wished she'd never said anything. The truth was, she didn't want to know. If Annabelle was better in bed than she was, she'd die if she heard it from Ruari's lips. That truth would hurt so bad that she'd never survive it.

"How do you compare with your sister? Do you really want to know?" Ruari want on.

Sophie tried to interrupt him and tell him that she didn't want to know, but he rode relentlessly over her.

"Well, I'll tell you—I don't know how you compare because I never slept with your sister!"

"What?" Sophie said, not daring to believe her ears.

"I know you won't believe me when I tell you it, because you never believe me about anything. But here's the absolute truth. I've been so besotted with you that I thought I could get you out of my thoughts and my dreams and my life if I slept with Annabelle. She looks enough like you that you two could be twins, but she isn't you. She doesn't have your softness and delicacy. For all that she looks like you, she wasn't the woman that I loved."

"Oh, God, loved?" Sophie asked, her voice anguished, but Ruari kept on talking.

"I tried to bed your sister and I couldn't. It was the first time in my life that I couldn't make it happen. I tried, I looked at her, I fantasized about it being you there with your legs apart, ready and willing to take me into you, but it wasn't you and I couldn't do it. I would have left immediately, but I was too drunk and I fell asleep."

He turned away from her too soon to see the smile dawning on Sophie's face. It wasn't past tense yet. It wasn't *loved,* it was *love,* and she could still salvage it if she worked hard enough to prove to him that this time his dream had come true.

"Shall we try that part about my legs apart, ready and willing to have you do all those glorious things again? I think I could be taught to make it the best that you've ever had, don't you?"

Sophie reached out and touched him on the shoulder as she pulled him toward her.

Slowly Ruari turned, and the smile that lit his face was so brilliant that it made the room brighter. "Do you mean it?" he asked.

"I mean it. And I was wondering if you've ever heard anything about a woman putting her mouth right about here?" Sophie pushed him back on the bed and began to kiss parts that she'd never even considered touching before.

"I don't think you need any lessons," Ruari managed to say, his voice choked with wonder as they sank again into the blissful state that both of them had only imagined before.

20

IT WAS BACK. THE CONNECTION BETWEEN Annabelle and Sophie was back again as if it had never gone. Right at the moment, the message was clear: *Come back; I need help! I've been caught and they're taking me to China. I'm aboard the* Mary Kathleen *with the other women. Please help.*

Annabelle? Are you all right? Sophie remembered the dream of her sister being knocked unconscious and taken away again.

Sophie, I'm scared. I can hear them loading stuff into the cargo and it's almost full. They're talking about leaving soon. I tried to work my way between the false wall and the bulkhead, but this time it didn't work; they've piled stuff up against the open space and I'm trapped. There was an edge of hysteria in Annabelle's voice that Sophie had never heard before. *I'm sorry that we fought; I don't want it to end this way, with us separated forever. Come get me, please.*

That was all that Sophie needed. She'd never been able to resist an appeal from her sister and she wasn't about to start now.

Sophie sat up in bed and shook Ruari until he surfaced from sensuous dreams of making love to small redheaded women.

"We've got to help Annabelle. I sure as hell hope that you weren't telling the complete unvarnished truth when you said that you weren't a pirate, because we've a desperate need for pirates right at the moment," Sophie announced.

Ruari opened his eyes and stared at her. It was obvious that he didn't believe her.

"Oh, God, are we back to that again? I thought I'd settled it forever with you." He rubbed his eyes, trying to clear his vision enough to see if she was joking.

"I think there's something I'd better tell you about Annabelle and me. You may not want anything more to do with me after I tell you, but there's nothing I can do about that," Sophie said, deciding that she'd better brave the worst part first. If he was going to walk away from her, better for him to do it now, before she'd fallen so blindly in love with him that she couldn't even begin to think of telling him the truth. As if she weren't already in love.

"Annabelle and I have always been linked, ever since we were babies. I know what she's doing; she knows what I'm doing. It's kind of a two-way communication that never stops. Except that it stopped when Annabelle got angry with me and turned it off, but she's back this morning and we have to go rescue her. The only way we can rescue her is by stopping the ship that's due to leave the San Francisco harbor before the day's over. That means that either we're going to stop them in the harbor or we're going to have to do a real pirate imitation and attack on the open seas," Sophie said, all in one breath.

"Right," Ruari said. "Are you aware that you aren't making any sense at all?"

"I am, too! I'm trying to tell you that Annabelle and I don't need to be in the same room, the same city, or even the same state to be able to talk to each other. It's something we've always shared, and right now Annabelle is telling me that she's been captured by the men who are shipping women out to China. She's on a ship that is going to sail out of the harbor this morning sometime. We've got to stop it or my sister will be lost forever."

Ruari took only a few seconds to digest the story and decide that he'd better believe her, because he'd hate to think that the woman he loved was crazy.

"It won't be on the high seas. I can't sail this vessel with only one other able-bodied hand. We're going to have to take them in the harbor. If that's what we're going to do, then we'd better get the anchor all the way up, actually secure it, and sail like Hades for San Francisco."

Sophie was surprised and gratified to find that Ruari didn't tell her she was a candidate for Bedlam. Instead, he climbed out of bed, looked back longingly at her naked form, and began to dress.

"Come on; if we're going to do this, we've got a lot of work to do. Pleasure later, love." He held out a hand and pulled her out of the comfortable warmth of the blankets. He dug out fresh, dry clothes for both of them, though the shirts and pants were woefully large for Sophie. The other clothes were still storm-soaked, and from the look of them, they wouldn't be dried for days.

Sophie did the best she could to cinch everything in tight enough so that she could work. A quick breakfast of hardtack and tea and they were ready to begin work.

Everything seemed to be moving in slow motion, Sophie thought as she looked up at the sun for the fiftieth time that morning. She'd been staring at the same piece of rock on the shore for hours, she was sure, and the *Flying Angel* wasn't flying fast enough to satisfy her with their progress.

Annabelle kept up a running commentary about what was happening on the ship. She hadn't heard the anchor being lifted yet—that meant there was still a little time—but Sophie had an awful feeling that they were going to have to try high seas piracy to save her sister.

It seemed to take days to reach the entrance to the bay. Sophie had kept an open line to Annabelle, but she could tell her sister nothing except to urge her to hurry.

Then, as suddenly as it came, the communication between them went dead. The *Flying Angel* was heading into the bay and had already reached calmer waters when suddenly, inexplicably, Annabelle simply wasn't there any longer.

Sophie stopped dead in her tracks and stared into the harbor, trying to find the link to her sister again. She was getting very tired of the communication switching off at the most inconvenient time.

Ruari talked to her, but she didn't hear him. Frantically she probed, hoping to catching something, a clue, some idea of what was happening to her sister. This wasn't like the angry retreat that Annabelle had staged when Sophie insulted her. Even then there had been an occasional leak that let Sophie know that they were still in communication, even if Annabelle didn't want it.

This was complete absence. There wasn't a sound, not an image, not even a thought from Annabelle, just like it had been when they knocked her unconscious.

There was nothing except . . . pain.

"Oh, God, they're hurting her!" Sophie wailed and ran to the bow of the ship, as if she could somehow make the *Flying Angel* go faster. She hung onto the rail, forcing herself not to plunge into the icy waters to see if she could swim faster than the ship could sail.

"Who is hurting her and what are they doing?" Ruari asked, grabbing Sophie around the waist and pulling her back to a safe distance from the rail. "Look, it isn't going to help her if you do something foolish and I have to stop and rescue you and her ship sails and I can't catch it." Ruari finally pulled her away from the bow.

Sophie took a deep breath, willing herself not to react to the pain that she knew her sister was feeling.

"I don't know; it's someone familiar, someone—the lady with the gun; I'm sure it is. That bitch is hurting my sister. If I get her alone, I swear I am going to carve her into fish bait."

"Perfectly reasonable. But right now, I need your help. We've got to get to your sister, and I don't know what ship she's on. We're going to have to search."

Sophie looked at him blankly.

"No, you're not. She's on the *Mary Kathleen*. I'm sure I told you."

"Not a word, but that does make my life easier. The *Mary Kathleen* hasn't raised anchor yet, she's sitting right where we left her, and she's going to be easy to pull alongside. The only question is whether we can get a clear shot at her sails once they're raised. That's the best way to stop them, rip everything to bits so they can't possibly sail."

"A clear shot with what?" Sophie pulled herself out of her sister's pain enough to focus on what Ruari was saying, and at the moment it didn't make much sense.

"Help me lift this cover, will you?" Ruari pointed to two rope handles on what had looked like a simple wooden box on the deck.

Sophie grabbed the handle and hauled upward at his count, moving the unwieldy box up and over to the side. As she lifted, she caught a glimpse of shining brass.

"Put it down over here; we won't be covering this up for a while," Ruari said, smiling wolfishly as he petted the shiny brass of one of the most solidly efficient-looking cannons that Sophie had ever seen.

"What the hell is this doing on your ship?" she asked.

Ruari smiled, his dimples deeper than they'd ever been. "You should know that a ship always needs a good defense. This is ours. See; she rotates on the gimbals, so she can fire at almost any position. She's very efficient and most of the time one shot from her across someone's bow is enough to stop them dead in the water. After all, how many pirates in the Pacific have you ever heard about?"

"Pirate," Sophie whispered and then began to laugh. "You lied to me. You told me you'd never thought of taking over the ship, and look at you, a real pirate, with a real cannon, and I believed you."

"Oh, you can believe me. When I first saw you on that deck, I was ready and willing to take over the *Salud Y Amor* for salvage. I stayed with you to help if you asked for it and to salvage things if it went wrong. But you were right when you said I was a pirate. I would have taken everything in an instant, if you'd given me the chance."

"And now you're going to use this to shoot down the *Mary Kathleen*? Oh, love, you do have the best equipment."

"You're not angry with me?"

"Angry? No, how could I be angry with someone who is as devious as I am? Now let's get this armed and ready, because it's time to pounce on the *Mary Kathleen* before they do any more harm to my sister."

They sailed toward the *Mary Kathleen*, watching the movement on the deck through the spyglass, waiting for the right moment to strike.

"I'm going for the sails. A shot to the ship itself might not stop them if they thought they could repair it while out at sea. I've got to wait until they have the sails up, because that's what I'm going to rip through with the cannonball."

Quietly, stealthily, they maneuvered until they were directly across from the *Mary Kathleen*, with the cannon trained dead on the sails that were being raised to move the ship out of the harbor.

The people on board the *Mary Kathleen* didn't even notice the *Flying Angel* until she was almost on top of them. Even when they saw her, they didn't register the fact that they were in danger.

Sophie searched the people on the deck, hoping that her sister would be above rather than belowdecks, where she'd be difficult to rescue.

As Sophie used the spyglass, she focused on two faces, and let out a small moan.

"What's wrong?"

"Dominic is over there. So is the woman who was working with Dr. Mao. I never dreamed that he'd be one of them. I thought he was so nice." Old dreams died a hard death when presented with reality.

Still no one noticed the stealthy approach of the *Flying Angel.*

The anchor was up, the sails were raised, and the *Mary Kathleen* was ready to sail out of the bay when Ruari finally touched the light to the cannon. There was an instant of silence; then the cannon roared and the ball ripped through the *Mary Kathleen*'s sails, shredding them into long flapping pieces. The ship sailed a bit farther; then stopped dead in her tracks.

The roar of the cannon brought instant attention. The bay was suddenly alive with skiffs, rowboats, all manner of vessels bearing down on the two ships to see what the problem was. Several of the ships reached the *Mary Kathleen* within minutes, but there was no way to board her; the crew on board wasn't making the same mistake that Sophie and Ruari had made by leaving down the ladder.

Gunfire erupted from the *Mary Kathleen* and Sophie saw with horror that the people had been prepared for this possibility.

"Stop them; they're going to set fire to the ship!" she screamed. Oh, God, she'd thought about this, about being caught in the tiny hole with no way out and no way to be rescued and fire all around her. Her sister was going to die down there, and there was nothing she could do about it.

"Ruari, you have to make them let the women go!" Sophie was screaming for him to do something, but she didn't know what he could do to save her sister.

"Shut up!" Ruari shook her. "Where is your sister? Can you figure out her location? We might be able to stop them from torching the ship and rescue your sister at the same time, but you can't go all hysterical on me now!"

The sailors were holding fiery brands to the paraffined canvas, but miraculously, the sails did not ignite. Sophie willed the fire to stop, and for a few seconds it looked like her wishes were holding the flames back.

Sophie gulped back another scream when there was a flicker of fire, but it died almost before it started.

Someone was trying to stop them from setting the *Mary Kathleen* afire.

Dominic. There was no mistaking that huge figure. There wasn't another man as large as he was in all of San Francisco. He pulled the brands out of one man's hand, but the other one still tried to light the shreds of the sails that hung down.

If the *Mary Kathleen* survived and Annabelle got out of this safely and Dominic came ashore in one piece, he was going to have some explaining to do to Sophie.

The rowboats and skiffs and other ships that had surrounded the *Mary Kathleen* were still milling about below the ship, but several enterprising sailors were throwing hooks onto the railing. Eventually one of them would succeed before the crew of the *Mary Kathleen* could unhook the lines and throw them back into the ocean.

"Damn it, help me. Where is Annabelle?"

Sophie drew a shuddering breath. "Do you see that porthole, the third one from the left? She's directly below that in the hold."

The cannon was loaded, ready to go, and he held the fire above the fuse for the cannon.

"Now fire up that communication that you have with her, because this is going to save her life. Tell her to get the women out of the way. They've all got to get to the port side as far as they can and pray that I'm accurate with this thing. It's the only chance they'll have of surviving."

"You're going to shoot them out?" Sophie didn't like the sound of that.

"I'm going to open a hole that they can crawl through. Now

tell them, damn it. We don't have much time."

She closed her eyes, willing the fires not to leap up the sails when she wasn't looking. She reached out and found Annabelle. Her sister had gone quiet, almost unwilling to communicate. She had given up, sure that there was no way out now.

"Stop acting like a baby and do as I say," Sophie ordered her sister.

Ruari watched in fascination as Sophie's lips moved. He couldn't hear what she was saying, but he surely hoped that Annabelle could hear.

Face the ocean. Once you are facing the ocean, move to the right as far as you can. Pile up on each other; do whatever you have to do to leave us space. We're coming to get you by blasting a hole in the ship right into the hidden space, Sophie said. She didn't believe it herself, she couldn't see how it was going to work, but it was their last chance, the only one that they had.

"Ready to fire. Is she out of the way?" Ruari asked.

"They're ready."

The cannon boomed to life again, placing the ball neatly below the third porthole. The wood splintered and a ragged cheer went up from the crowds that had gathered below. A hook grabbed at the edge of the hole, and while Josie and Annabelle looked out, a man started to climb up the side of the ship.

"Get the hell out of the way unless you want one of us landing on you!" one of the women yelled. The man retreated hastily.

She saw the rope and hook being tossed again toward the deck as she let herself down like a monkey using the rope and hook that clung to the side of the splintered hole.

"Go get those bastards. Teach them a lesson about snatching San Francisco's finest whores!" she yelled.

"Steal our women?" The cry went up, passed from ship to ship as two more women started down the rope.

"Capture the muckers and kill them all!" The first shouts went up as another anchor sailed onto the deck and hung fast in the brass railing. Before anyone on deck could toss the hook back, the men were already racing hand over hand to get to the deck. The torches were ripped out of the men's hands and thrown overboard, and the anchor dropped back into the sea, holding the ship prisoner in the bay.

Sophie was beginning to panic. She could see Josie coming down and she assumed that the other women were the ones that Annabelle had been looking for, but her sister hadn't left the ship yet.

Finally she saw Annabelle crawl out of the space and let herself down into one of the waiting boats. Sophie lost sight of her sister as the seamen rowed toward shore.

Within seconds of the first man hitting the deck, every person on board the *Mary Kathleen* had been taken prisoner and they were being let down over the sides like trussed ducks to be taken to shore and punished.

Sophie gasped as she saw Dominic being marched to the railing and then forced to disembark hanging onto a rope that threatened to snap with every roll of the ship.

"What the hell do you think he was doing on that ship?" she asked Ruari. "He wasn't part of this, was he?"

"On board the *Mary Kathleen*, set to sail with your sister being held prisoner, not trying to get them loose that we could see—yes, I'd say he's involved." Ruari didn't like Dominic too much; he was altogether too friendly with the woman Ruari loved.

"No," Sophie said emphatically. "I positively refuse to believe it. He's my friend; I know him and he wouldn't do such a thing. There is some other explanation."

"He's not going to get to give any explanation at all, I'd bet from the looks of the crowd. They're going to string everyone up and justice and explanations be damned."

"No, we've got to stop them. We got to save Dominic."

Ruari looked at her like she'd sprouted another head and a couple of extra eyes. "Go save him? You are joking, aren't you? Even if I wanted to, I couldn't stop those men who have got him.

Don't you recognize them? They're the ones who have started calling themselves vigilantes and swearing that they're going to stop the violence in San Francisco by hanging everyone they can get their hands on that they consider troublemakers. They're not going to listen to any explanations before they do their work."

"Then I'll stop them," Sophie said. She looked downward and saw that there was a skiff almost beneath the *Flying Angel.*

"Hey, get me off of here! I've got to catch those men!" she screamed.

The sailors looked up at her and pulled in closer so she could scramble down the ladder and into their ship. Ruari tried to grab her before she left, but his hands caught empty air. He'd never known that any woman could move so fast.

"Oh, shit, now I'll have to come after you," he said. He'd never thought that loving one of the sisters could be quite this much trouble. Then he thought about their night in bed and decided that it wasn't really that much trouble after all.

Once in the boat, she leaned forward, urging them onward so that no one could do anything before she got there.

Annabelle, listen to me! You're on shore; you have to make sure that they don't hurt Dominic.

Annabelle replied, *He was on the ship! He was going to sail to China with me and he didn't try to make them leave me behind.*

I don't care; he isn't at fault. There is some explanation—I know there is—all I have to do is talk to him. Please, don't let them kill him!

The communication faltered and then dropped to a hum in the background as Annabelle went to work, trying to convince the vigilantes, most of whom had been customers in the Painted Lady at one time or another, to listen to her.

She wasn't successful.

"Kill them!"

"Stealing our women, murder the buggers!"

"Hang 'em by their pigtails, the bastards."

The screams of rage echoed as the crowd dragged the crew through the streets toward Union Square. It was as if the entire town was reacting to the fires and the violence and the threats of more mayhem by focusing on this sorry band of Chinese who had been set to sail out of the harbor with the four women.

"Get Fry!" the cry went up as one of the crew members began to babble about the plans and about the women that had already been sent to China, where they'd never be found again.

"Fry's the one who decided which women to take!"

"Fry's the one who got his men to snatch the women off the streets!"

By the time Annabelle reached the square, there were already ropes hung from a couple of shop signs that hardly looked strong enough to hold up the sign, much less a man.

There were shots in the distance.

"What was that?" Sophie demanded as she pushed her way through the crowd. People around her let her through or they were left with bruised ankles and ribs and other damage as she fought her way toward Dominic.

"They haven't killed any of the crew, have they?" she demanded, but no one knew any more than she did.

"Fry's dead!"

"Shot himself when the men got to him."

"I'm glad the bugger's dead! Now let's get the rest of them and teach them a lesson."

Annabelle was the first to reach the square, and what she saw made her sick. Two of the crew were already dead, hanging from the signs. The vigilantes had tried to get a rope around Dominic's head, but it hadn't worked very well, since he was almost as tall as the signs themselves. Instead, they had the ropes tying him in place and someone was holding a gun to his head.

Dominic stared downward, giving no sign that he even cared what happened to him. Annabelle's heart lurched as she saw the beautiful face, the lively eyes, empty now, almost dead even before the bullet smashed into his head.

The man's finger began to squeeze the trigger and the crowd surged forward, eager to see brains blasted out against the brick pavement.

"Stop!" Annabelle screamed and launched herself toward the man holding the gun. He pulled the trigger just as she reached him. His hand wavered and the bullet grazed Dominic's temple instead of punching through bone and brains. He dropped like a deadweight to the ground and someone in the crowd kicked at him, until Annabelle stormed to the center of the crowd and whipped out her knife.

"That's enough, you bastards. Back off; he's the only one who tried to help us. Get away from him!"

"You and who else is going to stop us?" one of the men jeered, ready to kick Dominic again.

"Me and my sister," Annabelle said as Sophie finally reached her side. As they always had in dangerous times, they worked back to back, watching every moment as they guarded their fallen friend.

"Get the hell out of the way, woman," the man said, reaching out to push her aside.

Annabelle struck first, bringing her knife upward and skewering his hand before it reached her. She yanked the point free, ready to knife the next person who thought of taking liberties.

"Watch him," Annabelle said, so low that no one except Sophie could hear it, nodding toward a man that they both knew.

"You want someone to kill, kill him!" Annabelle yelled. "He's the one who snatched me right out of the Painted Lady and turned me over to the Chinese!" She pointed her knife toward the man with the red suspenders, who had been trying to kick Dominic.

As the crowd turned, Sophie knelt beside Dominic, trying to see just how badly he was hurt.

"Come on, friend," she pleaded, despairing of ever seeing those eyes open again. He was bleeding so badly that she was sure he had just lost half the blood in his body, and she couldn't see any way to stem the flow.

"Watch it!" Annabelle's warning came almost too late, as the crowd surged back toward them, almost trampling them to death as more shots were fired.

"That's enough. Get out of here; it's all over!" Ruari's voice boomed louder than Sophie had thought possible. "Let me through or I swear I'll fire into one of the buildings and start another fire. That'll clear you out in no time!"

"And I'll help him. I don't have anything to lose; everything I own went up in flames a couple of days ago anyway." Abernathy stepped forward. Even in the midst of a murderous, crowd-numbing rage, his voice was sepulchral. The crowd began to move back.

"Good," Abernathy said, grinning. It was a scary grin, especially when the man smiling was also holding one of the biggest guns anyone had ever seen. "Now, leave my artist alone, do you hear?"

The crowd moved aside reluctantly, until Ruari was able to reach the sisters with a cart that he and his friends were pulling behind them.

They picked Dominic up, six men lifting him, and laid him gently on the cart.

"Where to?"

"The *Salud Y Amor*. It's the only safe place for now," the women said in unison and began clearing the path for the men. It was amazing, Sophie thought, how easy it was to clear people out of the way when a nice shiny knife did some of the talking. A little tick here, a wave of the blade there, and the crowd parted much more easily than it had on the way in.

The vigil started when they reached the *Salud Y Amor*.

They laid Dominic on his bed in the two cabins that had been joined into one that was sufficient for his length. The bleeding had almost stopped, and the sisters set to work to see what the damage was.

"Boil water."

"Bring me soft cloths from my cabin."

"Come on, love; you have to wake up," Annabelle said, gently washing away the blood. The skin had been torn away, leaving a jagged edge, but the bone underneath wasn't even creased.

"Hmmm. Love?" Sophie asked so that only Annabelle heard her.

"I know. Isn't it the damnedest thing? He loves me. He was trying to help me. And now that I know, of course he's going to try and die on me, and I'm not going to allow it."

"Annabelle, when did he have time to tell you all of this?"

Her sister looked up at her innocently. "He never did. I just kind of picked it up when I heard him trying to stop that awful Chinese woman from hurting me. You'll see; I'm right about this, the same way you're right about all the people that you 'know' about when you meet them."

She kept working on Dominic, willing him to be all right.

Together they cleaned and bandaged their friend.

"Annabelle?" Sophie said quietly. "We were both wrong."

"We were both stubborn."

"But when you disappeared and wouldn't let me back in—"

"And then you didn't need me like I thought you would," Annabelle said, grinning wryly.

"But Josie?"

"A friend, not a sister. Cristine?"

"Not even a friend. I'm not like her, never will be."

"Ruari?"

Sophie stopped and smiled. "Almost as good as a sister, but I like a couple of his extra appendages more."

"I told you so!"

"Yes, you did. Now I understand. Couldn't pay me enough to stay away from it either," she said, laughing.

"Dominic?"

"I knew he wasn't a part of this. I heard him trying to stop one of the people, the woman who ripped the necklace off my neck. He was pleading with her, but my Chinese isn't nearly as good as yours, so I couldn't tell exactly what he was saying."

"You're sure you couldn't be mistaken?"

"No, and I'm so glad. But he was in an awful position—he was trying to save the women and not get himself killed along the way. He was damned if he did and damned if he didn't. The Chinese were going to kill him because they thought it was his fault that you came back and fired the cannon. And then the mob got him." Annabelle shivered at the thought of what would have happened if they had arrived just a few seconds later.

"I hope he survives. I have a couple of things I need to talk to him about. Like love. I was so stupid! He kept coming around and I had a grand time talking to him. He's like you—I can tell him anything and he doesn't get shocked."

"Well, almost like me, except when I'm trying to be too much like Cristine," Sophie said. "And I'm still sorry. You were right about her and a couple of other things, too."

"Well, of course I was. I'm the older one; you're supposed to listen to your older sister." Annabelle did her best to lighten the mood, but they were both too tired to laugh as she looked down at Dominic and tapped him lightly on the cheek.

"Wake up, damn you. It's not that bad," she ordered again and was rewarded by a flicker of Dominic's eyelids. Another fifteen minutes and he sat up, leaning against every pillow that they could find.

"Why didn't you let me die?"

The words hung starkly in the room; neither Sophie nor Annabelle could believe that they'd heard him correctly.

"Let you die? For what?" Annabelle asked.

Dominic closed his eyes. "Because it would be easier to die than have to live with this disaster."

Sophie thrust a cup of rum and tea into his hand and waited until he'd sipped a little of the mix before she demanded to know what the hell he was talking about.

"Did anyone go belowdecks after you were rescued?" Dominic asked.

Annabelle and Sophie looked at each other. "We don't know," they said at the same time. "Why do you ask?"

"Because my mother's body is down there."

"Your mother?" Annabelle's eyes narrowed. "You don't mean the woman who ripped the necklace off my neck, do you?"

Dominic nodded and then winced as it hurt his head. "Yes, I mean her."

"Oh, Dominic," Sophie said sadly. "You finally found her after all the searching and now she's dead?"

"It's better that way. I am disgraced; my family is disgraced. I should have been allowed to die."

"Oh, do shut up. If you say that again I swear I'm going to slap you until you begin to make sense," Annabelle snapped.

Dominic sat up a little farther, reached into his pants pocket, and pulled out Annabelle's necklace.

"I knew the instant I saw this around her neck that she was involved in the same kind of thievery that she had been a victim of. She was taking women to sell in China. All I could do was try to keep you four women safe until I could figure out a way to get you back home again. I was going to do it even if I had to sail to China with you and then come back for reinforcements to go back and ransom you all."

He handed the necklace to Annabelle and slumped back against the pillows.

Annabelle looked at him quizzically, as if she really couldn't figure out what was going on in his brain.

"Let me get this straight. Your mother was the one helping Fry pick out the women and snatch them off the streets to be taken to China?"

Dominic nodded.

"You were trying to help us?"

Dominic barely inclined his head.

"And you think you've done something wrong and deserve to

die? Boy, that bullet to the head may not look like it did any damage, but you are definitely sick. Lie back down and I'm going to check things again, because you're not making sense and I hate it when people I love don't make sense; it makes me go all funny inside."

For the first time Dominic actually opened his eyes and stared up at Annabelle.

"Love?" he said, his voice barely a whisper.

"That bullet didn't even come close to your ear. Yes, I said love. Now, if these other people will leave, I'm going to do a detailed examination and we'll see just what we find at the end of it," Annabelle said.

"Well, that was a dismissal if I ever heard one," Sophie said, catching Ruari by the hand and pulling him out of the room. She closed the door behind her.

"Actually, I caught an elbow in the ribs back in that crowd. Are you sure you wouldn't like to do the same kind of examination for me?" Ruari asked hopefully.

Sophie pulled open the door to the cabin and ushered him inside. She was about to kiss him when two frenzied balls of orange fluff launched themselves at her, mewing and scratching in their desperation to reach their mistress.

"What on earth?" Sophie caught one cat while Ruari caught the other. They were thin and their skin was flabby. It was obvious that they hadn't eaten in days, and they were wailing in fright and anger.

"That bitch," Sophie said, her teeth clenched. "Quick, get me some tinned milk and crack a couple of eggs into it. I'll open the oysters. Oh, you poor little babies, Mommy will take care of you," she crooned.

Ruari put the milk down just seconds before Sophie had the oysters chopped and ready for the kittens. They ate like they hadn't eaten in days, and then, tired from their ordeal, they tumbled against each other and slept.

"Here's a note," Ruari said as he looked at the captain's desk.

" 'Sophie, I've left some food for the kittens. I'm going away with Jacques, the new French baker. We're leaving for the gold country. Hope everything is well with you. Cristine.' "

"Is there a date?"

"December twenty-fifth. These poor kids have been without food or water for two days. It's a miracle that they're still alive."

"If I ever find her, she's dead meat," Sophie said.

"I'll help you. But, Sophie, for now, just for now, could you come over here and lie down beside me and make me the happiest man in the world? This has been a hell of a couple of days."

And Sophie did just that and would keep on doing it for the next forty-two years.